I0768322

Praise for A Good Rush of Blood

"Matt Phillips writes a seedy mystery full of unique characters who expose the unwashed underarm of the pristine Palm Springs. Phillips drags his heroine through the dirt and grime as she searches for the truth regardless of the consequences. You don't want to miss this latest noir installment."

– Travis Richardson, Derringer Award winner and author of *Bloodshot and Bruised*

"Noir virtuoso Matt Phillips' *A Good Rush Of Blood* is as hot as a Palm Springs sunburn, strong as a kamikaze shot, and always alive to the hard sweetness of destinies unfolding on the edges. His places pulse. His people breathe and kiss and ache. His writing is the kind of poetry that kicks you in the head. Rough, dangerous, sexy and sweet, *A Good Rush Of Blood* stuns and exhilarates."

–Jo Perry, author of *Pure* and the Charlie & Rose Investigate series

"This the latest page-turner by Matt Phillips, is a great crime novel with an evil conclusion. Or two."

– Rob Pierce, author of *Snake Slayer* and the Uncle Dust Trilogy

"*A Good Rush of Blood* confirms Matt Phillips' status as one of the finest practitioners of noir fiction writing today. Phillips provides an engrossing mystery populated by grime-coated, three-dimensional human beings. The prose is terse, to the point. No words wasted. The reader's eyes glide across the page, eager to reach the next shocking revelation. This is noir the way the Good Lord intended— simultaneously brisk and complex. A thrill ride for all fans of the genre."

– Alec Cizak, author of *Nobody's Coming Home*

Praise for Matt Phillips

"Phillips...in a just world, will someday get his due alongside some of those more celebrated Gold Medal authors. Because there's still an audience for storytelling that marries propulsive darkness with painstaking skill."
–Jim Thomsen, writer and editor

"Slick, razor-sharp dialogue and realistic characters make Phillips The Crime Writer to Binge Read."
–Stephen J. Golds, author of *Say Goodbye When I'm Gone* and *I'll Pray When I'm Dying*

"I can't get enough of Matt Phillips these days, and hope a sh*t-ton of other readers will soon feel the same."
– Anthony Neil Smith, author of *Slow Bear*, *All the Young Warriors* and *Yellow Medicine*

"Phillips is a writer who should be on everyone's radar for his lean, taut prose, authentic dialogue, and mastery of noir."
– Sarah Chen, Derringer award-winning author of *Cleaning Up Finn*

"A master storyteller in this genre..." – Readers' Favorite

"Lucky for us...Phillips knows his way around the dark recesses of the heart..." – *Tough Crime*

Editor: Krysta Winsheimer of Muse Retrospect

Book Design: Gary Anderson

Cover Photograph: Matt Phillips

Cover Design: Garth Jackson

ISBN: 979-8-9869930-5-8
Run Amok Crime, 2023
First Edition

Printed in the USA

A GOOD xx xx RUSH of BLOOD

MATT PHILLIPS

If you've ever run from anybody or anything,
this book is for you.

1/How it Starts

When Creeley started, she didn't know a damn thing.

It was a way to make money.

Small risk. High reward. Just drive—that's what Animal said. Drive, Creeley. Not too fast. Not too slow. No drinking. Maybe a little herb if you want to stay cool. So that's what Creeley did. She smoked a bowl and drove to Grants Pass from Portland. Summer then, and the highways were filled with Subarus, yuppies headed to the mountains for a taste of what it was to sleep outside under the black, rainless sky. An easy trip—no snow or ice. Her first time picking up Animal's product. A few hundred thou worth of cocaine, the bag so small it surprised Creeley. The whole payload in a gray Under Armour backpack that a redneck named Murphy jammed beside her Volvo's spare tire.

She remembered Murphy's weasel voice and cigarette breath. "I like these old Volvos. You could jump this fucker off a cliff and live to see Christmas." He slammed the trunk and leaned against her car with his arms crossed. "I ain't never seen you before. You Animal's girl?"

Creeley scratched her sunburned neck and shifted from one foot to the other. Her flip-flops were wearing through, and she felt the heat of the parking lot asphalt through the cheap rubber. They were standing outside an auto body shop, the chemical smell of paint making Creeley want to sneeze or cough. What Creeley was: thirty-nine years old, unwed, poor as shit, and somewhat proud to be a second-shift waitress at Walburn's in downtown Portland.

But no, she was not Animal's girl.

Creeley shook her head.

Murphy lit a cigarette, squinted at her. "Hey, look," he said while blowing smoke through chapped lips, "I'm just asking. I don't want to step on Animal's toes."

"Like, how?"

Murphy ran his tongue across his upper lip. He took another drag. He wasn't a bad-looking guy, but he had a neck tattoo—a small black raven—and a black spot of rot between his upper front teeth. Body slim and hard beneath a greasy white shirt—sculpted by labor and bad luck. He stared at her for a beat too long and said, "By asking you out. I don't want to step on Animal's toes when I ask you out."

"I have a long drive tonight. Back to Portland." Creeley looked away from him and stared at the slow-moving traffic on the roadway. Lifted pickup trucks and tractor trailers carrying uncut lumber. The sun was in the late stages of its arc and dense manzanita and pine glowed purple across the distant mountains. "And besides, I'm not dating anybody. I just got out of a relationship."

Murphy stood there and finished his cigarette, flicked it at her. He raised his left eyebrow when the glowing butt missed Creeley's unguarded feet. He shook his head and curled one side of his mouth. "Well, a bitch says she has to go—I ain't got a mind to stop her. Have a good one," he said, "and don't get caught on the way back." He shoved off from the Volvo and walked toward the auto body shop. Over his shoulder, he said, "See you next month, bitch."

The treatment didn't surprise Creeley. She expected it because being a woman meant being seen as a possession—men thought they deserved her. Or wished they deserved her. At her age, Creeley found this dynamic amusing. She'd stopped being afraid of men a few boyfriends ago, and now she steered clear of them. She'd given up on love.

Didn't exist. Not for her.

Her relationship with men was controllable, under her power and her power alone. Like everything in her life, by-the-fucking-way. That was how she could take a job driving cocaine from one city to another without a second thought. It was how she climbed back into her Volvo—a casual smirk on her lips—and idled out of the parking lot and onto the highway.

But not everything was in her control.

She had a panic attack during the return trip. Forty miles outside town when she looked in the rearview mirror and spotted a Ford Explorer bearing down on her. It was dusk and she recognized the headlights and familiar silhouette of the make and model. Creeley looked at her speedometer, noticed she was eight miles per hour over the limit. They say ten over is safe, but not when you have a load of cocaine. She tapped the brakes and started breathing in uncontrollable bursts. The headlights got closer, and Creeley's hands tinted white as she squeezed the steering wheel. She'd been through panic attacks before—a spat of mental fatigue during her late twenties. She had an abusive boyfriend and got sick of getting her ass kicked. One call and the cops decided Creeley's face was proof enough to put him in the joint. She ran off and never looked back, but a year or so later she got a call from him at her restaurant job. There was no mistaking the voice and the rage. She hung up without speaking, but for months she fought off panic attacks every time a phone rang. So when, at seventy-three miles per hour on an Oregon highway, her breath quickened and her chest tightened like a crushed sheet of tinfoil, Creeley had enough experience to keep her head, to realize she was having a biological response to uncontrollable stimuli. She flipped on her blinker and turned into a gas station, pulled her car beside an open pump. The Explorer—not a trooper, in fact—sped by without slowing. She unlatched her seat belt and put a hand to her chest, tried to bring her breathing under control. By the time the pump attendant reached her window, Creeley could squeeze out instructions for him. A few minutes later she was headed north again, her eyes darting back and forth to the rearview mirror. And with the cruise control set at a hard sixty-eight.

Three more hours and she was parked outside Animal's house in northwest Portland, her Volvo's engine ticking as it cooled from the long drive.

Her first run—a success.

When Creeley started, she didn't know a damn thing.

But she knew a whole bunch after finishing that first run. She knew all the risk was hers, that Animal didn't give two fucks about what happened to her.

Nobody did.

She knew that staying cool was everything, and that her panic attack was a one-time event—Creeley was done being afraid and on the run in her life. Or so she thought.

When Animal put three grand in her hand that night, she made an instant, irrevocable decision.

Creeley Nash decided to be a drug runner.

2/So Many Roads

Red Bull and Cheetos.

Chewing tobacco.

Hot Tamales and Bubble Yum.

5-hour energy mixed with Slurpee.

Limp hot dogs and stale pizza. Cigarettes.

Clove cigarettes.

Punk music. Heavy metal. Delta blues and classic rock. Stravinsky.

Wu-Tang Clan and Tupac. AM talk radio. Rush Limbaugh.

NPR and whatever jazz you can find.

You try it all when you're on the road.

Whatever keeps you awake.

For Creeley, that was the hardest part—keeping her eyes open and on the road. You do twenty straight hours to SLO on the 5 and it's like your pupils are glued to the inside of your brain. You pee at dirty rest stops and look over your shoulder while you fill your tank. You spend half the time praying you won't get a flat tire, the other half certain the highway patrol is on your ass.

The runs back to Portland were the worst. Six figures worth of coke or weed in her trunk and she's half asleep, her Volvo groaning into the mountains. A year in, Creeley invested in another car, a used Toyota 4Runner with 125,000 miles on it. She liked it for the four-wheel drive and high clearance, had too much experience bashing her Volvo through dirt roads and sandy washes.

Animal's people liked remote areas, as far from law enforcement as possible.

Easier to cut coke or cook meth. Easier to bury the bodies.

Or to strangle Creeley when she wasn't looking.

But Animal—well, her affiliation with Animal—protected her. She wasn't to be touched. In fact, it was known that Creeley was trustworthy, dependable. And she never got caught. Since she'd started, two of Animal's other drivers were put away, and it was all because of stupidity.

One guy drove drunk and slammed his Miata into a piñata store on the outskirts of Eugene. Made the local news. The other was picked up in South Dakota by some hot-shit state trooper. The trooper shot him in the leg as he tried to ditch the car near the Montana state line. Neither gave Animal up, but the run of bad luck did concern him. He started sending Creeley on longer runs, knew he could trust her not to fuck up. Creeley didn't stop at strip clubs or get shit-faced while on the highway. She smoked weed to stay relaxed, but that was nothing.

And she never complained to Animal about the money.

No matter where she went or how long it took, Creeley earned three grand.

That was her rate.

And she put it all into a savings account at Portland Credit Union. Creeley had a plan. For now, she was going to drive. But one day, when she had enough, Creeley was going to fly to South America and forget about every shitty thing that ever happened to her.

She was headed for the ex-pat life.

No more ceaseless Portland rain, and no more regret.

Her first long run was into Reno. She met a gangbanger named Rolo outside a rundown casino near the university. As soon as she stepped out of her car, she saw used condoms and empty beer cans.

Rolo drove a lowered Civic with shiny rims, leaned against the driver's side door with his arms crossed. He smiled at her below black Ray-Bans, his face tattoos nearly glowing in the hard Nevada sun. "Dang, Animal sent a girl to do a man's job. Fucking Portland—so progressive, eh?"

Creeley rolled her eyes, raised her chin at him. She had a roll of cash in one hand. "Animal put an extra G into it, said to call it gratuity."

"No shit?"

"It's what he said."

"Okay. *Okay.*" Rolo opened his trunk and lifted a small black rolling suitcase. He placed it on the ground and raised the handle for her. "Your luggage, miss." That smile again. Creeley passed him the money and started for the suitcase, but he caught her hand and squeezed. "My girls call me Rolo. I bet you think that rolls off the tongue, eh?"

"Let me go—now."

"C'mon, girl. Animal ain't shit. Me and you, we—"

The pepper spray hit him in his nose, sent him sprawling back against the car, the wad of cash popping out of his hand. Hundred-dollar bills flapped in the air, floated to the pavement like pigeon feathers.

"You bitch!"

"I told you to let me go." Creeley was back in the car before his vision cleared. Ten minutes later she was on the highway. She called Animal from the road and that was the last time Rolo did business in Oregon. Or Nevada. Animal couldn't have his number one driver getting harassed, not when there was so much money involved. Creeley didn't much like Animal, but he demanded respect—she liked that about him.

She did runs to San Francisco, SLO, eastern Idaho, and the Dakotas. He thought about sending her to Bullhead City, Arizona, but decided to pay two bikers to meet her in Northern Utah. They made the exchange at a Denny's off the highway. She drove a straight twenty-four that time, only stopped for gas and potty breaks.

Creeley liked the road. She loved the sound of rubber on the highway, the hum of her 4Runner as she powered through curves or bounced down a dirt road. All that movement made her feel like she was worth something, like there were people waiting for her somewhere. Never mind that they were drug dealers or smugglers or meth cooks—they were still waiting for her.

And she'd never had that before. Not ever.

No matter where Creeley was headed, there was always

somebody on the other end of the line.

Guaranteed.

That was her life. She watched reality TV and read shitty magazines. Did yoga on Thursdays and drank martinis at a dive bar named Mooch's. She never picked up guys or dated. When she had to, Creeley got off to a Whitesnake album—it was easier that way. And on the weekends she drove. To Reno. To San Fran.

To Boise and to Denver.

It didn't matter where Animal told her to go—Creeley went without protest. She drove. And she drove some more. And she put her money in the bank. At least, until a wet Monday in April, two days after her fortieth birthday.

This time was different.

Because Animal was sending her on a run to Palm Springs.

3/Running South

Crossing into Central California is when Creeley felt it, that emptiness running from her heart, up her throat, and into the back of her head. A few miles north of Monterey, she went blank—pure nothing behind her eyes. The 4 Runner caught road braille and she perked up, steered back into her lane. A tractor trailer passed with a brief honk, the driver looking down on her from the cab with a self-importance that reminded Creeley of attending Mass. She hated priests.

And she hated truck drivers.

Talk about entitled fuck heads.

Out her windshield, she noticed rows of strawberry plants unraveling like green ribbons to the east, rundown houses and trailers flanking the highway. The sky was gray and pockmarked with black thunderheads. The air flowing through the driver's side window—it wouldn't close all the way—promised a wet evening drive.

Fine, Creeley thought, *let it rain before I get to the hellhole that is Palm Springs.* She remembered the city as smothered in heat. No wind or night cooling—just heat and heat and heat. She remembered the motel, too. A dumpy two-story near I-10. One of those travelers motels popular with truck drivers and people on the run.

Creeley Nash left Palm Springs twenty-six years ago.

And she never looked back.

But now the emptiness had returned, what she felt as a fourteen-year-old sleeping on a motel room floor with reruns of *Tom and Jerry* filtering through the wall from the room next door. A callousness—like she had no feelings, no senses to experience the environment around her. She thought of a wind tunnel. Or outer space. What nothingness must be like.

She saw a billboard advertising a roadside bar. Creeley took the next exit and turned north on the frontage road, drove a mile or so, and pulled into the dirt parking lot. She needed to pee and smoke a bowl.

And for the first time on a run for Animal, she wanted a drink.

***

Not a bad-looking bar. Think Paso Robles meets downtown L.A. Stand-up cocktail tables and shuffleboard along one wall. The bar ran the length of the place and featured oiled oak with a brass foot rail. Creeley peed first and took a seat at the bar. It was three in the afternoon, and she was the only customer. The bartender—a short girl with black, boyish hair—handed Creeley a menu.

"Get you a drink?"

"I'll take a glass of red."

"You like Cab, or Pinot?"

"Whatever's fruity." Creeley studied the menu for a minute or two but gave up on it. She planned to eat Doritos and fast food all the way into Southern California. It was cheaper. She wanted one drink, and then she'd be gone.

"Here you go," the bartender said while sliding the wine glass onto the bar. "It's the Pinot. Tastes like raspberries."

Creeley sipped and said, "I get horse piss."

"That, too." The bartender gave Creeley a lopsided smile. Her left cheek had a dimple and it made her look mischievous, a bit like a toddler. "You headed into Monterey? Or going farther south?"

Creeley didn't talk about her drug runs, but the vacancy was spreading inside her, and she needed someone to talk to—a way to stave off her emptiness. And one conversation wouldn't get her caught. She had to drive another five-hundred miles and this would be long forgotten by midnight. "So Cal. I'm headed to Palm Springs."

"I love Palm Springs." Love was the longest word in the sentence. "I go down there with my girls sometimes."

"Oh, yeah? What for?" Creeley knew it was a resort town, but all she remembered was the ratty motel and her drunk mother's ceaseless antics.

"My kids love it. We play in the pool, sit around and watch TV. We just take it as time to relax."

"You have a daughter?"

"Two—six and fourteen. The teenager is getting a little testy, but I kind of love her for it."

Creeley nodded and said, "I'm happy for you."

"Thanks. You got kids?"

Creeley shook her head. "No, but the last time I saw my mom, I was fourteen and we were in Palm Springs."

The bartender scratched one cheek with a dirty fingernail. "Oh, shit. I'm sorry. Didn't mean to throw that at you. Are you headed back to see her?"

Creeley smiled at that. "Fuck no. My mom was a drunk. And she turned tricks. If I never see her again, that'll be the best thing that ever happened to me."

The bartender shrugged and said, "Shit, I hope you never see her again. Sorry for bringing it up."

"Don't worry about it." Creeley gulped her entire glass of wine, raised it in mock salute. "I've enjoyed your company."

***

Back on the road, night coming down like theater curtains, rain hitting the windshield, Creeley thought about the bartender. Here she was, working a blue-collar job, and she took her daughters down to Palm Springs for vacation. Creeley wasn't jealous, but it made her see the contrast—she'd had it rough as a kid and she didn't deserve it.

But it happened.

Like a lot of things in Creeley's life.

Well, look at me now, she thought. *I'm a drug runner for a loser named Animal.*

Oh, how the downtrodden do rise.

Ahead of her, a tractor trailer changed lanes, churned rain up into a thick mist. Creeley moved over and sped up, needed to jump the speed limit to pass. She made it and got back into the slow lane. She was trying to avoid it, but in her head a thought was churning like a final puddle of dirty bathwater. She kept thinking: *I wonder what happened to my mom.* But the thought made Creeley sick to her stomach. And it wasn't that she cared. She wondered, out of bitter curiosity, but that was it. And, no, she didn't plan on finding her mom. She planned to pick up the package for Animal. She planned to drop some money to one of Animal's network guys. And she planned to drive her ass back to Portland.

But the thought kept churning. Like a bad song on a hit record.

4/History Lesson: Running North

Creeley watched the wind turbines from the motel roof. She was sitting in a cheap lawn chair, curled up in a ratty blanket. A boy named Sly showed her how to climb from the motel's second floor—one foot outside the railing and a strong hand on the rain gutter, two pulls and you were over the top. He took her up there for a kiss, ended up with a hand job and a grin. Creeley didn't mind. She liked boys, and it was easy to make them happy. Sly was kind of a prick, but he liked The Replacements and knew how to roll a joint.

The hand job was worth it.

Besides, he left her alone after that.

Creeley spent her days at the motel. Her nights were spent on the roof or wandering the surrounding streets—mostly warehouses and offices for construction businesses. There was a biker bar two blocks north. Creeley spent a lot of time there, too. She hung around and watched for somebody who might buy her a six-pack or a bottle of cheap wine.

Tonight was no different. Her mom was in their room with some guy. A creeper. He wore his sideburns long, like an Elvis impersonator. Pulled up on a Harley. She didn't deny that he had a good body. His arms were thick muscle, and he wore tight blue jeans. And when he walked into their room, he ignored Creeley's mom.

It was clear—he was interested in Creeley.

Yep, another creeper.

Creeley grabbed her purse and walked out, slammed the door behind her. And she climbed onto the roof. In the darkness, tall wind turbines spun against a light wind. The motel was north of Palm Springs and Creeley knew from a TV show that this was one of the windiest places on earth. Some days the wind blew her hair into her face, and she couldn't hold her skirt down to cover her panties. Tonight it wasn't bad. A light breeze, but the windmills still churning against the rippled outline of mountains. She smelled cigarette smoke. Heard the hum of the interstate. It wasn't quiet here, but it was somehow peaceful. At least, it was peaceful until the boys climbed onto the roof. One of them, Ryan, was about ten—a little punk who stole from the convenience store. The other, Creeley's age, was called Paul and didn't talk much. Their dad was a truck driver and he was there for a training course. The boys ran wild no matter where he was. Creeley tried to ignore them, but Ryan said, "Are you that girl on the first floor?"

"No, I'm that girl on the roof." She saw the hint of a smile enter Paul's face.

The little one shrugged and said, "Whatever."

Creeley said, "What do you guys want?"

"You got any weed?" The little guy again.

"No. Do you?"

"Go fuck yourself." He flipped her off and climbed back over the side of the motel, disappeared. Creeley could hear his footsteps as he ran off to cause hell.

Paul cleared his throat and said, "I think you're pretty."

"Thanks."

"Sorry about my brother."

"I don't give a shit," Creeley said.

"My daddy says he's got some screws loose."

"No shit."

"He just eats too much sugar, if you ask me." Paul sat in a lawn chair next to Creeley, pulled his feet onto the chair and sat on them. He wore slip-on Vans caked in mud.

"Do you come up here a lot?"

"Nope. Saw you do it."

Creeley nodded and said, "I always try to come up when nobody's looking."

"I get bored and watch out the window. I saw you go past and we went ahead and followed you." Paul ran a hand through his black hair. He sneezed.

"That's creepy."

"I have allergies."

"Not that—you followed me."

He shrugged. "I don't know. Maybe. My dad says girls like it when you make them feel wanted. He told me I should go after any girl I want to bang."

"Wow. Any girl you want to bang?"

"Yeah, like, do it with her."

"I know what bang means, Paul. Have you ever had sex?"

"Have you?"

Creeley looked at him and rolled her eyes. "What do you think?"

Paul was quiet for a moment, but said, "Yeah, I guess."

"Too many times to count." In reality, Creeley was a virgin. She'd done stuff, yeah, but she wasn't a slut. She wanted her first time to be with somebody she loved. Somebody older.

"Sorry. I didn't mean to—"

"It's fine, Paul." She reached out and grabbed his hand. It was clammy. Cold. Caked with dirt. He squeezed her fingers. "Have you ever done...stuff?"

"Like, what?"

"I don't know, like, finger banged a girl?"

"No. I mean, yeah. I think so."

She looked at him again and giggled. "I think you'd know if you finger banged a girl. It's pretty obvious."

"I had a girlfriend in Indiana."

"Is that the one you finger banged?"

Paul grinned. "I think so."

She squeezed his hand. "Whatever."

"I did."

"Sure."

"If you don't believe me—"

"I believe you."

Paul cleared his throat. "Hey, what're you living here for?"

Creeley thought that was a good question. She didn't know

the answer, so she said, "My mom's a drunk and she has to bang guys to make money."

They were silent for a long time. The wind churned the windmills and stars blinked against the black sky. From below, sounds of motel life reminded them where they were: Car doors slamming. The bump of bass from a rap song. A woman's drunk laughter.

A loud big rig passed on the highway.

"You should run away," Paul said.

"Where to?"

"Anywhere. You can get on a bus for cheap. Or a train—that's free. You just have to hop on when they stop."

"I don't have money."

"Who cares?" Paul said. "You can steal food. Or just, beg for it. I know people who make money by the highway. That guy with the green sign? He makes, like, a hundred bucks every single fucking day."

"Bull. Shit."

"Ask him. A hundred bucks. I swear—he loaned my dad money for gas the other night."

That got Creeley thinking. She imagined herself on a Greyhound bus, the highway spinning beneath her as she headed for New York or Chicago. Florida, maybe. She saw pictures of Key West in a magazine and wanted to go there.

"Does the train stop here?"

"Sure," Paul said. "Across the interstate. Every once in a while they stop to let another train pass."

"How do I know when?"

"You just have to wait there overnight, I guess. You have to get lucky and have one train stop to let the other pass."

Okay, Creeley thought. *Okay. I can do that.*

I can wait.

***

Two nights later, Creeley trudged through the desert toward the train tracks. Sand spilled into her flats, and the wind kicked it into her eyes. Paul trailed behind her, his breath coming out in violent huffs. "Slow down," he said. "Come on, Creeley—I can't keep up."

Creeley didn't look back at him. Instead, she put her head down and tried to run. The desert air was filled with the fragrant scent of creosote. An army of windmills churned high above, at a height that seemed halfway to the moon. The power coursing through their foreign, mechanical guts buzzed like a cloud of mad locusts. It wasn't lost on Creeley that she could have been a girl running through the twisted world of a forgotten fairy tale. She still did not want to stop.

"Creeley! Hey!"

But Paul couldn't keep up with her. She grunted in anger and stopped, turned to face him with her hands planted on her hips. "What, Paul?" He was facedown in the sand, her other bag— the bigger one—weighing him down like a gray planet dropped from the sky. "Oh, shit." She trudged over, ripped the bag off, and helped him stand. "You know, Paul, if you want to impress girls, you might want to do some push-ups. I don't like a bunch of muscles or anything, but—"

"This bag is fucking heavy. How many magazines do you have in here?" He brushed dirt off himself, picked some cactus out of his bare elbow. "And why don't you just—"

"I told you. I'm not leaving my magazines."

He stared at her with his squinty green eyes and said, "Fine. I get it." He hefted the bag, swung it across his shoulders with a gasp. "We're almost there anyway."

She started moving toward the train tracks again. They'd hitched a ride over the interstate from a tow truck driver and had to run from the fucker after he laid a hand on Creeley's thigh. Paul dragged her out of the truck, grabbed her pack, and they hoofed it across an empty parking lot. When Creeley looked back over her shoulder, the tow truck was gone, its taillights blinking at her like an animal receding into the darkness. Creeley turned around and faced Paul again—he almost smacked into her. She grabbed him by the ears. "You know, I can take care of myself."

"I know that. I didn't mean—"

"You just wanted to be my hero."

"No—the guy was a creep. I just wanted to get out of there."

"Well, don't try to save me again."

"Okay, shit. How am I—"

Creeley silenced him with a kiss. It was awkward and wet, as pleasant as pulling off a leech. She turned and started running, heard his violent breath and footsteps behind her. Running that night in the desert was the first time Creeley felt free, as if she was her own person. It was the first time she had the sense that—no matter what she was born into—there was a way to something different, maybe better. Looking back, it might have been the surrealism of running through a forest of giant wind turbines. Or it might have been kissing Paul—she'd never kissed a boy before. Creeley had only ever been kissed and, in some way she couldn't describe, this felt different to her. As she ran, sand flew out in front of her and the wind pulled her ponytail free. By the time she got to the train tracks, there was sand in her mouth and hair and ears. She looked both directions down the tracks—there were two sets—and she saw nothing but darkness.

Endless darkness east and west into the desert.

Paul's breath came fast and irregular behind her.

"What the fuck?"

"What?" Paul coughed twice, breathed deep as he tried to catch his breath. "What's wrong?"

"There's no fucking train."

"I said around midnight. Usually. I mean, there's no guarantee that a train will—"

"You promised." She turned to face him, put one hand on her mouth. *Did I really kiss this boy?*

"I guess. I mean, if we wait long enough, I'm sure a train will come by." He dropped her big gray duffel and sat down on it. He looked up at her with squinted eyes, his shoulders moving up and down with his hurried breath. "All we have to do is wait, you know?"

"All we have to do is wait?" She was irritated.

"Yeah, look." Paul got down on his knees, put his head on one rail of the train tracks. "Like this."

"What the fuck are you doing, Paul?"

"I'm listening for the train."

"What the hell are you talking about?"

"This is how you know when a train is coming—you can hear it roaring through the tracks."

He looked like another crazy person to Creeley. Like her mother buying thirty cans of tomato paste at Pic 'N' Save because it was the cheapest thing she could find. Like the creeper who rode the Harley shouting at the news on the motel TV. And there was Paul, putting his head on the train tracks.

Why the fuck not?

"Are your eyes closed?"

Paul nodded without opening them and said, "Get down here and listen—I think one's on the way."

Creeley thought for an instant about running the other direction. Away from Paul and her bag of magazines. Away from the train tracks and the forest of wind turbines. Away from the train that—she was certain—would come at one time or another. But Creeley didn't want to run anymore.

She wanted to hitch a ride.

She got down on her knees and put her ear to the rail.

It took some concentration, but Creeley heard it: a low-pitched whir burning through steel—a solitary call reaching across vast acres of desert.

Miles away, from either the east or west, a train was coming to meet her.

✳✳✳

It came at them like thunder, the train from the west, one headlight hammering through the darkness. When she saw the light, the train was rounding a bend, and the sound coming through the rail filled her head. As it approached, Creeley stood, hefted her backpack, and swung it over one shoulder. She reached for the duffel, but Paul grabbed it from her. "Give it to me, Paul."

"You have to wait for another train."

"What? Why?"

"So they slow down. So one stops."

"Paul—I know I kissed you, but—"

"I'm serious. You need two trains."

Creeley wanted to punch him, but then she heard the horn: the rounded tone of a train horn. It came twice from the east. Both Paul and her looked toward the sound, saw the other locomotive coming straight at them by the yellow flame of its headlight. Creeley said, "If you're lucky, you might get another kiss. But I need you to help me get on one of these trains."

Paul swiveled his head to look at the other train. It hadn't made much progress toward them. "That's the one," he said. "It's stopping." He started to run.

And it was Creeley who followed.

They reached the stopped train as the other bore down on them, its horn filling the air with long blasts. The sound of all that steel and machinery was like a season of thunder. Creeley couldn't hear anything but the beast-like roar. Paul circled them outside the locomotive's powerful light. They stumbled through deep sand and head-high creosote, the wind turbines now a quarter mile behind them—steel blades still cutting at the air. Paul slowed, led her through the dark with the precise movements of a practiced thief. As the oncoming train began to pass on the far side of the stopped locomotive, he crouched and motioned her toward him.

He had to shout at her: "You see that car right there?" He dipped his head at a brown boxcar halfway down the line of train cars.

Creeley gulped, licked her lips. Sand got in her mouth and she swallowed it. "Yeah—I see that one."

The moving train—now invisible behind the stopped one—reached its end and shot east away from them. With it, the thunder subsided.

Paul said, "As soon as the train starts moving we run toward it. I can help boost you up. As soon as you get in, I'll throw this duffel up behind you. We have to move fast and once you start running, don't stop."

Creeley stared at the dark shape of the train and thought about where it was headed—she didn't know. "When do I get off the damn thing?"

"When you're far enough away and it stops."

"How far is far enough?"

Paul looked at her with steady eyes. "I don't know. Just ride it until you can't ride it anymore. Until it changes directions, runs north as far as it goes."

Creeley bit her bottom lip, felt tears on her cheeks.

The train began to creak and shudder. Bit by bit, the long snake of a machine began to move.

Paul said, "Now."

They ran.

Halfway to the train, Creeley fell and landed face-first in a small bush. Paul's hands grabbed her, lifted her to her feet. She pulled twigs from her hair and face as she ran. More long strides and she was running alongside the train, her backpack hopping back and forth across her shoulder blades.

The thunder-sound started, and the train's wheels sounded like gears crushing bird bones.

Paul screamed at her, "Get up! Now!"

She darted in front of him, put her hands on the wooden floor of the open boxcar. She felt Paul's hand planted on her ass, felt the boost he gave her as she twisted into the car. She rolled onto her side, looked back at Paul. The duffel flew up and landed next to her in a cloud of dust.

"Paul, wait."

"Go! Just go!"

She reached down for him, brushed his cheek with a hand.

The train was moving then, and Paul vanished into the darkness of the desert. Thunder in her ears, Creeley watched the sandy landscape and jutting wind turbines slip past her. When she fell back into the darkness of the boxcar and crossed her legs to rest, she saw something that surprised her: in the deep recesses of the boxcar, an orange pin of light burned and vanished.

It happened again.

Somebody was smoking a cigarette.

5/Destinations

After four hundred miles down the highway spine of California, Creeley's 4Runner rattled out of the Inland Empire, veered southwest toward the desert. She twisted the stereo volume higher, sang along to "Hotel California" for the fifth time in a row. She followed endless trails of red taillights, rubbed her eyes with sticky fingers. Now, an hour from her destination, the fatigue ached to her bones. She grabbed her phone from the passenger seat and pulled up Animal's text message, drifted into the slow lane so she had time to read.

She was supposed to pick up the package in Joshua Tree.

"Hey, Girl. My boy's address is in JT. 3274 Creosote Road. Get a package from him. Candy and bones. When you pick that shit up text me. I can hit you with the other place."

Creeley managed to punch the address into her map app while she kept her eyes on the big rig in front of her. She had forty-five minutes to go and as she tossed the phone aside, she saw the looming fingers of wind turbines up ahead. Their frames were illuminated by the blinking red signal lights along their tops—momentary warnings for helicopters. Like eyes in the night. The sight took her back to the night she hopped the train west and rode it until it headed north. She remembered sliding through a dark sandy night, past the looming San Jacinto peak. She saw the mountain now, a jagged pyramid reaching so high that she couldn't see the peak from her driver's seat. She remembered watching the mountain recede and, after a long time, vanish. She rode the train through the urban jungle of Los Angeles, and she made a friend—the boy who smoked cigarettes.

But that memory was for another time.

For now, she needed to get to the package.

Coke, for sure.

Weed, she bet.

Fentanyl, maybe.

The GPS sent her north onto Highway 62. She drove through a wretched wind, made a mountain pass of tight switchbacks. Soon, she was driving east through a one-stoplight town of gas stations and a few small convenience stores. Another long grade and she passed through a larger town—Walmart and Pizza Hut and Home Depot. She found herself again driving across expansive desert and made Joshua Tree with its cute antique shops and coffee joints. She passed the Joshua Tree Inn—didn't a rock star die there?—and the GPS turned her north onto Creosote. It was a dirt road and the 4Runner plowed through a sandy wash, climbed a berm without trouble. Creeley lowered the volume on her radio, flipped on her high beams. The road weaved through Joshua trees and creosote, climbed a steep grade, and descended into a ravine.

Fuck, Creeley thought. *Here I am paying a house call on another weirdo living out in Bumfuck, Egypt. Another weirdo in a long line of weirdos. Drug people. Fiends and fuck-ups.* Like her.

But maybe it was worth it—Animal said he'd pay her double for this trip.

That might make it worth it.

She bounced the 4Runner across another rutted wash and saw the outline of a house in the distance. As she approached, she noticed a single-wide trailer off to the right of the house, two lifted K5 Blazers parked at angles to each other. The house itself was one story, brick and mismatched stucco holding up a corrugated metal roof. There was no chimney, but instead, a black stovepipe spitting smoke. A wood-burning stove, maybe. The yard was strewn with engine parts and stacks of rotting tires. She also spotted a cord of firewood piled against the left side of the house, a chainlink dog run between the single-wide and the house. Inside, a large pit bull paced and barked. She flipped off her high beams and stopped beside one of the Blazers. She kept the 4Runner running and put it in reverse. After sitting for a minute, she watched the front door swing open—a skinny guy, shirtless, came out into the yard. He wore flip-flops and ripped jeans, a patchwork of tattoos covered his chest and shoulders. There was a pistol shoved into his waistband, just above the crotch. The pit bull kept barking and he turned and screamed at it to shut the fuck up. He squinted at Creeley's 4Runner, lifted a hand, and motioned her to get out of the truck.

She shifted into park and flipped the ignition.

✳✳✳

Tweakers.

Addicts.

Mutts.

Douchebags.

Creeley had seen it all, and these two fucks might be the worst. All of that combined. The skinny guy smirked at her and flopped onto a ratty pleather couch. He put his arms behind his head and laughed at a silent episode of *The Simpsons* playing on a huge flat-screen TV. The other guy, another skinny fuck in a flannel shirt and board shorts, nodded at her and pressed a joint to his lips. He took a long toke and held it for a minute, coughed out the smoke in violent spasms. He leaned back in his recliner and closed one eye to check Creeley out as she stood next to the half-open front door. Creeley said, "You got my package ready?"

The toker looked her up and down, lingered on her boobs. She was thankful for her dirty flannel shirt and baggy jeans. Just what she needed, another boner trying to dick her down while she was working. In her right hip pocket, she had a canister of pepper spray. She put a hand in the pocket, wrapped her fingers around the canister.

The toker said, "Damn girl. You fine."

Creeley rolled her eyes. "I'm asking about the package."

"I got your package right here." He put his hand to his crotch, gave her a gap-toothed smile and cackle.

"Leave her alone, Jimmy." The other guy sat up and squinted at her. "You want a beer or something?"

Creeley said, "I'm good. Look, Animal wanted me to—"

"Creeley? Is that you?"

She felt her stomach drop. She squeezed the pepper spray, brought the canister out of her pocket. "I don't know you." She tried to place his face. He was lean, gaunt, unhealthy as a street addict. His cheeks almost outlined his molars. His eyes were deep-set and dark, black hair falling loosely over them. She tried to discern his tattoos, but they seemed vaguely tribal—that was all she could see. Her sense of situational awareness heightened. The room smelled like burned pizza and beer. She didn't hear anybody down the hall or in the kitchen. Outside, the pit bull barked at phantoms of the night. Creeley moved backward toward the door, held the pepper spray out like it was a pistol.

"Oh, shit," the toker said. "You scared her."

"I'm just here for Animal's shit. You two fucks better—"

"It's me, Creeley," the skinny guy said. He stood and held his shaking hands out to her. "It's me. It's Paul."

***

They sat at the kitchen table, a lopsided candle burning between them. Creeley had a bottle of Corona in one hand, the pepper spray in the other. Paul was drinking Corona, too, his bottle emptying faster than hers.

"Sorry about the light in here," he said. "We got a short somewhere and the kitchen is fucked."

"Looks like this place needs some work." Creeley glanced at the dishes piled in the sink, brought her eyes back to Paul's.

He shook his head, tapped the Corona with his index finger. "Hey, I don't live here. I mean, this isn't my place. I'm just here because, you know, I'm watching the drugs."

Creeley shrugged and said, "I'm not here to judge you, Paul. Look at me—I'm in the same boat." She did recognize him, but the years did not wear well on him. He was missing teeth and the right side of his face was laced with knife scars. Somehow, his eyes seemed lopsided, or maybe it was something with his misshapen nose. Still, there was a handsomeness to him, like a pretty boy convict who'd seen better days. "To be honest, I just need the package and—"

"I always wondered where you got off that train."

Creeley closed her eyes, saw the boy with the cigarettes. His pale face, the sunken hollows of his eyes. She smelled his body odor and smoke spirit. She opened her eyes again and drank some beer. "It's a long story."

"I bet."

"Never got to thank you, though. For putting me on the train, I mean. Not sure I was better off, but you know how it goes." She leaned back in her chair, tried to relax. The toker was still in the living room. She heard him chuckle at a Spanish telenovela on the TV.

"Yeah. I know how it goes. Hey, you were the first girl I ever kissed. Can you believe that?"

"Bull...Shit."

He smiled, dipped his tongue over his bottom lip. "No fucking kidding. My first kiss." He laughed with a gasoline rattle in his throat. "Shit. Almost thirty years ago, man..."

Creeley couldn't believe it—almost thirty fucking years.

He eyeballed her then, his lips moving beneath his misshapen nose. "So, you get into the life?"

"You mean—"

"Matter of fact, don't tell me. I don't need to know. I did a few years upstate. Taxpayer-funded education, I call it. Studied the Bible while I was in. Waste of fucking time. Got out and found Jimmy." He tilted his head toward the toker. "We got set up with a guy and here we are, sucking down Coronas and watching Nick at Nite. You proud of me?" He gave her the grin and finished his beer.

"What was it?"

"Huh?"

"That put you inside."

Paul scratched the back of his neck, ran his hand to his tattooed stomach. Prison tats—the Grim Reaper and Jesus and a half-devil, half-Harley-Davidson. All connected by the tribal shit Creeley could see before she got up close to him. "Eh. I got in trouble with a girl. Big surprise. I did my ten, though." He put the empty Corona bottle to his forehead. "Did 'em like a heavyweight champ. Got the scars to prove it." He ran the bottle to his scarred cheek, set it back on the table. "You want another one?"

Creeley took a sip. "I got to drive and—"

"One more." He stood and got two bottles from the fridge, popped both caps with his teeth, handed her one, and sat. "Sorry they got warm—fucking house."

She finished her first one, started on the second. The beer was about room temperature, but it tasted good after so long on the road. She liked the tingle she felt in her knees. Too little food and too little sleep, she figured.

"Hey, I was sorry to hear about your mom." He said it without looking at her, his gaze pointed toward the TV noises in the living room.

"What? What about her?"

Paul's gaze swung back like a double-barrel shotgun, centered on her. "You don't know?"

"Know what?"

"Oh, shit."

"What the fuck—what is it?"

"Hey, look, I didn't know I was going to be—"

"Tell it to me. What happened?"

Paul stared at her with unsteady eyes. He twisted his Corona bottle in his hands and looked away toward the dark kitchen window. The pit bull was barking again. The noise from the television seemed louder, more frantic. A cop show now, with gunfire and shouting. Paul tilted his head to a shoulder, shivered. "It's not on me to tell you."

"What's that mean?"

"It means someone else should have said."

"Who the fuck else, Paul? Who?"

"Man, I never thought getting you on that train would lead to all this. I never thought I was doing something—"

"Lead to what, Paul? Be a man and spit it out."

The words got his eyes back on her. He chuckled under his breath, as if he couldn't believe his bad luck. "I can't believe you never heard about this."

Creeley waited.

"About a year after you ran away, that's when it happened. I saw it in the papers. Your mom got sent to the joint—murder one. Shit, Creeley. Your mom killed a teenage boy down in Palm Springs. Your mom murdered somebody. She's in the joint right now—hard time, and it's life."

6/The Joint

Creeley slept in a Walmart parking lot that night. Used the package—a black duffel that she didn't open—for a pillow in the back of the 4Runner. She woke up at least a dozen times. Gave up sleeping and ended up on the road at 5 a.m., a cup of hot 7-Eleven coffee burning her hand. Now she was headed west on Interstate 10—her destination the women's state prison in Chino. The night before, she didn't hang around and talk to Paul. He gave her his cell number, but she got out of there without saying much.

Truth was, she was shocked.

And she didn't know why, but hearing about her mom did something to Creeley. It scrambled her insides somehow, messed with her head. She pulled into the Walmart lot and a quick internet search on her phone gave her the details.

Blossom Nash, 36, apprehended for the murder of a boy, 17, in Palm Springs, California. The year was 1996 and the murder occurred at a trashy motel off the strip—South Palm Canyon. She couldn't get many details because most of the information was in archived newspaper articles, and back then they didn't hit the internet as hard as they did these days. She found a few article excerpts on the *L.A. Times* website.

The kid was strangled with his own belt.

Blossom was picked up on eyewitness testimony and connected to the kid by other physical evidence.

Bottom line? She did it.

And Creeley found out one other thing: Blossom Nash was a permanent resident of the women's state prison in Chino.

It surprised Creeley to be drawn to see her mother, but she was. Part of it, she had to admit, was the vengeance in seeing her mother locked up, put away for life without parole. But there was also the magnetic pull of wanting to see and know the woman who gave birth to her. Creeley didn't want to think about that as the 4Runner screamed down the interstate, but the thought circled her head like a fly spinning inside a glass of piss. *You knew your mom and she was a whore. A slut who worked for crack cocaine and cheap boxed wine. Sure, she got her share of rough stuff, but she treated you like a second-rate pet—she treated you like a dog.*

And that's why you left her.

And it's why you never went back.

But still, you always had a longing to know her.

Didn't you?

"Shit," Creeley said as she switched on the radio, searched for classic rock. She heard Kenny Wayne Shepherd and stopped searching. Listened to all the ways blue went onto black. She remembered the bruises her mom wore like tattoos—ink stains on her neck, her shoulders, her inner thighs. A collage of stains twisting and transforming and shifting across the cream-white surface of her skin. But Creeley thought, too, of her own life. *You make this world whatever you want. It's up to you. And if you're a whore? Maybe you chose to be a whore.* Of course, Creeley wasn't sure that was true for everybody, but for her mom? Yeah, it was the case.

So what was this? What was she doing?

Creeley watched the highway and felt the fly spinning in the piss of her thoughts—*you never said goodbye.*

And that's what you want to do.

You want to say goodbye.

✳✳✳

She got Animal's first text at 7 a.m.

"Hey girl. You get my package?"

Creeley read the message and tossed the phone into the passenger seat. She didn't know what to tell Animal. *I'm taking a personal day, motherfucker. You'll get your shit when you get it. Say it like that? Yeah, right.*

Her phone buzzed again.

"Connect said you been gone a few hours. WTF?"

Fuck you, Animal. I'm going to handle some personal shit.

"You supposed to text me when you pick that shit up."

I know that, but I'm about to—

"I need you to take some shit to Palm Springs."

Fuck.

"If you're on the road, turn your ass around. And get back at me. Girl, I ain't trying to send nobody to get your ass."

Shit. Creeley shifted lanes, pulled off at the next ramp. She parked at a Shell station and spent ten minutes writing and deleting texts back to Animal. She settled on:

"Had to rest. Just got up. Everything's good. You got an address or what?" She watched the empty gas station while waiting for a reply. The guy who ran the gas station store walked out and limped to the sidewalk. He lit a cigarette and watched the station while he puffed. Creeley's phone buzzed.

"I told you to get at me after you picked the shit up."

Creeley rolled her eyes and responded, "Told you I got tired. I'm sorry. Where you want me to go?"

"Them guys fuck with you?"

"No."

"You tell me if they did?"

"Yeah. They were all good. Just needed to rest." The smoker took a deep puff and exhaled a cloud of smoke. A big rig came down the ramp, stopped with a long squeal of brakes. The rig made a right, shuddered away down the street. Creeley added, "Where you want me?"

"Alright girl. Go to Palm Springs. South Palm Springs. Text me when you're in the area. I'll get you more info then. That cool?"

Shit. Now he was going to micromanage her. *Fuck.* Creeley was going to have to make up a lie. What, she didn't know. For now, she'd put it off. "Okay. Will text when I get there. Sorry about last night." Radio silence while the smoker limped back into his store. Creeley sighed and licked her chapped lips. She was going to need an energy drink, maybe more. This was going to be a long fucking day. Maybe she should abandon her plan to see Blossom, follow Animal's instructions instead. That would put all this shit behind her.

But no. She couldn't do that.

This day was going to be the closing of the loop.

It was the end.

For real.

She looked at her phone as Animal's last text hit. "Cool. Talk soon girl. Be safe."

I'll try, but no fucking guarantees.

***

"I didn't do it, Creeley."

Imagine it. You haven't seen your mom in a quarter century and the first words out of her mouth declare her innocence. Because in some parallel universe, maybe, your mom never made a mistake. Never left you in a motel room with snack bags of Cheetos and a liter of cheap wine. Never made you sleep on the floor so she could turn a trick with a lumber trucker from Reno. Never gave a blow job in a dive bar bathroom stall while you played with your dolly on a dirty tile floor. Never shot her arm full of crank while you watched *Tom and Jerry* on a black-and-white with no sound.

Never strangled a teenager in a rundown road motel in Palm Springs, California.

Never. Never. Never.

Because she's innocent.

Creeley held the phone receiver to her ear, watched an old woman run a wrinkled hand through chicken-wire hair. They were sitting opposite each other, nothing but glass between them. Blossom had crow's-feet around her eyes, smoking wrinkles stretching from her thin lips. She was missing an upper incisor, black rot growing between her other teeth. Her eyes were the same—green and darting and fearful.

Like a vagrant dog's eyes.

Like a crook's.

A whore's.

"I should have guessed you'd say that." Creeley sighed,

adjusted her flannel shirt. She was still uncomfortable from her journey into the prison—metal detectors and probing hands and bland eyes looking at her with vague pity.

"You the one that ran off." Blossom's eyes bounced from her daughter to the beige walls, back and forth. Pinball eyes. She was jittery like a crackhead. "Didn't even tell nobody."

"Why would I tell you?"

Blossom coughed hard, wiped her mouth with the back of her hand. She spit her next words into the receiver. "I'm your momma, girl. Don't matter you like it or not."

Creeley leaned back in her chair, wrinkled her nose at the smell of body odor. She was in a row of other visitors, and she was the only woman. All the other women were prisoners. She looked back at her mother and said, "Why'd you even have a kid, Blossom?"

"Like I always told you—it was a happy accident."

Creeley nodded and bit her bottom lip. What in the fuck was she doing here? What in the living fuck was she thinking? She scratched the back of her neck and said, "The only reason I came, it's to say goodbye. Forever. I never got the chance back then and I—"

"You might not want to face it, but you need me."

"I need you?"

"I'm your momma. A girl always needs her momma."

Creeley smirked. "I did just fine without you."

"The fuck you have."

Some fucking people, Creeley thought. *Some fucking people.* She put her elbows on the booth, got her face up close to the glass. "Everything I ever ate, I got it myself. And I never fucked for a high, Blossom. Shit, I never even fucked for money. I bet you can't get your head around that."

Heads turned toward them.

Blossom laughed as if she had no conscience, let it run out of her like a worship song. When she was done, she said, "Ain't you just a good little girl? Never fucked for a fix, huh? What the hell you even fuck for then?"

Creeley squinted, shook her head. "For the fun of it, bitch." She crossed her arms, held the receiver with a shoulder pressed to her ear. The room was quieter. A bit like a church confessional. Or a hospital room.

That gave Blossom another chance to laugh.

Creeley said, "Jesus Christ."

Blossom nodded and crossed herself. "Look, girl—I know what you think of me. And that's just fine. I guess I treated you pretty bad. But I did my best, as bad as that was. But that ain't the thing that matters no more—"

"Not to you, maybe."

"Or to any-fucking-one, Creeley. You still living back there, twenty-five, thirty years ago? Here's what matters, what's going to make a difference in your life." Blossom crouched, put her cracked lips to the window. "I didn't fucking do it."

"You're innocent."

Blossom leaned back in her chair, shrugged. "As a virgin bobbing for apples. I didn't fucking do it."

"Sure you didn't, Blossom."

"It wasn't me."

"They set you up."

"Fuck yes, they did."

Creeley chuckled. She replaced the receiver, shook her head in disbelief. She stood and spun toward the door without looking at her mother. She walked toward the guard standing there who opened the door for her. When she got halfway through the doorway, Creeley turned for one last look at her mother.

Blossom mouthed a last sentence with the exaggerated lip movements of a stage actress.

I. Did. Not. Do. It.

7/Animal Control

On the highway again.

Biting her nails as she drove, Creeley watched the cell phone on the passenger seat, waited for it to light up with a text from Animal. At this point, she'd been missing in action with Animal's shit for, what, twelve hours? Enough time for him to think Creeley was fucking him. Enough time for him to think she was down in Mexico. Or headed across the country for some small southern town. A place where she wouldn't be recognized. A place where nobody asked personal questions.

Creeley thought about doing it.

That was for damn sure.

She thought about it a lot.

But she got the sense—for some fucking reason—that she wouldn't be running from anything for quite a while. Her whole life had been running. And now it was time to stop, to get through this last trip and call it. Take her money and find a place to knuckle down and suffer like everybody else. Be a regular person. Or close to it.

This thing with her mom—fucking Blossom—brought Creeley to realize: No matter what it is that got you running, you can't escape it. You can bet it'll come back around to peck you on the ass, maybe take a big fucking bite.

Like never escaping her fuck-up of a mother.

A highway sign told her Palm Springs was thirty miles east.

And her cell phone lit up, dinged at her.

She picked it up and scanned the message:

"Girl, you better call me."

"Alright, fuck," Creeley said. The next off-ramp put her at a Mobile station in some highway town. She didn't know where she was, but it was time to get this shit out of the way. She switched off the 4Runner, took a deep breath, and tapped the number for Animal's current burner phone. He answered after one ring.

"I'm sorry."

"Creeley—what the fuck?"

"I told you—"

"Palm Springs ain't that far from Joshua Tree. I know this: You better have my fucking money. And you better have my fucking drugs."

"Have I ever not had your shit when I got back to you?"

He chuckled. "I've heard that before. It works okay, until you don't show up. Am I right?"

"I'm not stupid, Animal." Creeley spun her key ring around her index finger. He sounded pissed, but not pissed enough to put a hit on her. No, Animal preferred to have his shit. And it occurred to her that she—in a way—had the upper hand on him. She had his stuff, and he didn't know where the fuck she was. Her burner phone wasn't easy to track—that was the whole point. In case the cops picked her up or went after phone records or whatever. "You know I'm honest," she said. "I just want my end, as soon as I get back."

"Tomorrow afternoon," he said. "Early. You're going to drop the money and drive your ass up here. Straight through the night. That's the only thing I can—"

"I might have to stop somewhere."

"The fuck do you mean, you might stop somewhere? You stop where I fucking tell you to stop, Creeley."

"It's family business."

He was silent for an abnormal duration of time. But then he repeated, deadpan, "Family business."

"Yeah—a place I got to see."

"A—"

"One of the tweakers from yesterday...I knew him from way back. He knew me when I was a kid and—"

"All you got to do," Animal interrupted with a growl, "is drive your ass back down there. After, mind you, I get my shit delivered. Only reason I'm still talking to you, the way you did this, is because we've done good work together."

"I hear you."

"Do you, Creeley?" She could hear him biting and sucking on his lips. He did that when he was pissed. "So one of my guys, a hardcore tweaker by the way, feeds you some line and you're all up on him like a riverbank slut—"

"Animal—that is not what the fuck this is."

"Okay. What then? I've known enough bitches in my life to catch on when one gets hooked on a dick."

"Fuck you, Animal."

"Fuck you for carrying my drugs and money around with you, who the fuck knows where."

Creeley unlatched her seat belt, pulled her bare feet up under her butt. "He knew my mom—he told me something about my mom. It's not what you think."

"Where the fuck have you been?"

"Chino. The women's correctional center."

Animal laughed, said with a tinge of curiosity, "You been in the joint today?"

"Yeah."

"For what?"

"I went to see my mom." Creeley saw Blossom's wrinkled face, remembered her mouthing the words declaring her innocence. *Yeah fucking right. Innocent my sweet white ass.* "She's inside—she's doing a life sentence."

"Oh, shit. What'd momma Creeley do to catch a life bid?"

Creeley sat there for a moment and stared at the cars gassing up, watched a little old man shuffle to the rear of his pickup truck. He unscrewed the gas cap and went to work trying to get his credit card into the pay kiosk. Creeley imagined this old guy—at least seventy—being killed as a teenager, strangled to death in a motel room. Imagine: No pickup truck or loose jeans. No kids of his own or weddings or ex-wives. No nothing. Just the grave. *Man, fuck Blossom.*

She answered Animal, "She murdered a kid."

"Fuck. Well, how about that?"

"How about it," Creeley said.

"And you went to see her for a last goodbye?"

"Something like that, Animal."

He sighed and made more sounds with his lips. "Alright, look—you pushed it with this fucking thing. But, given the circumstances, odd as shit as they happen to be, I almost kind of get it. That ain't a fucking excuse, but I'm not a shit head. I'm a true asshole, but I'm not a shit head. I'm about to text you that address. You get there and hand over the bag. My boy will hand it back to you after he takes a look. You get back in the car, get some Red Bull, and drive your ass back to Oregon. You do that—and no fucking side trips—I'll pretend this never happened. Do that, and we're good."

The old man got his pump into the pickup, started pumping. He adjusted his greasy cap, rubbed a hand along the back of his neck. Creeley thought it was a funny thing, being alive. Made you wonder why you were here. *I mean, what's it all for?* She nodded and said, "Thanks, Animal."

"Look for the text."

"Okay," she said and ended the call.

She sat there thinking about nothing for a few minutes. The text came through and she didn't look at the address. Instead, she watched the old man pull away, pilot his truck onto the highway on-ramp. Creeley nodded again and said to herself, "I might just find that motel."

The one where her mother killed a teenage boy.

8/Palm Springs

Palm trees whispering against a dark sky. The *chip-chip-chip* of lawn sprinklers. Yellow light bouncing off cacti and mission-style walls. The street empty, all the Beemers and Land Rovers packed away in their garages.

Fucking rich people.

So goddamn perfect, Creeley thought.

But here she was, about to walk into one of these multi-million-dollar homes with a bag of drugs. Times like this confirmed for Creeley something she'd long known—poor people don't commit crimes any more than rich people. In fact, the opposite. But you'd never see a cop cruising these streets on a regular beat. Poor people got caught committing crimes because they didn't have million-dollar homes to hide the crimes they were committing.

And the more money you make, the easier it is to get away with shit. Make no fucking mistake about that. Creeley got out of the 4Runner, pulled the duffel bag from the passenger seat. She stood on the street for a moment, listened to the sprinklers as they shut off and left the soft buzz of insects hovering in the air. Before she walked up the drive, she texted Animal, "Going in now." She shoved the phone into a front jeans pocket, marched up the concrete driveway with the heavy duffel swinging from her right hand.

She rang the bell and ten seconds later a white chick with pink hair opened the door. "Who the fuck are you?" She poked a dangly earring with one long pink fingernail. "We didn't order anything."

Creeley didn't like the way the white chick looked at her, but she smiled anyway. "Animal sent me."

The white chick rolled her eyes, walked away, and left the door open. Creeley entered and heard rap music playing at low volume down the hall to her left. Ahead, there was a living room with a giant flat-screen TV playing *SportsCenter*. She counted three frat-bro types lounging on the plush beige sofas. The white chick flopped onto the couch beside one of the bros and said, "Is this over yet?"

"It doesn't end, man," came the reply.

A door opened down the hall and Creeley swung her head to see—a head poked out and a hand motioned her to approach. She walked down the hall saying, "You Animal's connect, or what?" The head vanished into a room.

Creeley reached the doorway and entered the room.

It was a master suite, light coming from a closed bathroom door to Creeley's right. The bed was one of those pimp beds—round and with a fur cover stretched tight across it. The room smelled like women's perfume—an expensive brand—and the music was louder, a rapper Creeley recognized—Nas. The head that popped out of the door was a body now, a skinny guy lounging on a chaise. Blue carpet and a blue chaise. The guy wiggled his finger for her to approach. "Let me get at my shit. I thought you ran out· on us."

"I don't run on anybody," Creeley said as she crossed the room. Behind the chair, a sliding glass door revealed a lighted blue infinity pool. Beyond that was darkness, but Creeley knew it was a golf course blanketed by perfect green grass.

She dropped the bag at the foot of the chair.

The skinny guy leaned forward and scratched his bare chest. He was wearing boxers—a shiny gray fabric like silk. He unzipped the duffel, put his hand in and came out with a stack of cash. Hundreds, from what Creeley saw. The stack was as thick as a trade paperback. The skinny guy thumbed through it, tossed the stack into the center of his pimp bed. He went in for another stack, had to dig a bit, then tossed it. Did it twice more. He zipped the bag closed and leaned back in the chair.

"That's it?" Creeley was trying to count the money in her head. *Eighty thousand, maybe? More?*

"That's it."

"Well, that was easy." She picked up the duffel and started out of the room, but the guy's voice stopped her.

"You want to make some side cash, sister?"

She turned, studied him for a second. Cool customer. A bit douchey. But serious, too. Like with a look on his face that meant business and real money. "How much?"

"I like that," he said with a grin. "Not how...But how *much*."

9/Side Money

"It's not what you think, this thing." He cringed as he sipped from a glass filled with cheap sparkling wine. They were standing in the kitchen, the lights off and only the lighted blue pool through the sliding glass door making it so Creeley could see his facial expression. "I mean, it seems like what it is, but it ain't that. It's so simple."

"You're asking me to make an old man think I'll fuck him." She downed her own glass of wine, nodded at him to refill her. She took another sip when her glass was full. "That is, if I heard you right."

"Yeah, sure. But here's what's cool: you actually don't have to fuck him. You don't, shit, you don't even have to touch his thing, okay?"

"His thing?"

"You know...His...Lizard."

Creeley shook her head and sighed. She looked out at the glistening blue pool and wondered why she was even considering this. *For another two grand? That's it?* She looked back at Hero—that's what he called himself—and raised a hand to her chin. "You're saying I get two Gs?"

"Yeah. That's right. You get into his place and leave the door unlocked—yes, two Gs."

"And how much are you going to get?"

Hero shrugged, took another drink. He leaned against the kitchen island with a nonchalant hand on one hip. Shirt still off and hair dangling across his ears and eyes. "Look, sister. I'm the guy who put this thing together. If you don't like the cut you can kick rocks."

"Why won't she do it?" Creeley pointed at the living room with her eyes. *SportsCenter* was running back again.

"You mean Isabel?"

"Pink hair?"

Hero scratched behind one ear, mocking deep thought. "You think an old man gonna fuck a girl with pink hair?"

"She's got a decent body."

"And the personality of a doorknob."

Creeley forced a smile. "I guess I should take that as a compliment, right?" She downed her second glass of wine and shrugged him off when he raised the bottle.

"You're just what I need to pull this off."

"Is it only money?"

"Only money? Don't insult money, okay? Look, I know Animal's got somebody down here, she must be legit. I see you come in, how you walk and talk, I know you got what it takes to get this done."

"But is there anything else I need to know? Like, does he have a gun?"

"Sure, man's got a gun. I assume he does. Like I implied, he's got some money. And I happen to want it."

"Can I have a gun?"

Hero bit his upper lip and shook his head.

Creeley nodded, thought for a minute. She looked down at her dirty, wrinkled jeans and flannel peppered with soda stains. God, she looked like shit. Smelled like it, too.

Hero said, "We'll get you cleaned up. Get you something pretty to cover those hips and tits."

"I want three Gs."

Hero pretended to contemplate. He didn't try for long before saying, "You got it, and it's still a bargain."

***

Walking into Merv's, Creeley saw herself in the full-length mirror next to the bar: black dress to above her knees, three-inch fuck-me heels, and her hair pulled into a bun. She liked the dress, how it hugged her hips and tugged her belly in a bit. She was bare-armed though, and she felt goosebumps rising, knew her nipples would poke through the thin fabric. *Well, shit—it might make this job a bit easier.* She nodded at the hostess and scanned the dining room. Rows of round tables with white tablecloths and sterling silver. One of those joints for retired executives and trophy wives. The bar wasn't quite as swanky, but most of the people at the bar had glasses of red or white. She spotted the guy—Hero had described him to her—at the end of the bar.

Monty Emeril.

Alone.

Black, curly hair and a three-piece suit. Baby blue with darker pinstripes.

Had a glass in his hand that looked like a Manhattan or plain bourbon. Funny thing to Creeley—he was decent looking. And slim for a guy in his fifties. She crossed the bar and sat next to him, waved the bartender over, and said, "Can I get a Manhattan, please?"

"I'll get that for you," Monty said, but not with the tone of a standard creep. He sounded like he was just being nice.

Creeley turned to him and smiled. "Thanks for that."

"Just something nice to do, that's all."

She tried to get him to meet her gaze, but he was staring at the TV above the bar, a baseball game running late. "You always doing nice things for people?"

He shrugged and said, "Only when it's easy."

"I can respect that." She got her Manhattan and enjoyed it for a few minutes. Why not let him come to her? Would that work? Creeley had no idea. She was about to turn and flash him some leg when he twisted in his seat.

"I've never seen you here."

Creeley looked at him, brought her cold glass to her lips. "I'm not much of a late-night girl."

"Is that right? What do you do for work?"

She dragged a thumb through the condensation on her glass, ran the same wet thumb across her lips. She decided that being honest might do the trick. "It might sound funny, but I'm a delivery driver."

"Whatever pays the bills, right?"

"Something like that." She looked into his eyes then and saw something that scared her. It might have been a coldness, or a blank emptiness—she didn't know how to describe it. In that moment, Creeley wanted to get this over with and didn't understand how she found herself here. Was she committed to ruining a simple, good thing? All she had to do was get the drugs (and money) back to Animal. But instead she ran off to visit her murderer mom and, now, she was sitting across from who the hell knew, trying to flaunt her twat for three Gs.

"I respect working people."

"Good to know," Creeley said. "They're the salt of the earth."

"Amen to that." He waved at the bartender. "Give us a couple shots of Patrón, Vince."

The shots arrived and they took them, neither Creeley nor Monty asking for lime or salt. Nothing to it. She was starting to feel a buzz coming on and she did flash a bit of leg, upper thigh that was way too pale from her northwest lifestyle.

Monty's eyes crossed down to look, shot back to her face. "I never paid for a piece of ass."

Creeley nodded, licked her bottom lip.

"Just so you know."

"And now I know," she said.

"But if you want to have a good time tonight..."

"First, I want to ask you something."

He tilted his head, invited the question.

"What do you do for a living, Mr. Salt-of-the-Earth?"

He took his time with the answer, and he patted his right side when he finally gave it to her. "I thought you had it figured," he said. "I'm a cop."

✳✳✳

A modern studio apartment off Palm Canyon. A sliding glass door and balcony overlooking a pool and hot tub. Palm trees waving everywhere and happy laughter in the courtyard. His bedroom was up a short staircase—a kind of loft. Monty mixed them each a bourbon and Coke, motioned for her to join him on the leather couch.

She said, "You do okay for a cop."

"It is a studio apartment."

"But new. And pretty damn nice. No kids? An ex-wife?" The bourbon made her grimace.

"Both, matter of fact. We get along."

Creeley thought of her mom for some reason, saw Blossom's tired eyes again. "Hey, what kind of cop are you? I mean, are you a detective?"

He nodded. "Homicide. Eighteen years, if you can believe that." He looked her over, but again not in a creepy way. More like somebody appreciating a fantastic piece of art.

Creeley admitted it to herself: she was attracted to him. She put a hand on his knee, let it fall back into her lap. "Can I ask you something about your work?"

"Work is all I am—go ahead."

"You ever put somebody in prison, somebody that...You know—"

"Somebody innocent?"

She nodded.

"No—not innocent. Sometimes we get caught on somebody. Yeah, they might not have done what we think. And maybe they get put in for it. Shit, once or twice that might happen. But I promise you this: they fucking did something."

"But how can you say that? If I didn't do it—"

"I can't explain it if you're not a cop. All I can say is that there's a lot of people out here...They get away with shit. I never do anybody wrong if I can help it."

Creeley was getting used to the bourbon. And liking it. She ran a hand along the top of her cleavage, left a streak of moisture from holding her glass. She watched his eyes land there and linger. "But you're saying it's possible. People do get put inside for shit they didn't do."

"It happens."

Creeley wasn't certain why, but she leaned forward and put her lips against his neck. He smelled like cut grass and dill, tasted like sweat. She leaned back and smiled. His turn to lean in and kiss her left ear. She squealed, started moaning as he trailed down to her neck. The fuck was she doing?

She was attracted to him, but what the fuck?

She was here for three Gs.

Creeley put her hands around him, kissed his jaw. "Go upstairs and meet me. I just need to use the little girl's room."

"This one's a little boy's room," he said, joking with her.

She ran her hand across his thighs as she stood. In the bathroom, pulling a gray hair from her left eyebrow, she heard him climb the stairs, remove his belt. He fell into bed.

Remember, Creeley, you're ripping off a cop.

She exited the bathroom, heard his breathing above her. Creeley turned and walked toward the front door, turned the deadbolt. She grabbed the handle, pushed it down, and swung the door inward. She heard him ask where she was going, but Hero and the other two were already rushing past her, handguns in front of them like pitiful searching cocks. After that, Creeley heard an unmistakable sound again and again: the thud of fists smacking bone and flesh.

10/Next Steps

A cruddy motel room off South Palm Canyon. Smells of dog piss in the carpet and the sound of bass-heavy rap coming from the room next door. Creeley sat on the bed and counted her three grand. Twenties and fifties—a lot of wrinkled bills facing the wrong way. She finished counting, bound the stack of bills with a hair tie. She peeked into the black duffel. First time she'd ever done that, matter of fact. Found more stacks of cash, a couple bricks of what felt like cocaine wrapped in brown shopping plastic. Looked like Paul and his tweaker pal were sending cash and product back to Animal. She drove all this way—through Oregon and down the California coast—for that. And to pay Hero for some long-ago favor. But that didn't matter to Creeley anymore.

Fuck it.

She was done with Animal's directives.

She drank from the bathroom sink using her hand, fell back on the bed, and switched on the local news. Small-time shit about Little League and city council feuds. Why did Animal owe Hero money? Why? What? How? Most times, Creeley dropped money and left with product. This was different. Part of her wanted answers, but another part of her wanted to forget everything and leave. Fuck Animal and the people he did business with. But she was pissed at herself for trusting Hero. Felt dumb each time the detective's flesh made that horrible slapping sound. Fist to bone. She didn't scream or protest while it happened—too much of a fucking shock. But she did see Monty breathing before she left.

Bloody and breathing.

On the nod, but hardly on the mend.

She paced the motel room, peeked out the window and watched the parking lot. Her 4Runner was backed into a spot along the fence that circled the pool. She saw two teenagers flirting in the blue water, the boy using his hands to squeeze a stream of water at the girl. The light from the pool broke around the palm trees and made odd shapes on the windshields of the cars.

Three grand and you got a cop beat half to death. What the fuck, Creeley?

She felt like a cluster of steel marbles was sitting in her stomach. She took more water from the sink, cleared her throat. She picked up her burner phone and dialed Animal.

"Tell me you're on your way back home."

"That drop—the money drop—was a motherfucking shit show."

"In what way?"

"They got me tied into a cop beating," Creeley said. "Real life *America's Most Wanted* shit."

The silence on Animal's end was louder than a jet. She could hear his tongue running across his lips before he said, "Tell the story."

"They forced me to go along, play a shill while they got this cop alone."

"Play a shill? What are we, in 1942?"

"They beat him to a fucking..."

"Bloody pulp?"

"Yes."

Animal clicked his teeth. "If he's a cop, he deserved it. Tell me you're on the fucking road."

Creeley fell back on the bed, stared at the peeling beige ceiling paint. "No—I'm not."

Another loud silence.

"I got a room. After they—"

"I don't give a shit if they ass-fucked Jesus Christ. I said I want you back, I want you back. It's my shit you have with you. And until it's in my fucking hands, there's a chance—"

"What was this deal?"

"Don't you fucking interrupt me, Creeley. You fucking—"

"What kind of fucking deal was this?"

"Girl, don't—"

"Why the fuck did you have me drop money to that asshole!"

He was breathing hard. And trying to keep himself under control. "Creeley, I've sent you on a lot of deals. This is just another deal—not a goddamn thing else. Hero did something for me a couple years back. This was my way of getting him the money. It was convenient."

"The fuck it is, Animal. The fuck it is."

She could hear his surprise. "I don't know when the fuck—"

"When you decided I was a fool," Creeley said. "Right now, I've got your money and I've got your drugs. I'm staying right goddamn here."

"What the fuck for?"

"Something to do with my mom."

"Your fucking mom?"

"She needs my help. And you're not telling me everything."

Animal's voice dropped an octave. "Creeley, listen to me. The drugs don't belong to me. The money doesn't either. I'm not fucking around when I say—"

"Why'd Hero want to hurt the cop?"

Animal sighed. His impatient voice—tinged with irritation—came over the line. "The cop is dirty, Creeley. And he's probably giving shit to the Feds."

"How the fuck do you know that?" She closed her eyes, thought about Monty bleeding in horrible pain a few blocks north of her.

"This is a thing for The Vandals."

"The motorcycle gang?"

"Yes—the fucking motorcycle gang."

Creeley sat up, an idea coming into her head. "I didn't know you did dirty shit for them, Animal. I thought you were the boss man."

"Where in the fuck did you get the idea that you could—"

"I guess it's up to you to figure it out. What to tell them."

"About what?"

"About why they aren't getting their drugs anytime soon. Or

their money."

"Creeley—"

"I'll see you when I see you, asshole."

"Creeley. You better fucking—"

She hung up and tossed the phone onto the bed beside her. She stood and walked to the window, watched the teenagers making out. She thought of skinny Paul sitting in that shitty desert shack and cutting drugs, sipping endless Coronas. She thought of kissing him when she was a teenager and almost—so many years later—felt his breath on her lips. The teens were going for it in the pool, enjoying each other. A feeling of nostalgia ran through Creeley while she stood at the window. Nostalgia for the teenage girl she used to be, for a childhood she never got to live. Creeley saw again that look in Blossom's eyes: certainty fixed inside rage and helplessness. And she saw those words spelled out on Blossom's lips: I. Did. Not. Do. It. Creeley felt odd for watching the teenagers and for thinking these thoughts. She closed the curtain. When she returned to the bed, her phone was buzzing. Texts and calls from Animal. Sure, she got the cop beaten half to death. But he was dirty. And he probably needed information. Shit Creeley knew. Like who Animal was and who he worked with—could this be a way to get Creeley some help with her mom's case? She was going to look into it.

She wanted help from the detective.

11/The Detective

Pink box of donuts in her hand, two paper coffee cups balanced on top, Creeley knocked on Monty's front door. She waited for a minute but heard nothing. She surveyed the courtyard, all the queen palms still and majestic in the warm desert air. The smell of watered grass tickled her nose. No other residents that she noticed. She pounded three times on the door and said, "It's me. We need to talk." She sighed and added, "About last night."

The deadbolt clicked and the door cracked.

"It's me."

"You got balls, coming back here."

Creeley said, "I didn't know what it was." Thinking about the sound of fists pummeling Monty's face—she felt the warmth of blood rushing to her head. More than anything, she was embarrassed.

"You knew it was something."

She sighed again, looked out at the courtyard and empty pool. She turned back to the crack in the door. "You're right. I knew it was something."

Footsteps shuffled away from the door, but it didn't close.

***

Monty stretched across half the couch, still in his nice suit. But it was wrinkled and torn, his face bloody and shaped with bruises and swelling. One eye was clear, but the other was closed into a blue-purple mound. Rays of sunlight poured through the slatted blinds. He tilted his head to escape the brightness. "I gave up donuts two years ago—had to drop the spare tire."

"Coffee?"

"I'll drink both."

Creeley set the cups on the coffee table within his reach, pulled the box of donuts closer to her. She took one of the sitting chairs opposite the couch. The apartment smelled of cologne and gun oil. "So."

"So."

"I'm sorry about last night. I didn't know it was going to be like that. I mean, I didn't think—"

"I'm a big boy. Maybe I deserved it." He grunted as he reached for a cup, fell back into the couch. The right side of his face got some light and Creeley got a better look at his eye—closed up into a blue plum. "Hurts though," he said. "That's for goddamn sure."

"I'm sorry."

"What's your name."

She hesitated.

"Give me your name. I'm not going to take you in. You know I'm not."

"Creeley Nash. I'm from Oregon. Portland."

"What kind of business are you into, Creeley Nash?"

She cleared her throat. "I run drugs for a mid-level guy—thinks he's fucking Scarface."

"I know the type. Across state lines then, huh?"

"Depends," she said. "But this time—yes."

He nodded, sipped the coffee.

"I didn't come here about that. Not all the way. I came here because I need some help."

"You? *You* need some help? The woman who runs drugs and works for some Oregonian shit head—she needs help from me. A cop. Do you hear yourself?"

"Help with a case," Creeley added, the words funny coming out of her mouth. She shifted in the chair, tried to sit up straighter but ended up feeling arrogant. That eye needed a bag of frozen peas. Or something like that.

"A case. Well, ain't that just a fuck-me development? I did not think I'd wake up this morning with a headache the size of Hoover Dam and some hippie chick asking me for help."

"Wrongful conviction." She gnawed the right side of her tongue.

"Baby, they're all wrongful. Especially when you get it straight from the loser's mouth."

"But I believe her," Creeley said. "For the first time." She watched Monty's non-reaction. "For the only time. My mom. She was a whore. Is...is a sex worker. And she never gave me one damn shred of true, but I saw it in her eyes. This time, it's not a lie. She didn't do it."

"Maybe not," he said. "But what else did she do? You ever put your mind to that?"

****

Monty wanted to walk.

They got outside the courtyard and started around the parking lot that circled his building. A slatted steel fence revealed a golf course next to Monty's building. The electric hum of golf carts captured Creeley's attention, along with the indiscernible chatter of the golfers. She walked slow to accommodate Monty's new limp and shuffle.

He said, "You get beat down, best thing to do is get up. Start walking around. You know, they tell you the same thing when you're in the hospital. The people who get up and walk around, they're the ones who make it. Keep laying there, letting people bring you food and drink, might as well die anyway. Every time I take a beating, I get my ass moving."

"It happens to you a lot?"

Monty sipped from his coffee, grunted. "Let's say I move in unappreciative circles."

"You a dirty cop?"

That stopped him for a second, but he limped forward after pausing to study her. "Every cop you ever met is dirty."

"Even I don't believe that."

"Well—tell me anybody who does it right every time. Give me one fucking name."

Creeley didn't answer. She had Blossom's face in her head again, her moving lips and that phrase. *I did not do it.*

"I do what I can to survive," Monty said. "But I do it by a code, and no dirtbag ever comes out ahead."

An old lady passed them walking in the opposite direction. She was leading a small poodle with crusted tears under its eyes. The woman kept her head down, wouldn't look at Monty.

"Detective Monty—keeping the dirtbags on the ropes."

"You got it."

Creeley scratched behind an ear, sneezed once. He didn't bless her. "So, are you a real detective, though? Like, do you try to solve murders for real? Or do you just walk around and pretend you do?"

"I solve murders, Miss Nash. You can bet your ass—I put them suckers down fast as they come up. You want to solve a homicide, it's about fear. You have to scare people."

"Intimidation," she said.

"Right."

They turned a corner, encountered a parking section that mirrored the first side of the lot. The cars were older Mercedes models, a few Lexus sedans—nice stuff that Creeley couldn't imagine driving. She said, "What kind of car do you drive?"

"Why?"

"I'm just wondering. See if you match up to my idea of a cop. I guess I just—"

"A Toyota Camry. Gray with tinted windows."

She stopped to look at him. "That's not exactly hot, Detective."

Monty bit the inside of one cheek, placed a hand on his black eye. He groaned, took a long breath. "It's inconspicuous. Whatever the fuck that means."

"Are you a drunk?"

"That's not the term I prefer, but I like booze."

Creeley chuckled now. "Perfect. I choose a drunk detective to work the case with me."

"I never said we were working a case."

"I thought you put murders down when they come up?" She watched his reaction, still wanted to know if her gut feeling about the detective was correct.

He started limping again. "I solve murders, Miss Nash. Already told you that. You can bet your ass."

Creeley followed him, felt for some reason she was chasing him. "Will you help me?"

"Why am I going to help a drug runner?"

Creeley stopped, watched him limp away from her. "Maybe I can help you somehow. Like, with information. About how it all works."

"I know how it all works."

"I can help you with The Vandals—be a witness or something. An informant."

Monty sighed, cracked the knuckles on his right hand.

"I'm more than a drug runner, you know. It might seem like that's all I am, but that's total bullshit."

Monty shuffled toward her a few steps. The sunlight hit his face and he closed his good eye to the light, stood there looking at her with closed eyes. "What are you then?"

"I'm somebody who never had a chance."

"You think that has to do with how good or bad you are?"

"Of course," she said. "How can it not?" She ran her hand through her hair, swallowed a bad taste rising in her throat.

"Your choices—that's what you are in life."

"As simple as that?"

He shrugged.

"You're wrong, Detective."

The detective turned and walked away from her.

Creeley parked the 4Runner in the library lot, watched two homeless men push squeaky bicycles into the park. The library was a large cement building, two stories with architecture that Creeley thought must be mid-century modern, though she wasn't sure. She had a vague remembrance that Palm Springs was famous for the style. It was 8:50 a.m. and the library didn't open until 9:00. She watched the homeless men pass a brown paper bag between each other. Four more cars pulled into the lot, their drivers waiting until just before nine to exit.

Creeley didn't get out of the 4Runner until the front door opened and a librarian waved everyone inside the building.

Inside, the air cool and crisp, she noticed a large bulletin board filled with flyers, advertisements, and two 'missing' posters—teenage girls. Didn't surprise Creeley. She spotted the kids' books section to her left, looked across an open area covered by a large skylight, and realized she had no idea what she was doing.

"Can I help you?"

Creeley walked toward the voice behind the front desk. A young girl—midtwenties?—with a mohawk and a nose ring. "Hi," Creeley said. "Can I be honest with you?"

Mohawk smiled and said, "You don't have to ask permission."

"I have no idea what I need."

"Don't worry about it. Why are you here?"

"I need to research a murder."

Mohawk nodded. "Something well-known, famous?"

"It happened here. Downtown. At a crummy motel."

"No shit—wild." Mohawk looked excited to help somebody research murder. Maybe it was the librarian in her, but it could have been something else. "You know how long it's been?"

"More than twenty years?"

"Shit—internet might not help. You can look at old issues of the *Desert Sun.* Our local paper. We'll get you a microfiche station. Ever used one?"

"God, no," Creeley said. "This is the first time I've been to a library."

"Glad I could pop your cherry," Mohawk said with a playful smile. "Follow me."

✳✳✳

It took about an hour, but Creeley hit on a series of articles in the *Desert Sun*. The same one she found the day before, after Paul told her what happened, plus a bunch more. She got pretty good at scanning each piece of film for relevant headlines, setting it to the side when she was done. She burned through almost a year before she found it—homicide in Palm Springs on March 20th, the first day of spring in 1996. A leap year. The headline read "Body found, murder likely." They had the murder from the day the boy's body was discovered. The articles were written by a reporter named Dawn Griffin. Creeley wondered if she could be found. Wondered whether she was still alive and in town. The first article was a main story, above the fold, a picture of yellow crime scene tape flapping in the wind outside the motel.

Body found, murder likely

By Dawn Griffin

A man was found dead—likely murdered—in Palm Springs early Wednesday morning. Investigators have not made the man's identity public, and they haven't provided details on age or ethnicity. In the early morning hours on Wednesday, investigators arrived at the Sunny Dunes Motel on South Palm Canyon. A crime scene investigation unit arrived within twenty minutes and staff were questioned in the parking lot. Officers canvassed the immediate area, mainly motels with the exception of some apartment buildings, but did not take any suspects into custody.

Through a public information officer, Palm Springs PD confirmed a body had been discovered and that homicide detectives were on scene. Palm Springs PD would not verify the scene as the location of a homicide, though anonymous police sources have indicated a homicide.

As sirens illuminated the south side of Highway 111, apartment dwellers drifted outside to watch the response unfold. "I see cops here all the time," said Morgan Haley, 33. "I swear they have prostitutes in and out of here, but I can't prove it."

Asia Bradley, 24, a night clerk at the nearby Motel Cactus, said she has called the police numerous times to respond to drug use at Sunny Dunes Motel. "Usually, what they do is shoot up out back. We share a common space for our trash dumpsters—it's always people from that place. I don't want to say it's a bad crowd, but they have a lot of issues over there."

Crime mapping data available in the public domain confirmed at least 43 calls to police for criminal activity at Sunny Dunes Motel, all in 1995. Twelve more calls have been placed this year.

Detectives did not respond to requests for comment.

Creeley found the following day's edition and slid the film onto the tray. The microfiche machine magnified the print, and she was surprised at what she saw. That day, Thursday, the murder was front page, above the fold, and Dawn Griffin had confirmed some facts.

Teen Found Murdered in Motel

By Dawn Griffin

Levi Mackey, 17, was found murdered Wednesday morning in room 23B at Sunny Dunes Motel on South Palm Canyon. Investigators today confirmed the victim's identity and provided key details related to the homicide—Mackey was strangled sometime between 8 pm Tuesday evening and 1 am Wednesday morning. Police have no suspects, but believe the perpetrator is likely female.

Details about the victim are scarce. Investigators verified his identification using an Arizona driver's license. Calls to Mackey's previous recorded residence went unanswered.

"It's likely we are looking for a local female, possibly a sex worker. Though we can't confirm that at this time," said Detective Sergeant James Ives.

Investigators have verified the existence of eyewitness accounts but stopped short of saying how valuable they are. The motel owner—Frank Soriano, 56, based in Las Vegas—could not confirm if the motel maintains security cameras and stores closed circuit footage. Soriano said he was disappointed and horrified at Mackey's death. "We always do our best to ensure guests have a safe environment at our motels. We run operations across the country, and it is extremely rare for us to have an incident of this nature," Soriano said. "My heart goes out to the family."

Soriano denied his motel is a magnet for vice criminal activity.

Police crime data detail the motel's recent struggles with crime. In the calendar year 1995, the motel recorded 43 criminal complaints. Of those, 28 were sex crimes, 12 were assault/robbery, and 3 were battery. Looking at citywide data, this ranks the motel as the leader in vice crime across Palm Springs.

Creeley found more articles written over the following two weeks, information trickling out from local police. Dawn Griffin had good sources in the police department and local government. Creeley printed each story to the copy machine and stapled everything together so she could review it back at the motel. But the story that most interested Creeley was the one published on April 25th, more than four weeks after Mackey's body was discovered.

Murder suspect caught, confession details sordid killing

By Jimmy Goffs

Investigators caught an alleged murderer Sunday night and, after a long day of interrogations, have secured a confession to the March 20 murder of Levi Mackey, 17.

"We have caught a killer," said Detective Sergeant James Ives. "With the help of our homicide investigative unit and the Riverside County sheriff, we have taken a murderer off the streets. Palm Springs and the Coachella Valley are safer today."

Blossom Nash, 32, of Parker, Arizona, will face capital murder charges for the killing of Mackey.

Ives said, "What I heard today is undeniable. Levi Mackey, a teenager, was killed in cold blood for the few meaningless dollars in his pocket."

In a press release, Palm Springs police said Nash confessed to the murder and provided key details about the crime scene and method of death. These details convinced detectives, including lead detective Ray Parks, that her confession was not only credible, but also enough to ask the district attorney's office for capital murder charges.

Nash, who is currently being represented by a public defender, appears to have resided at a motel in North Palm Springs. Management at The Palm refused to provide details about Nash, but residents of the motel confirmed she lived there.

"I know Blossom," said Ray Carl, 48. "She's been living here longer than me. At least a year, I'd say. She didn't have no work and I used to see a teenage girl with her."

According to records in Parker, Arizona, Nash may have one daughter, 14. But detectives have yet to locate the teenager.

Investigators plan to search Nash's motel room today. "We've got a host of tasks to complete here," Ives said. "For now, we're getting a lot of paperwork done, but we also need to collect evidence and do a thorough search of Nash's motel room. We collected a lot of physical evidence at the scene of the murder. We are waiting on the state lab to match the evidence to Nash. We are certain it will match. Essentially, this is case closed."

Nash is scheduled to be arraigned here in Palm Springs early this afternoon.

Funny—a different reporter on that story. Creeley wondered why. Was it Dawn's day off? How many crime reporters take a day off when a story they've been hunting for weeks reaches a climax? *Something odd with that,* Creeley thought. Had to be. The confession, too, seemed odd. They spend a day talking to Blossom and next thing you know—*bam.* Murder is boxed up and wrapped like a Christmas gift. Right away, Creeley was suspicious. Another two hours in the library and her eyes were dry and sore. She scanned another year of news—day by day— and came up with nine more articles. All detailing proceedings at Blossom's trial. All written by Dawn Griffin.

Jimmy Goffs was back on the political beat, like usual.

Creeley collected her printed articles and thanked Mohawk on the way out. "I might be back—maybe I won't have to bother you next time."

"Don't worry about it. That's what I'm here for." Mohawk smiled, a lip ring peeling back over her incisors. "Let me know if you need more help." She hesitated for a moment before adding, "Are you new in town?"

Creeley stopped at the door. "I'm here for a couple days doing some research—that's all."

"I'd love to hear about it."

Was Creeley getting hit on? Seriously?

"I'm interested in true crime—that's all. It creeps me out, but I can't, like, turn away or whatever."

"Got it," Creeley said. Her first instinct was to refuse—this was a personal thing for her. But then she had a second thought: *I need help and librarians are smart.* "Sure. Why not? You want to meet for a drink later? Downtown somewhere?"

"Sure. How about The Tiki Room at six? It's a little spot downtown."

"Sounds good." Creeley chanced a smile herself, walked out and jogged across the parking lot. She tossed her articles into the passenger seat, got the 4Runner started, and her phone started buzzing. She looked at the screen, expectant.

It was Animal.

13/The Cage

"**C**an't you take a hint, asshole?" Creeley held the phone to her ear with a shoulder and steered the 4Runner out of the library parking lot. She made a left and another left, headed down Sunrise toward her motel.

"You can't ignore me, Creeley—you have my shit."

"But it's not your shit, Animal."

"And that—there—is the fucking problem. Look, you got some family shit to handle. Fine. I don't give two fucks. Come back here, drop off my shit, and drive back to the desert."

A red light forced Creeley to slam on the brakes. She leaned back in her seat, dangled an arm out the window. The sun was high and hot and Creeley felt her skin start to burn. She had the sudden urge to sunbathe, thought about all her years in the Pacific Northwest and the vitamin D she missed. "What are you going to do, Animal? Send somebody to kill me? Because I don't think you have the balls for that."

His silence told her something.

"You don't have to do that—I'll be back in a few days. A week, at the most."

"Staying is not an option. Those guys from last night? I can pay them to find you. This is your last fucking chance."

The light turned and Creeley rolled along behind a late-model Lexus. Fucking rich people drove ten miles per hour below the speed limit. Creeley wanted to get back to the motel, lay out at the pool, and read the articles from the *Desert Sun*. But the old people had her trapped. And Animal was somewhat kind of threatening her life. Everything was moving slow, but she had to think fast.

She made a decision.

"I'll come back tonight, but I want double pay."

"Shit. You're the one who—"

"I've always done right by you."

Animal clicked his teeth over the line, settled on a number. "Five hundred extra. Because I want to be done with this."

She hesitated, sniffed. "Fine. That works."

"Call when you're on the road."

"I will." She hung up and tossed the phone out the window. *Fuck you, motherfucker.* The Lexus moved over and Creeley floored it—the 4Runner hummed with unleashed speed.

***

The motel pool was green and too warm. But the sun was still high and hot. Creeley didn't have a swimsuit, but she had jean cutoffs and a halter—the sun and heat felt good on her shoulders and thighs. She chugged three Coronas and read every single article she printed at the library.

It boggled Creeley's mind that all this happened—so many years ago—while she was hopping trains with gutter punks across the country...the oddities of life.

The trial went as the prosecution planned, but with one exception: the district attorney knocked the charge down to second degree murder. They had no evidence that Blossom planned to kill Mackey, and the sentence—twenty to life—was going to be enough for brutally strangling a teenager.

Parole unlikely.

The jury bought it all, including Blossom's confession. The physical evidence was there: Panties left in the room with Blossom's DNA. A receipt from a convenience store downtown and security camera footage to prove it was Blossom who made the purchase (vodka and condoms). And, worse, her hair and saliva in the bathroom sink—an easy conviction all the way around. Blossom never got on the stand. Her confession spoke for her. Coerced or not.

Creeley was so convinced by the articles that she felt stupid. Maybe this was just her mom lying to her again. Talk about the long con—if anybody was capable of manipulating a long-lost daughter after a quarter century, it was Creeley's mom. But there was something that nagged at Creeley. She'd learned over the years to trust her gut, and this was her gut speaking. It wasn't logic or stupidity or facts. It wasn't doubt or some magnetism to family or heritage.

It was her gut. Nothing else.

Creeley was alive because she followed her gut.

And she trusted it.

And now she had a list of names.

People to bother about the trial:

Detective Ray Parks.

Dawn Griffin.

Jimmy Goffs.

The public defender—Jenny Frost.

And the prosecuting assistant DA, a guy named Hector Alonso.

The library research had given her a start, but now it was time to get on a computer and scour the internet. Creeley figured a simple search would turn up information, but Mohawk could help her dig deeper. Have a drink tonight, sure. Or a few. But make sure to get Mohawk on board to help with research. She seemed interested and—more important—capable. Creeley tossed her Corona bottles into the trash can, scooped up her stack of papers. She was hopping barefoot across the hot concrete when a voice stopped her.

"You'll burn out here, girl."

Creeley saw the tiny man in pink shorts out of the corner of her eye. She got to a patch of grass near the fence that edged the pool, sighed as her feet cooled.

"That pasty skin will be red as a hickey."

Creeley glared at him. Slicked-back hair faded high on his head. Ray-Bans and botoxed lips. A Tommy Bahama shirt open to his sculpted abs. He wore a puka shell bracelet on his left wrist. His right hand dangled over the fence, showing off a silver watch of significant worth, even to Creeley's untrained eyes. He licked his plump lips and grinned.

"You got a nice body though, girl. I bet you get all the little boys. Don't act all modest, girl. Get a two-piece. You are in Palm

Springs, for fuck's sake."

"Who the fuck are you?"

"Kimmie."

"Kimmie?"

"Kimmie, girl! Don't act like you don't know me."

Creeley chuckled, almost dropped her papers. She moved closer to him, squinted behind her sunglasses. "Seriously, who the fuck are you, Kimmie?"

"Your neighbor. Duh." He sauntered around her, slipped the latch on the pool fence and held it for her. "We're going to be friends, girl. Kimmie loves to make friends."

***

"You want a cactus cocktail?" Kimmie eyeballed her with one eyebrow raised, pointed at her with a red Solo cup. They were in his room—he had two rollaboard suitcases opened on the second bed and piles of shoes in every corner.

"Cactus cocktail?" Creeley set her papers on the bed without all the clothes and took the wood chair near the window. "What the fuck is that?"

"Cactus Cooler and Absolut Peach, of course. I've got ice, too. Don't you worry your pretty little head." Kimmie scooped some ice from a bucket into the cup, poured from a half-empty vodka bottle. He topped it with soda—Cactus Cooler—from a two-liter bottle and handed her the drink. "This is my desert drink, girl. Gets me in the mood."

"In the mood for what?" Creeley sipped her drink, liked it right away because it brought a smile to her lips.

Kimmie poured himself a drink, sat on the edge of the bed with his legs crossed, one bare foot bobbing up and down. "My yearly desert soiree. I like to spend a couple weeks sweating and picking up big guys downtown."

"Slut," Creeley said.

"Mmm-hmm. That's right," he said and smiled.

"You come out here alone then."

"Not always—this year's been a little rough on Kimmie."

Creeley sighed, sipped. The soda was cool and refreshing after a couple hours in the sun. She pressed a finger to her right shoulder, watched the pale impression fill with red. She had a sunburn. "Okay—how is your world falling apart these days? I bet it doesn't compare to mine."

"Everybody's life is their very own special disaster. I had a breakup. A nasty one—my husband."

"Ex-husband?"

"When the divorce goes through." Kimmie wiped a hand across his brow in mock starlet fashion. "And there's the condo to sell. You know how it is."

"No—I don't."

"Don't tell me nobody ever put a ring on it, girl."

Creeley shrugged, tried to smile. "Nobody ever put a ring on it. They put a few other things on it, though."

Kimmie nodded and pursed his lips. "You like bad boys, huh? I should have known when I saw you."

"That, and I'm sort of dumb."

Kimmie bit both his lips at once. He had an expressive face— almost an actor but without the chiseled-from-stone profile. "All that reading you were doing? I doubt you're one of the dumb ones, sister."

"A drug dealer wants to kill me."

"Only one? You haven't lived yet, babe. Stick with me and we'll get in some real trouble."

Creeley laughed. "I'm actually reading about my mom."

"Ooh—she some kind of celebri-tah?"

"Kind of. The murdering kind. She's in prison for killing a teenager. In prison for life."

Kimmie hummed low in his throat. "I'm sorry, babe."

Creeley finished her drink, handed the cup to Kimmie and he poured her another. "We were never close. I ran away when I was a teenager."

"No shit? Me too. I just knew we were meant to be together, girl!" He twirled and handed her the drink, topped off his own and tasted it. "That's so good." He sat on the TV stand and lowered his green eyes on her.

"Why?" Creeley watched him while she drank.

He rolled his eyes. "Look at me, girl. You think Daddy liked what I had to tell him? Do you think he accepted it?"

"I'm sorry."

"You should be—I never got over it."

They laughed together.

"Why you reading about little old Momma now?"

Creeley hesitated in telling him, but wondered why she shouldn't. There was nothing to hide. "I went to see her and she convinced me that she didn't do it."

"Ah, the old, 'it wasn't me—it was the one-armed man' bit. And you went for that?" he said over his drink.

"My gut tells me it's true."

Kimmie wagged his head from shoulder to shoulder, scratched the back of his neck.

"I told you I'm a dummy."

"No. You said you were dumb."

"Same thing."

"Not really, girl. A dummy is forever. Being dumb, that's just once in a blue moon."

Creeley felt herself blush, but she couldn't understand why. She poured the drink down her throat.

"You poor thing—nobody ever loved you, did they?"

"They've loved certain things about me."

"Ooh. I know. But that's not love, now is it?"

Creeley glared at him, playing a bit. "Are you one of those super-sentimental queens?"

Kimmie rolled his eyes again. "Always a romantic."

"I like you."

"Like? That's such a wimpy word. Let's promise to love each other, from now until forever."

Creeley stood, walked over to him. She bent over and kissed him on the neck.

———

MATT PHILLIPS

"You're my new sweetie," he said.

"Thank you for saying something nice to me." Creeley moonwalked back to the chair and sat, swigged more cactus cocktail.

"You got some moves, babe." Kimmie pumped his shoulders. "You want to go dancing tonight or what?"

"So, I was serious about the drug dealer."

"Me too."

Creeley rolled her eyes back at him. "And I need to get my mom out of the clink."

"It can wait, sister. Let's do some blow."

"God, you're bad!"

"You know it," he said with a sheepish look on his face.

"I'm sorry about your marriage."

Kimmie said, "It was destined to fail. Young love."

"And your parents?"

"They love the phrase 'We told you so...'"

"But you..." Creeley didn't know how to say it.

"They accepted me? Yes—after a few years. They're good people. But like all good people, they're racist and out to get the fags and abortionists."

"Kimmie!"

"What? I told you I'm a good time. They love me at bingo night in Indian Wells."

"Stop it."

"I'm serious about dancing, girl."

"I know," Creeley said.

"And I'm serious about the coke."

"I feel like I just met a demon."

"You did, babe. I'm so bad it hurts—and I love a good goddamn time."

Creeley shook her head, clicked her tongue at him. "Your Palm Springs vacation, huh? Where are we going to get some blow? I don't have a hookup down here."

"Where else, girl? We'll ask the first black guy we see."

14/Mohawk

Downtown Palm Springs had its heyday in the fifties and sixties, being a short jaunt from Hollywood, but after a long hiatus starting in the eighties, the party was back in The Springs. Creeley was surprised to hear live music coming from a few restaurants on the strip. Sure, it was Friday, but it was still early evening, and she couldn't imagine there were many retirees out on the town. The rideshare driver dropped her and Kimmie on a corner. She peeked in the first restaurant they passed, and she was both right and wrong: Not a ton of retirees, but some. Lots of young to middle age gay couples and hipster types who Creeley figured must be out of L.A.—like Kimmie. She had to hustle to keep up with him. He strutted up the sidewalk, arms pumping like a power walker. Sweat beaded on Creeley's head and neck. Her sunburn was already starting to bother her. "Are we in a hurry?"

"Oh, yeah," he said over his shoulder. "We need a drink and we need some blow. Of course we're in a hurry."

"Okay, about the—"

"Don't try to get out of doing cocaine." Heads turned as Kimmie and Creeley passed the patio of a French bistro with sweaty, tuxedoed waiters hustling overpriced wine.

Creeley sprinted to catch up and said, "God, you're brazen."

"It's Palm Springs, girl. Not Catholic school. Nobody gives a flying fuck."

"How much—"

"There it is," Kimmie said as he veered off the main drag into an alley.

They reached a staircase outside an adobe-style building. Creeley followed as they climbed a first flight, swiveled, and climbed a second flight to a large wooden door with a repetitive relief of Polynesian masks glaring at them. They pushed their way in and a flush of cold air hit Creeley's face. The shaking of a cocktail tin got her attention. Along with Kimmie, she moved to the bar on the left. The right side of the restaurant featured a teak host stand and three ornate booths covered by palm frond shadings. The motif was general tiki, but not overdone or tasteless.

Mohawk was already at the bar and deep into a drink.

Creeley said, "Hey—I missed you." She took a bar stool on one side and Kimmie took the other. "This is my new friend, Kimmie."

"We just met, but we're meant for each other," he said.

"That's exactly how I feel. I'm Amber."

"Thanks for your help this morning." The bartender lifted his chin at Creeley, and she said, "A mai tai?"

"Me too, cutie," Kimmie said. "So, let's get down to business, Amber, babe. Who do you know that can get us some..." He peeked around the bar—about half-full—and pressed one nostril with a finger, sniffed.

"Ooh," Amber said while pulling her phone out of her purse. "I don't usually partake, but..." She started scrolling through her contacts.

Creeley met Kimmie's gaze and he gave her an I-told-you-so expression.

Amber texted while she said, "Let me try this guy I know from Palm Desert. I haven't seen him in a while, but he's definitely the type."

Kimmie and Creeley got their drinks.

Kimmie slurped his mai tai through a straw, tilted his head at Amber and Creeley. "Do you two ladies like to have a good time? Or am I going to have to train you up?"

"Um—I just asked an ex-boyfriend for some coke."

"Oh," Creeley said. "Now he's an ex."

Amber grinned and said, "Or something like that."

Kimmie flagged down the bartender and asked for a round of kamikaze shooters. He leaned in as Amber messaged back and forth with her ex. "Tell him we'll come to him—if that's what it takes."

Creeley leaned over Amber and said, "I thought you said we should just ask the first—"

"Oh, hell no, girl—don't you dare. I'm only racist in private." He wagged his chin with pursed lips. "Don't try to shame me."

"What? You were going to say the first black guy you see?" Amber eyeballed them both. "Is that it?"

The bartender dropped the kamikazes, and they clinked glasses and drained them.

"My ex is black, you racist fucks," Amber said. "And we're the ones—us white people—who are doing the shit."

Kimmie laughed and Creeley shook her head.

Amber checked her phone again. "He says he'll be at the casino tonight to watch a fight. We can get something from him then."

"Perfect," Kimmie said. "For now, let's get drunk." He held up three fingers for the bartender.

Amber leveled a gaze at Creeley. "Tell me about this research you're doing. What's it all about?"

Creeley sipped from the mai tai, let the bitterness cut with sweet juice linger on her tongue.

Kimmie said, "Tell her about it, girl. You're following your gut. Maybe she can help."

"The case I was looking into, all those newspapers, it's about my mom. I mean, it's not about her. It's—"

"She's part of it somehow," Amber said.

Creeley hesitated while the bartender delivered three more kamikazes. She brought the rocks glass to her lips, sipped from it. Not a taste so much different from the mai tai. But more acidic. Lime and liquor and fruit juice. "My mom got put away for it, for the murder. They say it was her—that she did it. She's in prison for life."

Amber leaned back, crossed her arms. "Wow. I didn't expect that. Not at all."

"I know."

Kimmie threw back his kamikaze. "Creeley here is doing an investigation. Something tells her—it's a gut feeling—that

Momma didn't do a damn thing."

"I never said that. You can bet if my mom was wrapped up in this, she did something. I just don't think...I don't think she killed anybody. In fact, I'm positive she didn't kill anybody. It wasn't her."

Amber nodded, obvious that thoughts were running through her head. "Have you talked to her about it?"

"That's what convinced me. She said she didn't do it, and I believe her."

"And you're starting with the story, looking backward."

"Read the whole thing in the paper and got a sunburn," Kimmie said.

Creeley pressed an index finger to her burned left shoulder, watched the skin go pale and then reveal a deep-red hue. "I feel like...I don't know. I feel like I need to get past the news. I need to actually—"

"Talk to some people," Amber said.

"Yeah. Like, the actual people."

"Fieldwork," Amber said. "You need to do some fieldwork." She knocked back her kamikaze and looked at Creeley with the same unblinking gaze. "You know, I can help with that, too. Do you need some help with that Creeley?"

Kimmie said, "You don't have a crush on her, do you?"

Amber shook her head. "I like dick more than you."

"I doubt that, girl."

Creeley drained her own kamikaze. "Let's agree to all love dick equally—is that politically correct enough for you two?"

"Nobody loves it more than me," Kimmie said. "Let's agree to disagree about that. And, yes, Creeley needs some help with that other thing, Amber. That's why we're here. Plus, we want to get down and party."

✳✳✳

Creeley was buzzed by the time they reached the next bar, a dive serving mimosas for two bucks a pop. Rock 'n' roll was on the jukebox and she remembered swaying happily to the thrum of power chords. They walked two blocks to the casino after that, waited as Amber's ex got a few feels in before handing over a bag of coke—it cost them two hundred bucks. They split the cost and Creeley planned to replenish her expense by the next day—figured she'd pull it right out of Animal's stash.

Fucking Animal.

Her life was so much better without that phone buzzing her all the goddamn time.

They did a bump in the casino bathroom, all three of them giggling in a ladies' room stall. Kimmie so excited he was breathing hard. By the time they hit the street outside he was singing lines from *Hamilton* and glaring at passing cars.

"Where are we going?" Creeley chased after him.

Amber was close behind.

They reached the main drag again—Palm Canyon—and Kimmie flagged down a cab. When the driver pulled to the curb, all three of them hopped in the back and Kimmie said, "Take us to Toucans, bitch!"

Creeley said, "What's that?"

Amber patted Creeley's bare, sunburned knee. "Don't worry. You're going to love Toucans."

***

The thump of bass. Bodies pressed together. Sweat and the smell of booze and cologne and hard muscles. Creeley shook with the sound—power-pop mixed into electronic dance music—and held a drink above her head. Amber did the same. They rubbed together and laughed as the dance floor tilted back and forth in Creeley's vision.

Thump. Thump. Thump.

A beat going on forever.

Creeley leaned into Amber for support, but the music kept them both aloft. There were bodies everywhere, a DJ with a backwards cap bobbing up and down beside the bar. The bar was three deep with bartenders spinning past each other and tossing tips into a full bucket beside the cash register. Toucans was a gay bar—no doubt about that. And Creeley loved it. It felt good not to have the regular, predatory male gaze feasting on her body. She felt free and sexy and turned on. Not by a man, but by the joyous pull of the dancing and excitement of other people.

It might also have been the coke.

They did lines in the cab and right before they entered Toucans, a giant bouncer waving them in without checking ID. She didn't order a drink, but Kimmie somehow handed her one anyway as he spun into the arms of a shirtless man who made a receding hairline and thick glasses look sexy. Her and Amber let the beat take them.

Thump. Thump. Thump.

That beat going on forever.

Echoing in her head.

***

Another bathroom stall.

The thump still thumping outside, through the walls, in the chambers of her heart.

Amber was squatting on the toilet, her miniskirt pulled up around her waist. Creeley leaned against the stall, listened to the tinkle mix with laughter from outside the door.

"No underwear," Creeley said.

"So astute," Amber said and flushed. "You have to go?" She stood and tugged her skirt over her hips.

Creeley shook her head. "I want to do another line."

"I think we're out. Your little friend has been sharing quite a bit."

They stared at each other and Creeley smiled. "That's a bummer."

"I know, right?"

Creeley ran a hand inside her blouse, brought it out slick with sweat. "It feels so good to dance, you know? It feels really good." And it did—her heart was pounding, but her brain was calm... almost content.

"When's the last time you went dancing?" Amber's eyes probed at her.

"Like, never."

Amber rolled her eyes. "Come the fuck on."

Creeley blew air through pursed lips. "I don't know—my late twenties?"

"How old are you now?"

"Fucking forty—it's bullshit." Amber's bare knee bumped into Creeley's thigh, stayed there. Her skin was warm and wet, too soft somehow. "You know," she said again.

"Sure. I know." Those eyes still open and unblinking.

"Are you, I don't know, coming on to me?"

"Am I?" Amber reached out and grasped two of Creeley's fingers.

Creeley stared at her for a long minute. She could smell urine and perfume and disinfectant. The sunburn on her forehead felt raw, rough as lobster shell between her eyes. But somehow—maybe it was the drugs or maybe it wasn't—she was turned on. And she wanted to kiss a girl.

Amber said, "I will if you will."

Creeley pushed against her, felt those round boobs come up under her flatter ones. It was awkward reaching a hand around the back of Amber's shaved head, but their wet lips touched, and she felt Amber's tongue run across her top teeth. She tasted Vaseline and lime juice, pressed her own tongue back into Amber's mouth. Creeley expected to feel weird, but she didn't. She felt alive, like she was headed somewhere far off and tropical. It didn't feel right exactly, but welcome somehow. She pressed harder, felt Amber's hand brush the inside of her thigh—just under her wavy skirt. Creeley moaned to say yes, and the hand moved higher. More tongue and gasps—a bite on her lower lip. Something bigger than a moan now, but higher pitched. And a finger prying at her panties, skipping along the lips down there. She let a soft giggle come out, feeling that welcoming feeling still. And the finger was inside her—slick and wet and just saying hello. More lips and tongue and Amber breathing hard against Creeley. The finger moved higher, outside—wet and wanting. Somewhere more sensitive—always better.

Amber said, "Are you okay?"

"No," Creeley hissed. "I have a fucking sunburn."

15/The Smoker

Creeley opened her eyes to the sun shining through a sheet with the texture of a saltine cracker—her motel room bed. She rolled over, waited for the reactive weight of another body.

Nothing.

She pulled the sheet down, squinted into sunlight burning through her dusty window. Nobody but her in the room. A half-empty bottle of Beefeater sat on the TV stand, two clear plastic cups next to it. Both empty. *Thank God nobody stayed the night,* Creeley thought. She pinched the bridge of her nose, sensed a slight headache somewhere in the center of her brain. She spotted her sunglasses on the nightstand. She reached and snared them with two fingers, slid them over her eyes, and sat up in bed.

Naked. Besides her shades.

She cupped one boob, noticed red teeth marks ringing her purple nipple. *Nice.* The memory came back to her and she grimaced. Not that it was bad, but it was something she'd never done. With another girl, at least.

First time for everything.

As she got into a hot shower, Creeley decided to be proud of herself. Why the fuck not? She told Animal to shove it—though he was after her by this point. Or had sent someone after her. She'd taken up her mom's case. Followed her gut on that. And she had herself a nice sexual experience. Talk about living the life. Nothing to complain about. Except the headache, now that it ran to just above her eye line. Maybe they had Advil in the motel office.

She was drying off with those scratchy motel towels when somebody knocked on her door—housekeeping.

"Come back later! I'll be gone in a minute!"

Another knock.

Huh.

Creeley wrapped herself with a towel and went to the peephole, peeked through. *Shit*—it was Amber.

Creeley unlatched the chain lock, turned the deadbolt, and let the door swing inward. They stared at each other.

"Hey," Amber said.

"Hey."

"You said to come no later than ten."

"I did?"

"Yeah."

Creeley said, "You got some sharp teeth, sister."

"So do you," Amber said with a playful voice.

Creeley let Amber in, and they both flopped on the bed. There was no intimacy there—it was just awkward tension and the morning heat spilling over their bodies. Amber wore some capri shorts and a white tank top. Looked a little butch with her mohawk and satchel purse. Creeley said, "What are we supposed to be doing no later than ten?"

"Tell me that's all you forgot."

She turned to face Amber on the bed. "I had other stuff to remember. Or, to not forget."

"Fieldwork. We decided to talk to the reporter."

"Right," Creeley said. "The reporter. What was her name again?"

***

Dawn Griffin.

Amber used tax records to find out Dawn owned a home in Movie Colony, a historic neighborhood that used to cater to movie stars and lounge singers. Or so the real estate agents must have said. They got into Creeley's 4Runner and headed up South Palm Canyon.

"All it takes is a laptop and an internet connection."

Amber nodded in the passenger seat. "Just because she owns the place doesn't mean she lives there."

They cruised up the palm-tree-lined street, Creeley taking note of all the hip-looking restaurants and a few boutique hotels. Amber directed her east and then west, onto a wide street with homes mostly hidden behind tall hedges or adobe walls. They found the address and parked behind a late-ninties Honda Civic, silver with a rusted hood and roof. Of all the houses on the street, this was the smallest and worst kept. Red garden bricks made a walkway through dead grass to a door inlaid with foggy glass block. An aluminum awning covered a patio of cracked concrete. This house was your basic stucco exterior, a kind of off-brown with hints of charcoal. The windows on either side of the front door were covered with newspapers.

Amber said, "Looks promising."

"Does it?" Creeley pinched the bridge of her nose again and sighed. She reached out and pressed the doorbell.

They heard a hacking cough approach and the door unlatched, swung open to reveal a small old woman in a pink terry-cloth robe. She had a cigarette shoved between her lips and it moved up and down when she talked. A strong wave of cigarette smoke spilled from inside onto the patio.

"The fuck do you two dimes want?"

"Dawn Griffin?" Amber bounced in her Doc Martens.

"That's what it says in the papers," the woman said.

Creeley said, "I was hoping I could talk to you about some stories you wrote. This was back quite a few years."

"Had to be—I haven't written for the *Sun* since, what, since my pencil-dick ex-husband was puffing out his chest on the night copy desk. Which stories, honey? I got more bylines than a train station hooker has bug bites."

Creeley hesitated to respond. Looking at this old woman with her burning cigarette and ratty pink robe, she felt out of place. As if she didn't deserve any answers. Worse, as if she didn't deserve to try to get answers. Like she didn't deserve her own voice and thoughts. Creeley knew it went back to her childhood, to running away in the desert so long ago, to the long train rides that took her worse places than she wanted to admit or remember. At her age, she was only now doing what her gut told her to do. And she was doing it for her mother, who—honest to God—couldn't give two shits about her. But it wasn't about any of that, being here. It was about something else inside her clawing to get out—a creature digging at her insides that wanted more. More for itself. More from the world. More for her—more for Creeley Nash the drug runner. She blinked twice and cleared her throat. She thought about what to say, how to ask.

"Spit it out, dime score. *Judge Judy's* coming on in five." The old woman plucked the cigarette from her mouth with two fingers, dangled it at her hip. One knee bounced forward and back beneath the robe.

Amber said, "It's about the—"

"The murder," Creeley said, cutting in with too loud a voice. "The Sunny Dunes Motel on Palm Canyon."

Silence like smoke.

And then Dawn Griffin said, "Levi Mackey—it was 1996."

***

They sat in the breakfast nook. At one of those wrought-iron tables from the seventies, looking through thin glass windows at a lime-green pool. The house was clean but drenched in smoke—a worn leather couch faced an old box-screen TV, and news clippings were framed on the walls. Creeley figured Dawn Griffin for a shut-in. Didn't look like she entertained much. Shit, ever. She brought each of them a tumbler of gin with a splash of orange juice. "Let's start brunch," she said as she sat down and smacked a pack of cigarettes against her palm.

"Thanks so much," Creeley said as she drained half the drink. "I know we're—"

"Got a hangover, huh? Tell you what I used to do, when I was on the beat. I used to put pickle juice in my coffee." She lit a cigarette and puffed. "Sounds gross, I know. But don't knock it." She tapped her ash into a coffee mug in the center of the table.

Amber cleared her throat, drank.

"I guess, what I'm hoping, is you could tell me about—"

"What brings you into it?" Dawn puffed and squinted at Creeley through dense smoke.

"Me?"

"How are you connected to the murder?" The sentence came out slow, pointed. How you'd say it to somebody with bad hearing. Dawn's I'm-asking-*you* voice.

Creeley looked at Amber. She got a shrug.

"You know Levi? Or the hooker?"

"The hooker," Creeley said.

"Well, you look like her. You know that? I thought that might be it, and it don't surprise me."

"What's that?"

"She's got somebody convinced it wasn't her. I knew it'd never be nobody from the law. Maybe one of them projects they got at the law schools. But nobody besides that. Had to be family. I never did find you back then." Dawn snapped her fingers. "That's right. Creeley—isn't it? I remember your name. You still going by that?"

Creeley felt the surprise on her own face. "What do you mean, you never found me?"

"Shit—first thing I did when they hauled Blossom in, I got a jailhouse interview. She tells me she's got a kid, a daughter. A runaway. I made calls all around the country, figured you got picked up somewhere. Never hit, though. Nada. Zip."

"She asked you to find me?" Like her own voice coming out of somebody else's mouth.

Dawn sniffed smoke and sucked at her top teeth. "I can't say she did, Creeley. I was just doing my job. Following up on everything—all the leads."

Amber reached out and covered Creeley's hand with her own. Creeley pulled away, sat with both hands in her lap. The gin and OJ was calling her name, but she left it. Dawn noticed Amber's caring gesture, but it didn't faze her. She stared with the calm indecision of a veteran reporter.

No surprises in her world.

Amber said, "We have your stories, but is there anything that isn't there? Something you had to leave out?"

Dawn grunted. "Honey, there's always shit we got to leave out.

Or put in. Or both at once. Don't ever let nobody tell you reporters are neutral—it's absolute horseshit." She reached out and took Creeley's drink, finished it for her. She puffed and talked. "At the time, I was screwing a narcotics cop—decent piece, if you take my meaning—and they always sent word to me through him. I got so much shit on background it was embarrassing. That's how Chief Lopez got taken down in '98. But usually they were asking me politely to hold back on certain things. So they could use it in an interrogation. In case they ever caught anybody."

"Like my mom."

"Like Blossom."

Amber said, "When you say background…"

"Means I'm free to know it, to try to dig it up from other sources, but I can't use it. Not in the way I need to. Gives me facts, a way to get at the story."

"Facts about the murder? Weapons? Evidence?" Amber was jotting in a small notebook. "Or was it something with the cops?"

Dawn shook her head and said, "Lots of stuff like that. Key details. But all that comes out in the trial, for the most part. I'm talking something else. Shit people think won't make a difference, but it does."

"Like what?" Creeley's hands were still in her lap.

"Well, the relationships all these people had to each other, for one. Start off, what the hell is this out-of-town kid doing with some local hooker at a motel? Might seem simple—he picked her up. But Levi didn't have nothing like that in his background. Got me interested and I had a sit down with the homicide commander. Unofficial, one long evening at Melvyn's. He got a feel in on my left tit, but it was worth getting the info. I don't regret it. I knew it might help someday, but I wish it was sooner. And now here I am, giving it to you. See, most times with murder…It's somebody they know who did it. Cops, they start with the husband. Or the wife. They move in a circle from there—close relatives, friends, frequent people who the victim came into contact with. They do it like that. And, sure as dog shit on a flip-flop, it's somebody close. A surprise maybe, but not surprising."

Creeley felt her eyebrows pressing into each other. The headache was a ball-peen hammer now and her stomach was turning. She said, "What are you telling me?"

"Long way about it, I'm telling you what I think."

"And, what's that?" Amber was making ink circles in her notepad now.

"She didn't do it," Dawn said. "It wasn't her."

Creeley licked her lips, sighed. "How do you know?"

"Levi Mackey was tough. And he was about to become a Marine. He was a strong *man*—not a kid—and any asshole in this town would have struggled mightily to kill him. That"—she pointed at Creeley with a cigarette—"I can promise you. And besides, Levi Mackey was Blossom's son. You think she has it in her to kill your brother, Creeley? All the shit she did, you think that's in her?"

"I hear you," Creeley said, "but I don't understand."

"Levi was your brother. And his dad—wherever he is—was your daddy. Or so Blossom told it to me."

"This doesn't seem right," Creeley said.

"No—it's not. Same as being put away for what you didn't do...That don't seem right neither. But what the fuck do I know? I'm just a reporter. Neutral as a cock in a cold, cold shower."

16/Less Lethal Means

The dive bar smelled like wet towels.

Creeley poured a Negra Modelo down her throat and waved at the bartender for another.

Amber said, "Let's get two shooters of tequila."

The provisions hit the bar and they drank.

"I'm not sure what to say." Creeley stared straight ahead at a dusty Miller Lite mirror. She saw her own reflection broken up by the letters—eyes off-kilter from her nose and chin. Sunburned forehead red as all hell. And it hurt.

"Anytime you go after something like this, anytime you start to dig in, you're going to find stuff."

She wanted to look at Amber and tell her to fuck off.

You don't find out your only brother was murdered.

And maybe by your mom.

No—that's not the kind of shit you uncover.

"Dawn said she was sure your mom didn't kill him."

"Levi," Creeley said.

"Levi. I know. His name was Levi."

"My brother."

"Okay, look, I don't want to be a voice of doubt." Amber stopped and watched Creeley.

Creeley said, "But?"

"But this comes from somebody, and we haven't verified it. It could be wrong somehow, or more nuanced than what she described. As far as we know, she got the information from your mom."

"Blossom knows how to lie."

"Or maybe she lied for a reason."

Creeley nodded, thought about what Amber was saying. If it was true that Levi was her brother—*fuck*. If it wasn't, why lie? They needed to confirm Dawn's presentation of facts. Learn the truth.

Wasn't that why Creeley was here in Palm Springs?

Wasn't that why she was hiding from Animal?

Yes—for the truth.

"How do we figure this out?"

Amber pulled out her notebook, drew a square. Inside the square, she wrote 'Levi Mackey.' She drew lines out from each side of the square and wrote 'Blossom Nash,' 'Creeley Nash,' and 'Dad' next to each line. "First thing is, we need to find Levi's birth record—from that, we get his dad's name. And, we confirm whether your mom was his mom."

"He was, what, three or four years older than me when he was murdered? That puts him being born in Pasadena, I think. Or maybe Arizona—my mom lived in Bullhead City for a few years." Creeley waved for another round of beers. She took hers down to half, patted her stomach. Bloated already and it wasn't yet noon. "We need to switch to the hard stuff."

"We can go to my place for internet."

Creeley side-eyed Amber, nodded with pursed lips. "More internet shit?"

"More internet shit. Hopefully, the records are online. California and Arizona are where we start."

Creeley thought again about Animal, knew he had sent somebody—or paid somebody local—to find her. That got her thinking about the money in her motel room. And the drugs. "You know what," Creeley said, "I need to get back to the motel."

Amber stopped scribbling, looked at her. "Why?"

"There's something there—I should move motels."

"Or stay with me," Amber said. She flushed red, hesitated before saying, "Because, you know, it's cheaper."

✳✳✳

Creeley slowed on Palm Canyon as they approached the motel. She passed the parking lot entrance and peered past Amber out the passenger side window.

"What are you looking for?"

"I'll know it if I see it." The parking lot was half-empty, like normal. Creeley could see her second-floor room—the door was still closed, and the window curtain hadn't moved. She scanned the parking lot for any suspicious cars, flipped a bitch at the next stop light.

"You seem a little paranoid," Amber said.

Creeley made the left-hand turn across oncoming traffic. She parked the 4Runner but kept the engine running. "There's some shit I haven't told you."

"Okay."

"Do you want me to tell you?"

"I don't know—do I?"

"You're helping me," Creeley said. "I haven't had a lot of help in my life."

Amber nodded. She bit her bottom lip and squinted at Creeley. "This isn't about last night—why I'm here. That was just..."

"A night," Creeley said.

"A night. That's all. I'm here, and if you need help...I'll help you."

Creeley shook her head. She scratched behind her right ear, noticed her headache was gone. She was thankful for this small favor of the universe, wondered whether it was the tequila or beer that did it. She decided to come out with it—if Amber was going to help her, she needed to know about Animal. And the money. And the drugs.

"I never told you why I was here," Creeley said.

"Your mom?"

"No—I'm here for work."

"Like, what, a job?"

Creeley sighed and said, "I live in Portland. And I run drugs for a living. Like, I work as a driver—I pick up drugs and bring them back to the city."

"You're serious?"

"I work for a guy named Animal."

Amber let out a belly laugh, wrinkled her nose. "You're fucking serious?"

Creeley nodded, amused at her own voice saying these things.

"A drug runner?"

"Yeah—I run drugs."

"And this stuff with your mom—"

"It's all true. All of it. When I got here—for my pickup—I ran into a guy I knew. I mean, when we were kids I knew him. He told me about my mom and it just..."

"It scooped you up," Amber said.

"That's a good way to describe it. The thing is—Animal is coming after me. Or sending someone after me. And you need to know that because Animal does not fuck around."

"You have his shit?"

Creeley nodded again. "I have his shit."

Amber chuckled, ran black fingernails through her mohawk. "I know people like Animal. Or used to know some. If you're trying to warn me, consider it done."

"And you'll stay?"

"Girl, this is the biggest adventure I've had in years."

"This is exciting to a librarian—really?"

"Go fuck yourself, Creeley."

Creeley opened her door. "Why would I do that, when I could ask you to fuck me?"

Amber rolled her eyes. "Get your shit. And Animal's, too."

Creeley got out of the car, looked back in at Amber. "Watch out for thugs and punks. I'll be right back." She slammed the door and headed for the stairway to her second-floor room.

***

A rush of cold air hit Creeley as she opened the door.

And so did Hero's voice: "I wondered when you'd get back."

Creeley stepped back into the outdoor hallway, but she stopped herself—better to face this now. She stepped inside and slammed the door.

He was leaning against the wall near the bathroom, one of those clear plastic glasses in his hand. His lips were wet, arms bare in the wifebeater tank, and his skinny legs poked out of board shorts and ended at dirty feet in drugstore flip-flops. *A desert thug. How atmospheric.*

Creeley leaned against the door and crossed her arms. "You found me. So what? Animal doesn't pay enough to hurt a girl, especially after what you got me into the other night."

Hero shrugged, sipped. "I do appreciate our first project together. The cop deserved it—in case you had any guilt."

"I don't." He didn't need to know about her trip to see the detective. Hero knowing that would be bad for Creeley.

"But I did get a call from Animal."

"I'm sure."

"He just wants his shit back—said I could let you go on whatever dumbfuck journey you're on."

Creeley nodded, squinted in the dark room to see if he had a gun on him. Couldn't tell. "How nice of him to set me free."

"Animal ain't so bad."

"What are you? Some kind of desert-rat errand boy?"

Hero straightened, let his empty plastic cup fall to the carpet. His face shrank into a scowl, loosened as he let her insult pass through him. "I knew you were a tough bitch, right when I saw you. Had that look and tone to you. A smell, maybe. They call it pheromones."

"Thanks for the biology lesson."

"I didn't get my GED for nothing, right?"

Creeley rolled her eyes, noticed the empty bottle of Beefeater on the TV stand. "Day drinking, huh?"

"Something like that. Hey, look, I got no beef with you. I hooked you up the other night, right? I just want Animal's shit. Then I got to get on the highway, drive my ass to Oregon."

"It's not here—Animal's shit."

"I figured that when I couldn't find it." He looked around the room, empty except for Creeley's JanSport pack and a pair of cutoff jeans and a black bra. "You travel pretty light."

"I didn't plan on staying."

"I get it. Plans change, right? Do me a solid—let's go get

Animal's shit right now, end this before it gets ugly." He took a step toward her, hung his head over one shoulder. "I don't want to threaten you or anything, but Animal—"

"Yeah. Yeah. Animal wants his shit—I know." Creeley swung the door open and started out into the oppressive heat. Over one hundred degrees now. "Let's go get it."

Hero followed her onto the landing, walked slightly behind her. "Where the fuck is it?"

"A friend's place." Creeley pounded on Kimmie's door as she walked past—two doors down from her own—and shouted a greeting, "I'll be back tonight, Kimmie!" She was thinking, *Get your ass out here. I need you, Kimmie.*

They reached the staircase at the far end of the building and Creeley started down the steps, Hero right behind her. She heard the 4Runner's passenger door slam and caught a glimpse of Amber getting out, cell phone in one hand.

Come on, Kimmie. What the hell?

Two more steps. Slow and steady.

"Let's go, man."

"Fuck you. I have a killer sunburn. And a hangover." Two more steps. A third—the sound of a motel room door opening. She saw Kimmie peer over the railing and look down at them. He was shirtless, a bleary sexed-up look in his eyes.

"Where you going, girl? Who's that thing with you?"

Creeley stopped and said, "I'll be back tonight—let's get a drink."

Hero said, "Hurry the fuck up."

"Wait a minute—I got something for you, girl." Kimmie vanished into his room.

Creeley stopped, leaned into the railing. They were about halfway down the stairs, Amber watching them with a nonchalant gaze.

"The fuck is this? Go." Hero nudged her with a gangly hand.

"Wait a sec. He's my friend. It'll seem weird if we go."

"I got it right here." Kimmie jogged down the walkway toward the staircase. He made the turn and came down the steps saying, "I promised you I was here for you, girl."

Hero said, "A fucking fruit—" And got a stream of pepper spray in the face. "Ah, what the fuck!" He stumbled on the steps, crouched into the fetal position. The pepper spray covered his hands and head, started him whimpering.

Kimmie screamed: "This man is hurting us! He's trying to touch my friends! He's trying to touch my girlfriend!"

Doors opened and the motel clerk poked his head out of the office. As Hero stood and stumbled past Creeley and into the parking lot, his hands probing at his face, people started telling each other to call the police. Creeley followed him down the stairs, watched as he lurched to his car—a blacked-out Audi— and somehow drove out onto the highway. The car swerved as it accelerated, disappeared.

Creeley turned to the crowd and said, "We're fine, everybody. I think we're fine."

Doors began to close and lock. The motel clerk watched for a moment but disappeared back into his office. Kimmie came down the stairs and gave Creeley a hug. "You okay, girl?"

"Thanks so much."

"Ain't no thing."

Amber, leaning against the 4Runner, said, "You should probably switch motels, Kimmie."

"Who cares—this is a dump anyhow." He looked at Creeley with his I'm-so-serious face. "You want that other stuff you left in my room?"

"I do," she said. "And I think the two of us should stay with Amber. That guy is a problem for all of us now."

Kimmie looked at Amber, who shrugged.

"Alright, girls," Kimmie said. "Party at Amber's house tonight. I'm down with that." He jogged up the stairs, the muscles in his back rippling with sun and sweat. The canister of pepper spray, bright pink, dangled from his right hand.

Another party.

With the boy from the train car—the smoker.

Mr. Mohawk.

So skinny he looked like an upright cigarette and could slip through the chainlink fence where it slid under the bridge. He followed Creeley down to the riverbank. She pulled at the straps on her bikini top, sure the boy—older than her?—watched her fingers brush at the pale skin of her shoulders.

"Hey, wait up." His footsteps crunched behind her—a sockless street kid in dirty checkered Vans.

"Keep up, buddy," Creeley said as she jogged along the marshy shore. She lost her balance and stepped into the damp soil, soaked her sandaled feet. She squinted at the sunlight glinting off the dirty river water, heard traffic passing in an endless rush above them.

"Where are we going?"

"To a spot I found," Creeley said. She stopped and tried to rinse her muddy feet in the river, winced as small stones dug into her heels. The mud wouldn't rinse—it was fine, watery soil that needed scrubbing. Whatever. She still heard the boy as she found her trail, tried jogging along the path. It was hemmed in by green, reedy plants and they scratched the backs of her hands as she ran. Around a concrete bridge support peppered with graffiti, and Creeley saw it— the worn fold-out couch missing its middle cushion. Still shaded by the blue tarp she rigged between two trees.

She ran to the couch, lifted one of the cushions, dug her hand into the metal guts of the couch. She came out with a plastic baggie—inside she had a pink pipe of frosted glass and some pot. Maybe two bowls worth. She flopped onto the couch, pulled everything out, and started to pack a bowl. Fingers twisting and rolling and pushing and sticky.

Mr. Mohawk came around the concrete and graffiti and

stopped to watch her. "You don't want to hear Johnny play his new song, or what?"

"Fuck Johnny," Creeley said. "He only knows two chords."

"So?"

"So? You need three to make a song." She looked up at him and watched his shoulders slump. "Don't be such a baby—I think I want to kiss you." She looked back at the pipe, didn't care to see him blush or get sheepish. One thing Creeley didn't like about boys: they were so hopeful of her approval. And who gave a shit what she thought? If it wasn't her, weren't there a thousand other girls with pretty smiles and green eyes? Ten thousand?

And he plopped down beside her, in the middle spot without the cushion. "Nice spot. At least you can see the river from here."

Creeley glanced up at the ribbon of black that stretched out of sight behind a meatpacking plant. She sighed and put her attention back on the pipe. "It's just a place to smoke out—no cops. Hey, you have a lighter on you?"

"Yeah. And, hey, I never told you my real name."

"I like Rooster. Let's just keep it as Rooster." It was the name he yelled at her in the boxcar as they rode the rails out of Palm Springs. She didn't want to know much more.

"Right. Yeah." His mohawk was plastered with hair gel. It stood straight up off his head, ran from his neck to his brow. He dug into his denim jacket—patched with Reverend Horton Heat, Anthrax, Social Distortion—and came out with an orange Bic.

Creeley snatched it from him and lit the bowl, inhaled. She flipped the lighter into Rooster's lap, sucked all the smoke into her lungs, held it. She passed the pipe to him and spoke without exhaling, her voice light and breathy, "I just get sick of being at those things. I like to get away."

Rooster took a hit, passed the pipe and lighter back to her as she exhaled a cloud of smoke.

Creeley said, "Why'd you follow me?"

"I liked what you were saying about the president."

"Oh, really? I don't know shit about politics."

"At least you have an opinion."

Creeley shrugged, took another hit. She tried to pass the pipe to Rooster, but he waved it away. She exhaled. "Only one hit? I thought you were a punk rocker."

"I'm not a punk rocker—it's just, these are my favorite bands. Do you listen to music, or whatever?"

"Yes. I listen to music. Or whatever."

"Sorry, I mean...Like, who do you listen to?"

"Van Halen. AC/DC. I like the hard rock stuff."

"It's classic shit," Rooster said.

"Fucking A. My mom used to—" She stopped herself. "I used to listen to it back home."

"Where's that?"

"Nowhere. Here. Wherever."

Rooster nodded, pulled his Vans up under his knees. "I know how that shit works."

"You're not from California?"

"Fuck no. Texas. My mom's a dental hygienist."

"Why'd you leave then?"

Rooster stared at her without blinking. "My mom's a dental hygienist."

"What about your pa, Rooster?" she said it with a twangy southern accent, giggled as it came out from between her lips.

That got him to shrug, look out at the river as the sun sank and darkness came down over them. "I never knew him, but that's not something that bothers me—it is what it is, okay?"

"You call it. I'm just here to let you get it off your chest." She slapped his leg, felt the crisp denim feel of unwashed jeans. "I never knew my dad either—what an asshole."

"Yeah. Total asshole."

"You want more of this?" She held the pipe out to him.

"I'm good—thanks."

Creeley took the last hit, let the smoke fill her lungs and linger. When she let it out, a raindrop tapped the point of her nose. "It's raining again."

MATT PHILLIPS

"I love rain."

"How long have we been here?"

"Like, maybe a month."

Creeley laughed. "Trust me, you don't love rain. Nobody loves rain."

"It's kind of poetic, if you ask me." Rooster leaned closer to her, put his arm around her shoulders. "Is this okay with you?"

She leaned into him. "You're the first guy I've ever heard say that word. And, yeah, I like it."

"What word?"

"Poetic, doofus."

"Should I say it again? Poetic. Poetic. Poetic."

The rain came then, hard and fast and fat.

Creeley tilted her head into Rooster's cheek, kissed the side of his neck. "You're right. This *is* poetic," she said. And she kissed him on the lips.

18/The Interwebs

Amber—Creeley's newest crush with a mohawk—lived in a second-floor walk-up in north Palm Springs. A run-of-the-mill condo complex built with cheap lumber and covered with beige stucco. It had a Palm Springs vibe, though, with all the palm trees and bougainvilleas. Creeley smelled Tex-Mex as she walked in, saw the downstairs neighbor peek his head out—a hipster guy with a nose ring and Orange County stars tattooed on his bare shoulders.

"Hey, Amber—I just made tacos. You want to hang out?"

Amber shook her head and started to climb the stairs to her door. "Not today, Micah. Having friends over. Thanks for the offer."

Creeley followed her up, heard Kimmie stop behind her and say, "Hey."

"Hey, you," Micah said.

Creeley and Amber got to the top of the stairs, looked down to see Kimmie give them a ta-ta wave as he grinned and hopped a patch of wet grass onto Micah's patio.

Amber shrugged and unlocked the door.

Creeley walked in and tossed her backpack and Animal's bag onto the carpet near the door. She said, "What are you, a cat lady?"

There were two tabby cats curled up on the leather sofa. Another one spread out on a chair in the corner. There was no TV, but instead a huge bookshelf full to the edges. It was taller than Creeley. In the corner was a desk with a desktop computer. The open kitchen was quaint, the bar top covered by two wooden wine racks. One rack was half-empty, but the other was filled with bottles.

Amber said, "I have roommates—my cats."

"No TV?" Creeley perused the books, ran her finger from one spine to the next.

"I like to read." Amber opened the refrigerator, pulled out a bottle of white. "You like?"

"Sure." Lots of travelogues. A whole shelf of graphic novels. Lots of titles by Patricia Highsmith and Walter Mosley. Amber liked genre fiction including horror and fantasy. Surprised Creeley to see few titles she recognized—no Moby-Dick or Shakespeare or any of that old shit.

"You read a lot, or what?" Amber popped the cork, poured wine into some tumblers. She walked over and handed one to Creeley.

"Not really. I like magazines." Creeley sat on the couch, flinched as one of the tabby cats leaped off the couch onto the carpet and slinked down the hallway.

Amber stared down at her, swished wine in her mouth.

Creeley said, "We should just talk about last night."

"Okay. I'll talk about it."

"I never do that. I mean, I've never done that. It's like—"

"Creeley, I get it." Amber swirled her tumbler, took a sip of the wine. "I get it. It was a one-time thing, right?"

Creeley watched Amber for any sign of disappointment. Drooping shoulders. A hidden frown. Anything. But there was nothing—just her nice smile and steady green eyes. *Shit.* Being with a girl wasn't like being with a guy. *Way different.*

A better kind of different.

But Creeley still wasn't sure it was her thing.

It probably wasn't.

Amber said, "Are we going to find out whether Levi was your brother, or what?" The *thump-thump-thump* of bass came through the floor and Amber rolled her eyes. "Looks like it's only me and you for the rest of the day."

"Kimmie's lonely, I think. He needs people."

"Micah needs people, too." Amber sat down at the desk and tapped the computer keyboard. She started punching keys before Creeley could respond.

"You going to do some of your librarian shit, or what?"

"Something like that. I spend a lot of time doing research and—just so happens—I have a subscription to a family tree research service."

"Like, one of those ancestry websites?"

"That's it." She punched more keys.

Creeley stood and walked over, squinted at the screen. She could see the search fields in the dialog box and fed Amber some information. "Try the name, Levi Mackey. Give the location as Pasadena or Bullhead City. If he's three years older than me, maybe four, give the birth year as, what, 1978?"

"Plus or minus a year or two. Just to get broader search results," Amber said as she punched the search button. A spinning wheel popped up and they waited. Both women sipped wine and sighed in unison. The search results populated. "Almost a hundred records. Looks like birth records, school yearbooks, and—"

"A death certificate," Creeley said.

"Holy fuck. That's him."

Creeley's stomach churned as she read the card. Levi Branson Mackey. Deceased 3/20/96. Riverside County, California. Where was she in March of that year? The Midwest maybe. Riding rails into a hot summer in the desert southwest. Already trying to escape Portland for the first time? She couldn't remember—not for sure.

Amber clicked on the record for more information—nothing else was listed. "We go down to the county record office, and maybe we can get more. Let me try a search with his middle name added in." She punched a few keys, hit search again. "There it is—around forty birth records."

Creeley watched as Amber scrolled through the records and then she saw what she was waiting for. "There—that one. Mother is listed as Nash. Does it have a first name for her?"

Amber clicked on the record but there was no first name. And no name for Levi's father. "Doesn't look like it."

"And no father listed?"

"Probably didn't sign the birth certificate."

"Well, that doesn't fucking surprise me."

"But we have a birthplace, if this is him. It's Pasadena."

The thumping below them stopped for an instant, resurfaced twice as loud.

"It has to be him."

Amber dipped her head, nodded. "It's likely him."

"Okay," Creeley said. "It's got to be him and, yeah, he was my brother. Fuck. I'm not sure how I should feel about this."

"Feel empowered. You have more to go on."

Creeley wandered back to the couch, sank into it, and started to run her fingers through the cat's fur.

Amber swung around in her swivel chair and said, "Alexander likes his ears rubbed."

Creeley raised one eyebrow. "Does he like hand jobs, too?"

"No. He's female."

"I'm sorry?"

Amber shook her head and finished her wine. "I was in an equality-slash-gender-is-performative phase."

"So you named your female cat Alexander?"

"Yes. Yes, I did."

Creeley didn't know what to say—she felt the music pounding in her chest. "Does Micah do this a lot?"

"Only when he has company. The romantic kind."

Creeley nodded, rubbed the cat's ears. Breathed as deep as possible. "My mother is terrible—I mean, she was a total shit head to me. I only know one or two people worse than her." Animal's pudgy face flashed through Creeley's head. She glanced at her bags—squinted at the black duffel full of money and drugs. "She was a hooker and a meth head, but she wasn't a murderer. And her own kid—no fucking way. Not in this hell, or the next."

"Okay, you're sure of it."

"Fuck yes." She looked from the bag to Amber. She met those steady green eyes again and, for some reason, felt confident. She knew Blossom Nash was innocent. Now, she had to prove it. No matter what it took. It wasn't about her mom. No. It was about her. It was about running away at fourteen and never looking back. About how that tore her to pieces. How it churned her into a ground meat of a person. It was about shooting drugs into her arms, her thighs, the bottom of her ass. About telling a wife beater to fuck himself and suck his own cock. It was about serving shitty burgers and beers, trying to pull a hundred in tips a night. If Creeley could do this, if she could prove that Blossom was innocent, it meant one important truth—Creeley's life wasn't all shit and waste. It was for something. Forget that the something was fucked up. It was still something. *Let's do this,* she thought. *I need to do this.* "I want to introduce you to somebody," Creeley said.

"You have a lot of friends for being in town two days."

"He's not a friend. Not yet he isn't."

"Who is it?"

"A cop," Creeley said.

"A fucking cop?"

"Yep."

Amber said, "I'm not a fan of cops. Every cop I ever met was a total dick."

Creeley nodded and said, "So is this one. He's a homicide dick."

19/Dirty Cops

Same apartment, but Creeley didn't have the pink box of donuts this time.

It was hotter—near a hundred degrees—and both her and Amber were sweating after the walk from the parking lot.

Creeley said, "I hope he's running the air conditioning," and knocked twice. "It's me, Monty—the drug girl!" Creeley noticed Amber flinch and look around the apartment complex and courtyard. "There's nobody around to hear, and he won't arrest me." She knocked twice more. "Come on. I know you're taking a sick day. You have to be."

The door opened and cold air rushed out at them. Monty—shirtless in gray boxer briefs—stood there with a green smoothie in a glass. His face had slimmed down a bit from the beating, but the gray-blue bruising was still visible. He had red marks up and down both sides of his ribcage, a modest beer belly showing a boot-shaped bruise. "I thought I got rid of you, drug mule."

"I brought a friend."

"That, I can see." He examined Amber's mohawk and bronze legs below her mid-thigh skirt. "Looks like another troublemaker to me."

"Monty—this is Amber. Amber—this is Monty, the brave homicide detective I told you about." Creeley smiled with false joy. "Can we come in now?"

Monty sauntered back to the sofa, fell onto it. He threw back the smoothie, slurped, and licked his lips. "Shut the door—don't let my air out, troublemakers."

When they were seated across from Monty, Creeley cleared her throat and said, "I know you don't necessarily want to help me."

"I can't help you. You're a criminal, and I'm a cop."

"You're a dirty cop." Creeley noticed Amber shifting uncomfortably again, decided to soften her approach. "Or maybe I'm remembering wrong—wasn't it you who said all cops were dirty?"

Monty rubbed his belly, finished a last gulp of green. He sat up straighter, set the glass on the coffee table. "Broccoli, kale, and apple. Tastes like orange juice, if you can believe that. My doc says I need to eat more veggies. He also says I need to cut back on alcohol, but that's another goal spinning its way down the toilet." Monty cleared his throat and coughed. "Look, I appreciate that you're trying to do this thing...What, for your mom?"

"That's right."

"But, and I say this with the biggest 'but' in the world, I can't get caught up in every social justice warrior's agenda. If I did, I'd be—"

"This is just about justice, Detective. It's not some guilt thing on my part. Somebody's locked up for life. And for something she didn't do—that doesn't piss you off?"

"A lot of shit pisses me off. Doesn't mean I can do anything about it."

Amber said, "But you're a detective."

"Yeah. And you're a groupie to a punk band. You think—"

"I'm a librarian, dickwad. With a master's degree."

"Whoop-dee-doo. You think that matters in this world? I'm a detective, but I have to do what people tell me. I can't just run off and take up random cases."

"That's not what we want," Creeley said. She tried to stare Monty straight in his eyes, get it into his head through telepathy that this was about law and order. It was about making sure justice did the world right. "We just need you to connect us to the right people."

Monty looked at them in silence. He sniffed hard through his nose. "You want me to put you in touch with some cops."

Amber said, "That's right. Homicide cops."

"Say I buy this, that I want to help you. I need some reason to put you in touch. I call up some old homicide dick about this, he's going to want to know why. I mean, it's me questioning the work. You see that, right? It's not about what I want—it's about professional courtesy."

Amber crossed her legs. "What do you know about the Mackey murder?"

"What I remember. A sex worker"—Monty's eyes touched on Creeley for a second before swinging back to Amber—"strangled some teenager down at the old motel off Palm Canyon. What I remember from the papers—I was on patrol back then—was that it was open and shut. Easy to close, right? Nothing weird or odd or, shit, mysterious even."

Amber nodded, looked at Creeley before responding. When she did respond, she did so with an even tone. Not pleading or passionate. A simple voice of reason and logic. "This case may seem simple. The basic evidence, from news reports, appears straightforward. But we've uncovered some information that doesn't appear to have been considered by investigators or the DA's office. That's why we're sitting here in front of you. It's not about guilt or innocence even, but about investigating all leads. It's about due diligence."

Monty chuckled. "What you see in the news reports—that isn't all there is to it."

"We know that," Creeley said. "That's why we need you to introduce us to Detective Ray Parks. He led the investigation, and he did most of the legwork from what we can tell. It's not us wanting to toast him. We're trying to get every piece of information available."

"You said you found new evidence. What is it?"

"Levi Mackey was my brother," Creeley said. "That means—"

"Your mom killed her own son." Monty watched her as he said it.

Creeley showed no emotion. Her response was to nod—once. No use fighting the conclusion now. This was about getting to the truth. And she needed Monty to help her. Getting introduced to Detective Parks by a fellow detective would urge him to speak to her. "That's a fact—whatever really happened—that should have come out. Don't you think?"

Monty rocked back and forth on the couch, shoved his tongue into his right cheek. He scratched his chest and watched Creeley for a long few seconds. He seemed to be thinking hard about what to do, and he appeared to make a decision. "How do you know this?"

"Birth records," Amber said. "You know, research?"

"Ray Parks—he's kind of an asshole."

Creeley said, "That's another reason why we need you to introduce us. If he knew, then he knew. He'll know why it didn't come out. And he can't know why Blossom didn't say anything. If she did say something, it's not on Parks."

"It's on her defense," Amber said. "Right?"

Monty shoved his tongue into his bottom lip. "Might be true. Unless what I said is true."

"What's that?" Creeley leaned back into the couch, felt confident Monty was on her side in this. Or moving over to her side, at least.

"Unless he's dirty," Monty said.

They sat in silence while the air conditioner hummed around them.

Monty the homicide detective lifted his cell phone from the coffee table, punched a button, and put it to his ear. It didn't take long until he said, "Ray—how you doing? This is Monty. I got an old case that came up on me. Hoping I can swing by for a chat."

20/Polo Shirts and Golf Gab

It took Monty twenty minutes to shower, shave, and slip into a beige polo shirt and above-the-knee shorts. He wore boat shoes and stinky cologne. Creeley and Amber followed him downstairs to his mailbox, watched him toss junk mail into a blue recycling bin.

Creeley wondered how she found the detective so attractive two nights before—he looked old and beat-up and addicted to country club brunches. He didn't carry his gun or badge. When they got into Creeley's 4Runner—Amber riding in back—she couldn't help asking, "No gun or badge for this, huh? What about what happened the other night?"

"That's all paid for now," Monty said. "Nothing to worry about. You're going to take a right out here. Make a left onto the next street. Ray's all the way out in Desert Hot Springs."

Amber said, "What about, like, crime and stuff? Don't you need your badge?"

"I'm off today—here's the left."

Creeley made the left turn, cruised past some residential office buildings and another apartment complex. She made a right onto a four-lane and they headed north. The road crossed a series of dunes, shaggy creosote bushes waving at them in the desert wind. To their right, gray power-line poles stretched beyond where Creeley could see, and the oncoming traffic ripped by with the sound of air and sand.

Amber said, "Desert Hot Springs? Shitty place to live. I guess a cop's salary isn't too great."

Monty checked the side-view mirror and shrugged, "Ray does okay. He's just a cheap bastard. Lives in one of those trailer parks. The mobile home's small, but he likes the spa and pool they have in the place. Tell you the truth, I don't know Ray too well. We'll drink together, talk shop, but I know jack shit about his personal life."

"What's that got to do with this?" Creeley checked her mirrors, wondered what Monty was searching for.

Monty said, "Nothing that I can see from here."

"What's that supposed to mean?" Amber leaned over the seat, rested her chin next to Creeley's headrest.

"It means what it means. I don't know anything about what happened back then...with the Mackey homicide."

A few miles after they crossed the 10 freeway, Monty directed Creeley to a trailer park called Hideaway Dunes and she took the dirt entrance road. Most of the mobile homes were rundown—flanked by rusted work trucks or secondhand sedans missing hubcaps.

Amber said, "There's a pool here?"

"Hot tub, too," Monty said. "And a sauna. They got a three-hole golf course, if you can believe that. All par threes. It's just that way." He pointed down one of the dirt lanes and Creeley swung her head to catch a glimpse of brown grass curving into a gold sand trap. "That's his place—right there." It was a newer model home. Blue vinyl siding below white trim and a patio layered with cheap green carpet. There was a black Cadillac parked beside it—a newer model with a sporty look to it. Dark tinted windows.

Creeley parked behind the Cadillac and they got out, met a short, muscular guy as he came out onto the patio. He had a polo shirt on—just like Monty—and short green golfing shorts. His head was shaved and he sported a long goatee. *White-trash country-club chic,* Creeley thought.

Ray Parks said, "You didn't say it was a double date."

Monty laughed and trudged up the patio stairs, met Ray Parks with a man-hug and a slap on the back. "These two are friends of mine, looking into an old family tragedy. A murder you caught." They met gazes for an instant before Ray centered his beady eyes on Creeley and Amber. "Plus, I wanted to pick your brain about my golf swing. My back's tweaked and I need to adjust the way I attack the ball."

That got Ray's attention and he opened the trailer door. "Get in here, partner." He looked down at Creeley and Amber. "Come on, ladies. I guess you can have a drink with us. I got some rosé in the pantry. Might not have turned just yet."

****

Thirty minutes of golf gab before Ray Parks refilled Creeley's tumbler of rosé. Amber got a refill, too, and both women thanked him as he settled into a La-Z-Boy across from them. Monty was in a wicker lawn chair pulled up to the coffee table from the same wicker patio set. A large flat-screen TV hung on the wall above the couch, where Amber and Creeley sat. It seemed to her that Ray Parks spent his money on immediate gratification: A Cadillac. A big-screen TV. A nice gold watch. And hookers, she bet. Ray was the type—a dirty old fucker. She saw it in his eyes. In how he curled his lips at her. In that crooked tooth smile and the hands behind his head.

"Now that we got Monty's golf swing out of the way, what's this about a family tragedy?"

Creeley leaned forward, held her glass between her bare knees. She knew that would draw Ray's eyes to her twat. That was okay—if it got her some answers. "The Levi Mackey murder. Turns out he was my long-lost brother. All I wanted was to get what happened straight from you. Just to complete what I got from the old newspapers and family lore." She felt Monty's eyes on her, knew the way she presented this would piss him off.

"Hmm. Way I remember, the kid was strangled. I come into the motel room, he's upside down on the bed—face up, that is, but with his head pointed in the wrong direction. Ligature marks on the neck and throat, clear signs of a struggle. Everything in the place kicked to shit. Neither of you is law officers, from what I can tell. But Monty here knows, you walk into something like that and it's like walking into another dimension. Shit, you're walking into somebody's last seconds. It's like a story that froze right on the worst part of it. No moving back and no going forward. That's us, me and Monty, we're the next part of that story. We found women's clothes on scene, used that later to put her with the kid.

A few witnesses and we had us a suspect. Didn't take too long before she confessed. Surprised me, that it was a woman. You say the vic was your brother, huh?"

"That's right. We have the same mom."

"No shit? Well, I hate to be brief, but there wasn't much to it. He didn't deserve killing, but he's dead just the same. You understand that's how it is? I don't sugarcoat it for people."

"How much did you know about the woman who killed him? How much did you know about Blossom Nash?"

"The hooker? I knew enough. She did it. No doubt."

Amber said, "DNA evidence? Anything from the struggle like blood or skin under his fingernails? What about—"

"Hey. The fuck is this?" Ray Parks looked at Monty.

Monty poked a tongue into a cheek and said, "These aren't tough questions, am I right? Basic stuff."

"These aren't tough questions? Shit, Monty." Ray narrowed his eyes at Creeley. "You got something to say about the woman. What is it?"

Creeley bit one side of her bottom lip, tasted the insides of her mouth. A dry texture—like dirt or cardboard. "Turns out Blossom Nash is my mom. Does that surprise you?"

Ray stared at her, began to nod. He breathed slowly through his nose and the corners of his mouth turned down. He looked to Monty and back to Creeley. "You mind I show you something?"

Creeley leaned back into the couch. "Happy to see whatever you have to show."

Monty nodded at Ray, eyeballed Creeley while the retired detective went into a bedroom. Creeley shrugged and widened her eyes at Monty. A sarcastic face. Like, what did he want from her? She was here for the truth—fuck his dodgy fucking police buddy. Her and Amber and Monty traded dirty looks while they waited. The trailer's air conditioner kicked on and Creeley sighed. And then Ray Parks put a .38 to Monty's head and said, "I guess it's time for you and your girlfriends to leave, pal. My professional courtesy only goes so far—and you just hit the limit."

***

Monty took them to a small bar on a road called Twilight. The bar shared a white adobe building with an army surplus store—a horse was tied up out front, next to all the work trucks. It was a Raiders bar from what Creeley saw walking in—all the flags on the wall and the bartender in his jersey. Flat screens on all the walls, but the bar was an old-style top with a vinyl armrest running along it. Monty took a seat, and the bartender brought him a Cuba libre. "Two more of those."

Amber and Creeley, perched on each side of Monty, drained their drinks to half.

Creeley said, "I guess you two aren't friends."

"Yeah—you can say that shit again."

Amber was still shaking, but the liquor got to her fast. "That guy is fucking crazy. And he's hiding something."

Creeley glanced at Monty. "Is she right?" The buzz of a sports talk show distracted her, a white guy droning on about quarterbacks and wide receivers. "Is your old detective pal lying?"

Monty nodded.

"Say something, Mr. Badass Detective."

Monty sipped his drink, sighed. He licked his upper lip. A few seats down, an old guy demanded a refill. He got a dirty look from the bartender and Amber, but got what he wanted and drank it down as fast as possible.

"You come here often?" Amber sounded sick of following Creeley's problems around town. She sounded sick of Monty. Likely, she was sick from the gun Ray Parks pointed at them.

"I got to give the two of you credit. You either got to something Ray didn't know, or you got close to something he doesn't want anybody else to know."

"What do you think it is?" Creeley finished her drink, nodded at the bartender for another.

Monty said, "Make it three," and they watched the bartender top them off. "I think it's something he doesn't want you to know, but I think you don't know what it is yourself. Not yet."

Creeley closed her eyes as she tasted the lime and soda and rum, a welcome taste after the long day of heat.

"We're onto something," Amber said.

Monty nodded.

"He's hiding something about the investigation," Creeley said. "He knew about my mom. About Levi. And he kept it quiet, got somebody put away for a murder they didn't do."

"That might not be it," Monty said. "Look—"

"What the fuck else could it be?"

"It could be she did it and he knows she did it. But he couldn't prove it. I know that may seem fucked up, but I've had a few times when—"

"It's all about the evidence." Amber was turned toward him now, leaning into his ear. "If you can't prove it, they fucking get off. That's all there should be."

Monty laughed, turned to stare at her. "You try telling that to someone, you just found their kid shot in the back of the head. When you ask them? Evidence has shit to do with it. It's all about—who did it? And I can tell you, most of the time we know who did it."

"But that's not how it works," Creeley said. She had something else bouncing around inside her head: What if Monty was right? What if Blossom killed her own son? Did she have that in her? *No*, Creeley thought. But she remembered the nights in the motel, the dirty men, and crumpled bills. The condom wrappers. Murder? It didn't seem like Blossom could get there, but Creeley never saw herself running drugs. Or trying to get a prisoner freed.

Life takes you to unexpected places.

Monty chuckled. One of those halfhearted chuckles that isn't about humor, but about surprise or wonder. "Look, I'm a homicide detective. The way I put cases down? I listen to the streets. And believe me, a place like that motel? A life like your mom had? The streets know what happened. If Ray did his job—I'm assuming he did—there's a reason your mom's in the joint. Trust me on that." He held up both hands. "I'm not saying it's right. I'm saying there's a reason."

They sat in silence for a few minutes. The drinks diminished and more appeared. Creeley said, "I need to make a call." She got up and headed toward the bathroom, found a pay phone next to the guy's shitter. A vomit smell made her gag, but she figured the scent fit the call. She dialed Animal's number collect. The call was accepted.

"And now you're charging me to talk to you."

Creeley said, "How's it feel?"

"Like I need my fucking money and my drugs."

"Hero got fucked up—you shouldn't have sent him."

Animal sucked air through his teeth. "Creeley, this is getting on my nerves. Me and you had a good thing. We were making money. And now you go AWOL on some momma's-girl bullshit? That seems really fucking dumb to me."

"You know what seems dumb to me?"

No answer.

"Do you?"

"No, Creeley. I don't. Not unless it's hiding my shit from me because—"

"Sending another trashy drug dealer after me. Next time, I'll kill him."

"Girl, you better—"

"I have a gun. And I will shoot whoever you send."

Animal breathed into the phone. He thought for a minute before saying, "It's like that. Okay."

"Okay," Creeley said.

"Let's say I'm good with that."

"You are?"

His lips made a chirping sound. "We do it like this, when do I get my shit?"

"Never."

"I beg your motherfucking pardon?"

"You never get it—I keep it," Creeley said. "That's what it costs, Animal."

A GOOD RUSH OF BLOOD

"What what costs?"

"Me not going to the cops in Portland. Or to the Feds. The DEA. Whoever the fuck. I bet they'd love to crush you, make you turn on your suppliers. They'd love to know about the Mexican connect."

"You don't know shit about—"

"I know enough that a big boy will be pushing your shit through your scrotum before you can say 'defense attorney.'"

Animal said, "This doesn't work for me."

"It doesn't have to."

"You realize, you're asking me to find you. You're asking me to kill you. That's what this conversation is."

Creeley said, "You're going to leave me alone. Or whoever you send will get plugged. One by one and with you at the end of it."

"I don't know what uniform you think you're wearing, girl. I mean, what the—"

"The one that says I'm sick of your shit. Don't send Hero. And don't send any other trashy bastards. Leave me the fuck alone. We're done here."

"Okay, Creeley," Animal said. "Whatever you say."

"Should I hang up first?"

Animal ended the call and Creeley hung up the pay phone, leaned back against the wall breathing hard. Monty came around the corner, stopped to look at her.

"I got to take a piss," he said.

"Good for you."

"Everything okay?"

"Tough phone call," Creeley said.

Monty hesitated for an instant, began to nod. "Our friend up north," he said.

"I handled it."

Monty grinned in disbelief and said, "I hope so. Either way, me and you are going to be hanging out some more. Maybe that'll help keep your friend at a distance."

"We are? How's that?"

"We're going to the Inland Empire tomorrow. I want to talk to your mom myself...In person."

21/Alone Time

After dropping Monty back at his apartment, Creeley and Amber found Kimmie passed out drunk on Amber's couch. He was shirtless with hickeys and bite marks trailing up and down his rib cage. Amber went to bed—gave Creeley the offer to follow her.

But Creeley needed time to think.

Time to wade through everything.

Outside, she strolled through Amber's apartment complex, nursed a glass of white wine while she thought about seeing her mom again. The air was still warm, and the sounds of traffic filtered through the brush of palm fronds. Something relaxing and comforting about the Palm Springs air. Even in a mid-grade apartment complex. What would it be like, telling her mom—after all these years—that she believed her? That Creeley trusted her about this. All the past behind them, and this is the thing that brings them together. But Creeley didn't see it being about them—she saw it as a wider purpose, a quest to clear her name. She wanted to free Nash of its poor history. The prostitution. The murder. And, with her, the drugs. That was the reason for her call to Animal—she was telling him to fuck off.

For good.

She heard music coming from a second-floor window. Electric guitar. She stopped in the center of the parking lot, tilted her head to listen. AC/DC—"Hells Bells." Creeley listened to the song and bobbed her head along with the guitar riff, mouthed the lyrics. She remembered lying in a homeless shelter in Seattle listening to that tape again and again on her Walkman. Those bells to start everything—ominous and foreboding and pulling her into the music. The thump of the bass drum. Like a rock 'n' roll symphony playing only to her heart.

The music gave way to more thought: If Blossom didn't kill her brother, who did? How did he get out here and why? Seemed like he wanted to see their mom, to talk to her for some reason. And she didn't know how in the hell her mom never told her about him. That lie—the unsaid lie—is what bothered her most. *She hid my brother from me, and now he's dead. Maybe she didn't kill him, but she killed what me and Levi could have had.*

Creeley walked around the parking lot again and again, trying to work everything out in her head. Who killed Levi, and what did Ray Parks know that made him find a way to convict Blossom? If it was bullshit—why was he so intent on putting Blossom in jail? Because it solved his case, got the papers to shut up about it? She thought back to the look on his face that afternoon, how he held the gun to Monty's head with a slight smirk. Ray Parks was a bad, bad man.

She knew that from hearing him speak, from seeing how he looked at her.

Not good. Not good at all.

As she circled the building, the same apartment started blasting another song—"Runnin' with the Devil" by Van Halen. Another one Creeley loved. And, God, it was all about her life right now. No love—from anybody or from anywhere.

She stopped to listen again.

Headlights swept the far side of the parking lot, showed her the license plates of a few dusty sedans. The headlights swung toward her, came down the center of the parking lot's lane. Eddie Van Halen's mean guitar riff was crushed by the throttle sound of a big pickup truck. The truck stopped, the engine switched off, and Creeley shielded her eyes with a forearm. "What the fuck, dude?"

Doors slammed. Two silhouettes blacked out the headlights, moved toward her.

"There's an open spot right there," Creeley said, pointing at an empty space.

A man's voice: "Animal said you got smart with him today."

Fuck—here it was again. She guessed Animal didn't take her seriously. In part, he was right about that. After all, Creeley didn't have a gun. And she didn't plan on killing anybody. All her words today were empty threats. An effort to escape Animal's grasp.

The man said, "All we want is the shit you have. It's an easy thing."

Creeley said, "I told Animal he could fuck off. I'm not sure what he's not getting about that."

"He's not getting the stuff you were supposed to bring him."

Creeley squinted, tried to see the man's face. Tried to see whether he had a gun. Or a knife. Or a fucking bat. It didn't look like it. He was bigger than her, though. And stronger. So was the other guy. No way she could fight the both of them. The silhouettes moved toward her, grew like the long shadows of a late day. "I'm sick of Animal," she said. "Fuck him and anybody who works for him."

"That's not an answer we're willing to accept. We weren't paid to let you get away with this."

"What did he pay you for?"

"To get his shit."

"And that's all?"

The men were silent.

Creeley watched them as they took small steps toward her. Another guitar riff burned through the night, seemed to call forth some devil from the deep, or from another dimension. The pleasant night air seemed hotter now, oppressive. The swaying palm trees felt ominous and foreboding. She gulped, bit her bottom lip, and took a couple steps backward.

"All we want is Animal's stuff."

"I don't believe you." Another step. Creeley turned and started to stride away from them. She heard footsteps closing in on her. "Leave me the fuck alone! I don't have Animal's shit!" They were coming for her—the footsteps increased, got closer. Creeley started to run. She felt her hair kick out behind her and the warm air turned cool, dried her eyes as she picked up speed.

"Hey! Don't run!"

But Creeley was running. For her life. She pumped her legs

and arms, rounded one end of the parking lot, dug in for the automatic gate that led to the main street. *Get there,* she thought.

Get to the street.

22/Dodging Traffic

Creeley reached the gate, her breath coming hard and fast, and chanced a look over her shoulder. The two men had gotten back in their truck, and she saw the headlights swinging toward her. Heard the big, throaty V8. The automatic gate was a swinging panel with some flex to it—she pulled herself through and made it to the sidewalk outside the entryway. Activated by the truck, the gate clinked as its mechanism engaged and it began to swing outward.

The driver revved the truck's engine.

Creeley looked both ways down the street, saw headlights closing space to reach her in both directions. Across the street, she saw one of the boutique hotels common in Palm Springs. The parking lot was full and there were lights on in the small lobby structure. Palm trees angled above everything like tall, gangly fingers. As the truck accelerated through the open gate, Creeley darted into the street. A horn sounded to the right—Creeley sprinted as fast as she could, the truck's loud engine straining behind her. As she reached the farthest lane from the sidewalk, she heard the screech of brakes, another horn, and a horrendous sound like sheet metal wrapped into a lawnmower. She jumped the curb as the visceral noise hit her and ran through her bones.

Creeley turned to look.

Cars coming from both directions squealed to a stop.

The truck was bent in half along its horizontal plane. T-boned by a beer delivery truck, a single-cab semi pulling a trailer with 'King of All Beers' painted across it. The semi's driver opened his door, toppled out onto the asphalt. Headlights illuminated his face, and he looked like a man walking through a nightmare. Blood ran down the center of his face, but he appeared unharmed beyond that. He sat down cross-legged and put his head in his hands. People exited their cars and began to trot toward the accident. Creeley stepped into the street, walked toward the

T-boned truck. A middle-aged guy in a tank top and flip-flops reached the truck. He poked his head in and said, "Can you hear me? Can you guys hear me? Hey, can you hear me?" He backed up two steps as Creeley approached and said, "Jesus Christ. They're dead."

People began murmuring about calling 9-1-1, but sirens were already moving toward them through the night.

Creeley reached the truck and stared at the two men who tried to abduct her. Both wore gold earrings and had tattoos on their necks and faces. There was blood splashed on all the windows and shattered glass covering everything. The steering wheel was pressed into the driver's right ribcage, a splinter of white crossing through it from inside the man's body. Creeley's stomach turned, and she gagged. Behind her, she heard the semi driver mumbling to himself.

It was clear to Creeley that both men in the truck were dead.

She backed away from the truck and sank into the small crowd of onlookers. A couple people kneeled next to the semi driver and soon two police cars arrived. Each patrolman ran to the truck, but both turned away while speaking into the radios hooked to their shoulders.

The circulating red-blue of the lights flashed in Creeley's vision as she watched the fire engine and ambulances arrive. There was a flurry of action that seemed rehearsed before patrol officers began questioning the crowd. One asked her if she witnessed the crash and Creeley said, "The pickup just pulled out—I couldn't believe it. I was standing right there." She pointed at the sidewalk opposite the apartment complex. She motioned at the semi driver. "No way he could have stopped in time." The officer asked her to sign a form with his writing on it and she did.

It took about thirty minutes, but firefighters extracted both dead men, and their bodies were put into ambulances on stretchers. By then people were back in their cars and traffic was alternating on one lane. Creeley stood with a couple onlookers from the apartment complex and watched as a tow truck arrived and the driver began to coordinate with the police officers.

She thought of Animal back in Portland—imagined him smoking out on his couch, waiting for a call from his thugs. Imagined how he was waiting to hear Creeley's pleading voice through the phone. She walked back to Amber's apartment and let herself inside, found Kimmie's phone on the coffee table. His snores filled the apartment with a high-pitched warble. *Funny, he even seems gay in his sleep.* Creeley was glad to see his smartphone used the fingerprint access app. She crawled over to him and pressed the screen to his index finger. He twitched and turned into the couch cushions, but the phone unlocked and Creeley sank into one of Amber's chairs, dialed Animal's cell number.

"Yeah. Who is it?" That drug-dealer voice trying to say "I'm a badass and you better be scared."

Creeley said, "I told you not to send anybody. I warned you. Didn't I warn you, Animal?"

He didn't have an answer, but instead panted slowly into the phone.

"They're dead—both of them."

"I think you must be fucking with me," he said.

"Would I joke about something like that? This thing, you can chalk it up to a loss. Do that and walk away. I told you I'm out and that's what it is—I'm out."

"Ain't no goddamn way you killed my boys."

"You go ahead and check in with their mommies sometime next week. See about it."

"I'll believe it when I see it. Or when I hear it."

"Well," Creeley said, "what is it they say? Streets will talk?"

"Yeah, they will."

"How'd you ever get into this, Animal?"

"You're asking me my life story now? God, girl—you got stones."

"I just wonder...That's all."

"You know what, you bitch?"

"What?" Creeley said it with a half grin.

"You can stop wondering about me unless it's you wondering about sucking my dick."

"Wow, you have a dirty mouth, even for a big bad drug dealer."

"Man, fuck you."

"Don't call me man, you little punk. I'm a woman. You know what? Send somebody else. Let's keep playing this game, see who comes out on top."

"Only motherfucker on top is—"

Creeley hung up and set the phone on the coffee table. She leaned back in the chair, closed her eyes.

She slept without dreaming.

23/The Joint

Monty got nods from the correction officers as they rolled through security at the women's prison. Creeley got the man-gaze from everybody—the COs and the prisoner's moms and kids. Checking her out, like, who the fuck are you? They got seated at one of the booths with the glass wall and the phone. Creeley said, "They like you because you're a cop?"

"It's like an aura," Monty said, a sly grin coming to his face. He looked smart in a tailored suit, clean-shaven with a badge clipped to his belt.

"Oh, fuck you."

"Maybe it's the way I walk."

Creeley shook her head and gave a slight wave as Blossom trudged through a door and nodded at them. She picked up the phone as her mom sat down and rushed to speak. "I know it wasn't you and I'm going to do everything I can. I brought a detective with me and he's going to help us figure out—"

Monty's big right hand covered the phone receiver. He gently pulled the phone away from Creeley and put it to his ear. "Ms. Nash?" he proceeded after her nod. "My name is Monty Emeril. I'm a detective with Palm Springs PD, and have been for close to twenty years. I'm not necessarily here in a law enforcement capacity. You might say I'm here for personal responsibility. I introduced your daughter here"—he glanced at Creeley—"to a colleague of mine. A former detective. His reaction was—to my mind—a tip-off that something was...not on the level when it comes to his investigation of this case."

"Ray motherfucking Parks," Blossom said. Her lips were pursed so tight that her smoker's lines looked like deep knife scars. Her eyes glared through the glass.

Creeley could hear her through the phone but tilted her head closer to Monty.

"That's right. Detective Parks."

Blossom chuckled and said, "You call that small-dick mother-fucker a detective? Please. You know, the first time he questioned me, he actually wanted to pay me for a blow job? I'm not kidding, he put fifty dollars in my hand and asked for a knob job."

"I doubt that," Monty said.

"I'm sure you do, Detective. But it doesn't change my truth—that it happened. That blow job—if I did it—might have paid for my freedom. Instead, I'm in here. And it's Ray Parks that's responsible. There's lots of other people who screwed up, but it starts with him."

"And the DA was crooked, too, right?" Monty's smirk was as demeaning as a slap in the face.

"Let me ask you something, Detective Emeril. If you—"

"Call me Monty. Because we're friends now."

Creeley glared at him.

"Sure. Monty, then. If you wanted to fool the DA, or an assistant, could you do it? Could you find a way to get somebody convicted if you told yourself—if you rationalized—that it was them who did it? Even if the evidence, all of it, didn't add up to that person?"

Monty pressed his lips together and sucked air through them. The smooch noise turned heads in the room. "I could do a lot of things—that doesn't mean for one fucking second I do them."

"Next time you see Ray Parks, ask him about The Vandals MC."

"What about them?"

"Just ask him about The Vandals MC. See what his reaction is."

Monty nodded and moved his jaw back and forth. "Did Parks assault you?"

"You mean sexually?"

"That or any other way."

"Parks was handsy, but he never got what he wanted. I did it with one of the other cops, though. But that was just for fun."

Creeley sighed and shook her head.

Blossom said, "You need to get laid more, Creeley."

"Who?" Monty watched Blossom with the trained, steady eye

of a detective. Looking for a lie.

"Why should I tell you?"

Creeley pinched her tongue between her teeth, gave Blossom the evil eye.

Monty said, "So I can interrogate him."

Blossom said, "It was a her."

That surprised Creeley and her jaw dropped.

"In the jail? Or some other place?"

Blossom tilted her head from shoulder to shoulder. "In the jail, yeah. Sometimes. But we did it in the evidence room, too. If you can believe that."

"I'm not sure I do," Monty said.

"Like I said—it doesn't matter. It's my truth."

"You going to give us the name, or keep fucking around?"

"Stacy."

"Detective Brewster?" Monty couldn't contain his surprise. He was breathing hard and getting red in the face.

"She wasn't a detective then," Blossom said.

"Well, she is now. Narcotics."

Blossom laughed and shook her head in disbelief. "Stacy knew how to get a line down that snoot of hers. Maybe she was working an undercover thing with me, huh?"

"Another thing I doubt," Monty said.

"Being in prison has taught me a lot. I have to admit that. I do admit that. The biggest thing I learned in here? There's this idea that some people are better than others. Smarter. More levelheaded. More fair. And that's absolute and total bullshit. We're all pretty much alike. It's just about where we are and who we're with when we go the wrong direction. That's what puts us on this side of the glass...Or that one."

"I'll write that down and send it in to Hallmark."

Blossom shook her head, aghast at his response.

"After all," Monty said, "you're the one serving life."

She shrugged and said, "I guess you're right. People like you always are."

———

✳✳✳

On the drive home, Creeley said to Monty, "Do you believe her?"

"It's too bad, but I do."

"Why?"

"I believe her because she wasn't lying—I know that for a fact."

"How?" Creeley checked her mirrors and squinted into oncoming headlights.

"Lot of practice. And my gut. But it's more than that—it's my own experience."

"I have to ask you, okay...Are you going to help me?"

Monty thought for a minute before he responded. "No," he said. "I can't help you. Not like how you want. I can help somebody else though—I can help Levi Mackey. And that's what I'm going to do."

24/Chasing Tail

Wind and dust.

An endless wave of heat.

Creeley lifted her hair from her neck, desperate for some way to cool off. The radio was playing low while blowing sand tapped at the underside of her 4Runner. They were parked about a mile from the trailer park where Ray Parks lived, waiting on a street of ramshackle trailer homes enclosed by low chainlink and protected by untrained pit bulls.

They were talking rock 'n' roll.

Monty favored the psychedelic stuff: concept albums and lofty lyrics. Makings of Pink Floyd and Meat Loaf. Creeley liked garage band shit: Van Halen and AC/DC and The Stones. She said, "I just like feeling like, you know, I'd hear it in a bar somewhere on some Saturday night."

Monty slurped another energy drink, sighed as he said, "Yeah—I get it. Like, it has that down-and-dirty feel to it. But you can't beat a Pink Floyd album. How it all goes together and it's one big thing to just, you know, absorb."

"But you can't fuck to it. That's why I like Van Halen."

Monty looked at her and laughed, shook his head. He crushed the can with one hand and tossed it out the window. "You fuck to Van Halen? That's some weird shit."

"I fuck to real rock 'n' roll. How it's meant to be."

"But Van Halen? David Lee Roth Van Halen or Sammy Hagar Van Halen? That's the real question."

"Both," Creeley said, liking how she had an easy way with this guy, the moody fuck-up of a detective.

"Both? Even Van Hagar? You're an animal."

"Fucking A," Creeley said.

She watched traffic zip by while Monty put his thoughts on that. Probably on her. But she didn't mind, not in the way she might mind another guy thinking of her. Or thinking of her fucking to Van Halen.

After another few minutes, and another song by Boston on the local rock station, Monty said, "I wonder if Ray's going to leave today. That lazy-fucking-ass."

"Tell me again why you think we should follow him?" Creeley didn't quite understand—it seemed to her they needed to go after Stacy Brewster, the detective Blossom talked about. Question her. Try to gather evidence or proof that the jailhouse love affair happened. From there they get a lawyer involved—leave the rest of the investigation, and Blossom's eventual appeal, to the lawyer. But Monty wanted to solve the case. The way he told it to Creeley over a two-egg breakfast, they needed to forget about proving that Blossom was wrongfully convicted. That didn't matter—not to anybody. What they needed to do was solve Levi Mackey's murder. For real. And beyond any doubt. She wanted to know why.

"Because nobody in the justice system, or the general public for that matter, gives a good goddamn about some murderer in prison."

"She's not a murderer, though."

"Yes. She is. She's in prison, and in America that means she is what the system says she is. Because that's how it works. No judge cares. No lawyers care. No sobbing mom sitting on a couch watching midday talk shows will care. No reporters care either. What they do care about, though, is a detective and a private citizen solving a murder that the public—whether right or wrong—thought got put down back in the day. It's not about your mom. It's about Levi Mackey, and it's about the motherfucker who got away with killing him."

And Creeley believed all that—she understood it. But that didn't lead to following Ray Parks. Not in her mind. She wondered about Monty, shoved away the vague feelings of discomfort he gave her. Odd, to be drawn to someone who—in some way—repelled her, too.

Monty chewed another piece of gum—they'd stocked up at a nearby 7-Eleven—and blew a large bubble. When it popped, he chewed faster, teeth mashing together like the gears inside his head must have been mashing together. It took a minute, but he said, "Ray's a little prick. And he likes to think—he needs to feel—that he has power over other people. That's how he gets up in the morning. If I'm right about that, Ray knows what happened between your mom and Stacy. He knew then and he's still going to hold it over Stacy's head. I promise you that. My guess is—and I'm guessing, okay—is he's going to remind her not to talk to you, to me, or to any lawyers who start digging around."

"So, we want to catch the two of them together."

"You could say that. Yes."

Creeley wrinkled her nose as a funny thought came into her head. "For a cop, you have a lot of time off."

"I got sick leave for this," Monty said while pointing at his face. Still bruised but fading closer to normal color every new day. "Do you remember the beating you so gracefully arranged for me?"

That made blood rush into her cheeks and Creeley turned away from him. She was rolling her eyes when his voice changed.

"Start it up—now."

Creeley watched the road as she started the 4Runner and saw the black Cadillac—Ray Parks's Cadillac—zoom past them twenty miles per hour over the speed limit.

"He still drives like an asshole," Monty said.

She turned right behind Ray and sped up, passed a slow-moving pickup truck.

"Hang back a little. This is a long stretch and, if he turns, we'll see it."

"What about when he jumps on the freeway?"

"Then, too. Trust me, we're good."

"Are we?" She steered with one hand while the Cadillac cruised in front of her by about three football fields. Beyond the road, San Jacinto Mountain stretched eleven-thousand feet above, its peak shaded with the white gleam of snow despite the heat of Palm Springs and the surrounding valley. "He is getting on the freeway," Creeley said.

"Looks like."

"Headed east, too." Creeley followed the black Cadillac as it entered the circular on-ramp headed east into the deeper Coachella Valley. The mountain swung around behind them, and flat beige desert stretched out ahead of them.

"Palm Desert, maybe—or so I hope," Monty said.

"Why? What's in Palm Desert?"

"Stacy Brewster lives there," Monty said. "And she just so happens to have the day off."

***

They exited at Monterey—a main thoroughfare into the desert—and drove past a large shopping center and a few golf resorts. Creeley hung back, followed Monty's instructions—he was adamant that Ray not spot them. Ray reached Highway 111, crossed it, and turned left after a couple blocks into a condominium complex. As they drove up on him, he was punching a gate code into a booth for entry.

"Keep going," Monty said. "We'll park somewhere and walk in."

"Let's turn around and follow someone in after him."

"No—he'll make your car later on if we give him a clear look at it. Trust me."

He directed Creeley to take the next left onto a residential street. They parked on the street, the 4Runner out of place among immaculate luxury cars. They locked the car, jogged along the sidewalk back toward the gated condo complex. Monty pointed and they crossed a grassy drainage ditch and approached the wall. There was a break in the oleanders there and he said, "Let's hop over here. Find out where he parked."

Monty helped Creeley up onto the wall—it was about five feet high—and she toppled over it into wet grass. Monty came next and she followed him as he found the nearest sidewalk, marched along as if he was a resident.

The complex was well-groomed, all grass and bright flowers under the windows—it was a grid layout of two-story buildings, four units each.

The black Cadillac was parked in visitors' parking. They began to approach it, but Monty shoved her onto a nearby patio. "Shit, get back—out of sight."

"What?"

"He's still in the car."

They both chanced a look and saw Ray Parks sitting in his car, looking down at his smartphone.

"Texting her, maybe?"

Monty looked at the Cadillac again and said, "Let's get back to your truck."

"Why?"

"I think they're going somewhere together."

They hustled back the way they'd come, toppled over the wall and into the drainage ditch. Creeley jogged ahead of Monty as they made it back to the 4Runner.

"Do me a favor and flip a bitch, but roll up on the corner slowly."

Creeley made the U-turn, idled to the curb.

"Let's just watch." Monty flipped the radio off—some new band raised on emo and Instagram. "They're shit."

"Agreed," she said.

"Here we go." The black Cadillac rolled through the gate, made a slow right turn. Sped into light traffic. "Roll out, but hang back like we've been doing."

Creeley put the 4Runner into traffic, made a left after the Cadillac, rolled past as the Cadillac made a right into a shopping center. "A lunch date, or what?"

"Could damn well be. Let's circle back from the other side of the parking lot. We'll see if we can watch where they go."

Creeley turned at the next entrance, drove through the parking lot past a grocery store, and slid into a spot. "This okay for now?"

Monty ignored her, squinted as he examined the lot. His head stopped swiveling and he said, "There they are."

Creeley squinted herself and saw Ray Parks walking with a

short, butch-looking woman into a small taco shop. "And what do we do now, Almighty Detective?"

Monty patted his stomach beneath his Hawaiian shirt. "What do you think—we put a gun on him."

✱✱✱

Creeley was trying to tell Monty this was a bad idea, but he was two steps ahead of her and not slowing down. They jogged across the parking lot, sweat now showing through Creeley's blue tank top. As they entered the taco shop, Ray Parks and Stacy Brewster were taking a table. A small number stand—lucky number thirteen—stood between them. Parks saw Monty approach and started to rise, but Monty closed the gap and had his gun in Ray's stomach as both men took seats in rickety wood chairs. "Shut up, Ray."

Creeley smiled at Stacy Brewster and took a seat next to her. "Hi," she said, "I'm Blossom's daughter. We never met." She held out a hand, but Stacy didn't take it.

Monty had a big grin pointed at Ray Parks and he said through it, "How's it feel to have a gun pointed right at your dick, Ray? You like that?"

No answer.

Stacy said, "The fuck are you doing, Monty?"

The taco shop was empty except for the movement in the kitchen, behind the front counter. Looked to Creeley like the cook was the lone employee this early in the afternoon. Somewhere in the back a flattop grill sizzled, and mariachi music floated out to the table.

Monty didn't look at Stacy, but glared at Ray Parks as he said, "I'm returning a favor Ray did for me. Isn't that right, Ray?"

"What favor?"

"He put a gun to my head two days ago."

Stacy swung her gaze to Parks, sniffed hard through her nose. "Well, I can't say I'm surprised."

"You're fucking up, Monty," Ray Parks said.

"Let's talk this through, Monty." Stacy leaned over the table, got Monty to look at her. "What exactly is this about?"

Creeley smiled big at Stacy and gave it to her: "My mom's locked up for life and you were the one fucking her while she was in lockup. That's what this is about."

"I don't know what you're talking about."

Ray Parks said, "Blossom Nash killed that kid. Doesn't matter what you think, girlie."

Monty shoved the gun harder into Ray's crotch.

"Fuck, Monty."

"You and me both know you're crooked as a Reno strip club owner. You going to tell me why you pinned this on the lady? Or do we have to take you somewhere, beat it out of you?"

"Torture is your game now, Monty?"

Creeley smelled carne asada, burning green peppers.

"Maybe it is."

"Monty, come on—this kind of shit is going to get you canned." Stacy reached across the table, put a hand on Monty's shoulder. "Let's talk through whatever this is."

Monty stared bullets into Ray Parks.

Creeley watched with a helpless feeling. Part of her wanted to take control, to let Monty know this was her case—a thing she was supposed to be doing. But she also saw the fear emanating from Ray Parks. And she liked that.

Loved it.

From the counter, a cook in a white apron said, "Number thirteen—it's ready."

Monty licked both his upper and lower lips, sighed. "Para llevar, por favor," he said. "We got somewhere to go."

***

While Monty munched carne asada tacos next to Ray Parks in the back seat, Creeley negotiated red lights and slow-moving old-people traffic on Highway 111. They were headed back to Palm Springs, but Monty wouldn't give them the exact location. Instead, he was riffing on Mexican food after putting the guns he took from Parks and Brewster into a duffel bag between his feet.

"I get your carne asada addiction. I do. But me, I'm partial to the al pastor tacos. You know, with that diced pineapple on top. You know what I'm talking about, Ray?"

Silence from the detective.

Stacy, in the passenger seat, shook her head and said, "Are you going to eat my carne asada fries, too, Monty?"

"I'm going to save those for later. Warm those suckers up after I have a margarita or three."

Creeley dipped her nose out the window, cleared her sinuses of the meat scent and cigarette stench that seemed to hover around Ray Parks like an invisible cloud. She said, "Where are we taking these two, Monty? Seriously—this is kind of fucking weird."

Monty chewed and chewed without responding.

Ray Parks said, "Monty's taking me to get my ass beat."

Stacy kept shaking her head.

Monty gave Creeley instructions to turn at the next light. She made a right, drove across a bridge spanning a dry wash, passed through more gated apartment complexes and a residential neighborhood.

"Left up that way," Monty said. He crushed the taco packaging into the bag and put it on the floorboard.

"Don't get my truck all dirty," Creeley said, her eyes darting to the rearview and settling on him.

"Be calm, Creeley Nash. Be calm."

As Creeley made the left, Stacy said, "Little Amsterdam, huh? Looks to me like you're about to be part of a crime, little sister. You might want to consider, you know, getting out of this before it gets too big for you."

Creeley rolled her eyes as the 4Runner slid past warehouses and office buildings. Given the weekend, many parking lots were empty or almost empty—a ghost-town feel to the place adding to its rundown looks. "What's 'Little Amsterdam'?"

"First pot shops in Palm Springs," Ray said. "It's a euphemism."

"But kind of a gold mine—if you know how to work it." Monty patted Ray's shaved head. "Especially for a little entrepreneur like you, Detective Parks. Hey—up here, Creeley. We're going into that office park."

Creeley turned into the parking lot, drove through two sets of gray buildings with reflective windows.

"It's at the end here—the storage facility."

Ray said, "What are you doing, Monty?"

Creeley pulled up to the kiosk outside the electric gate. "We're going in here?"

Stacy said, "This is fucked."

Monty cleared his throat. "Let's have it, Ray."

"Four-eight-two-four-five, and then press pound."

Creeley followed his instructions, and the gate swung open to let the 4Runner pass into the complex.

"Two rows down," Monty said. "Make a left—what's the unit number, Ray?"

"Fuck you, Monty."

"That's fine, Ray. But what's the unit number?" A rustling came from the back seat and Monty said, "What's the unit number, Ray? What's the unit number?"

"God. Fuck. Okay—it's 119. Get your fucking gun out of my ribs. It's unit 119."

Creeley stopped the 4Runner outside unit 119, shut the engine off, and said, "What now?"

"What now?" Ray Parks leaned toward Creeley from the back seat. "What you should be asking is—why this? What the fuck does this have to do with your mommy being locked up?"

"It has to do with you being dirty," Monty said.

"But it isn't about the Mackey case."

"It will be."

Creeley twisted in her seat, gave Monty her full-fledged this-is-me-being-a-bitch face. "Are you fucking with me, you prick? Because if you are, I swear to fucking—"

"Didn't I tell you this is about Levi Mackey?"

Ray said, "Oh, here it goes..."

"Didn't I tell you that?"

"Yes," Creeley said.

"Then hold tight—we're going to solve this thing. What happens with your mom, that's not up to us. But we can solve the murder."

"Already did it," Ray Parks said.

Creeley turned around, put her eyes on Ray Parks in the rearview. She saw Monty put the barrel of his gun to Ray's cheek.

"Get out and open it, buddy," Monty said. "And let's not have any trouble."

***

It surprised Creeley when Ray Parks didn't fight opening the safe. It was a large safe, the size of a dresser, with a big combination lock. He could have held out and they would have never got it open—no way in hell.

But when he did open it:

Some automatic weapons.

A small filing cabinet.

And a pile of cash.

"How much is it?" Creeley tried to count stacks of bills, but abandoned the attempt when she reached double digits. The storage garage smelled of dust and bug spray. She wanted to sneeze but put the back of a hand to her nose and mouth and stopped it. "It looks like a lot. A lot, a lot."

Monty said, "Maybe half a million, right? Lots of small bills."

"Give or take," Ray Parks said. "More, I think."

Stacy stood silent next to Ray, eyed the gun in Monty's hand.

Monty said, "We're going to put it in the truck. And then we're going to visit Slide Raymond up in your neck of the woods, Ray."

"I see what you're doing."

"Do you?"

"You can pay Slide what you owe him, I could give a fuck. But don't take it all. This is my retirement, man."

Stacy said, "Jesus-fucking-shit."

Creeley didn't understand what was happening, or where she found herself. Things had spiraled since the second visit with

Blossom. She watched Monty—saw the targeted look in his eyes—and wanted to know how she'd ever wrestle control back from this batshit-crazy detective.

Monty wouldn't take his eyes off the money. After what felt like a long time to Creeley, he managed to say, "Get it in the truck. Let's make it happen."

***

A tract home in Desert Hot Springs.

Red tile roof and stucco—that two-car garage and a black Escalade on big-ass rims sitting in the driveway.

Small neighborhood nestled against sand-colored hills covered with creosote bushes.

Creeley parked on the street and the four of them walked to the front door of the house. Monty forced Ray Parks to press the doorbell. He and Stacy were in front—Monty and Creeley stood behind them. Stacy carried a gray duffel with some of the money. More than a hundred grand, in fact. The gun in Monty's hand—pointed at Ray Parks's kidneys—made Creeley more nervous with each passing moment. She'd been around guns a lot in her life. Her penchant for bad boys assured that, but Monty had a different way about him—it was clear he had training and experience. He wasn't some junkie waving a gun around for show.

The door swung open and a hefty guy with a goatee and a shaved head stood with his arms crossed. The soft thump of hip-hop bass filtered into the alcove and the guy smirked. "I answer my door and I see three cops and a chick who thinks she's tough. What am I supposed to think?"

Monty said, "Don't think. Instead, you better pray we don't have a search warrant."

"Fuck you, Monty. Search warrant for goddamn what?"

"I'd like to put your dirty thoughts into evidence, lock your ass up, Slide."

That got a laugh from him, and he said, "Let's see what trouble you're in now, Monty." He led them into the step-down living room with brown leather couches and the biggest TV Creeley had ever seen. The thump of bass came from speakers in the ceiling and the TV was tuned to silent *SportsCenter.*

Ray and Stacy sat down at Monty's direction.

Creeley stood next to Monty, saw Slide's surprise at the gun as he sank onto the squeaky leather. He laced his hands together behind his head.

Monty nodded at Stacy and said, "Give him the bag."

She tossed the bag at Slide's feet, and he bent forward to dig into it. After rustling around inside, he leaned back into the couch. The fat arms went behind his head again.

Creeley smelled pot and Hot Pockets. There didn't appear to be anybody else in the house. She noticed the framed movie posters on the walls. *Scarface. Goodfellas. Ghostbusters.* It appeared that Slide Raymond was a cinephile.

Slide said, "Is that all of it? The whole bill?"

Monty put the gun back in his hip holster. "That's all of it, what I owe. A little more—for all the trouble and wait."

Slide pointed at his own face. "That from the boys they sent?"

Monty nodded.

"It's not permanent, I guess. You understand why it happened?"

"It's business," Monty said.

Creeley interrupted them with a sarcastic tone. "And this has to do with my brother's murder how?"

Slide didn't look at her. He kept his eyes on Monty. "Why are these two here?" He waved a fat finger between Ray and Stacy.

Ray said, "That's my money at your feet, you cocksucking crook."

Stacy said, "Christ, Ray."

Slide's head swung to the left and he tilted it to examine Ray. "You must be one of the blue boys who made a living playing a hard ass. I bet you think everything should go your way. That's how you play it."

"It goes however the fuck I say it goes," Ray said.

Slide sighed, labored to his feet, pivoted to face Ray Parks.

Ray said, "What are you going to do, you fat fuck?"

Slide Raymond pulled a fist back over one shoulder and punched Ray Parks in the nose. Ray slammed backward into the couch, blood spurting from his nostrils. Creeley swore she heard a crunch as the fist met pay dirt. Ray struggled to sit up again, but Slide hammered down with the same fist and more blood spurted from Ray's nose. He took a long time to recover with Slide standing over him. He somehow straightened, hung his head with a loose neck—appeared slightly conscious. Slide Raymond looked down at Stacy and said, "Your boyfriend likes to talk, don't he?"

"He's not my boyfriend, you—"

"Shut the fuck up." Slide fell backward onto the couch, laced his fingers behind his head. "Go ahead and tell him, Monty."

"I had Slide here do some checking. That's from the streets, you understand."

"So-the-fuck-what?" Stacy's mouth twisted into a nasty sneer. She had age lines running along her forehead and her crow's-feet enlarged with her anger.

Creeley said, "Yeah—so-the-fuck-what?"

"So," Slide said as he rested one Nike sneaker on a plump knee. "Boyfriend here has been paying off a guy I know for, what is it, the last twenty years, plus? That's the-fuck-what."

Stacy's sneer shrank into pursed lips.

Ray sat there and bled.

Creeley cocked an eyebrow. "What's that mean?"

Monty took a step toward the couch, bent at the waist to stare Stacy in the eyes. "It means these two paid somebody to lie—for what, I'm not sure—and they kept paying that somebody all the way until today."

"Fuck you!" Blood sprayed from between Ray's lips as he yelled. He teetered and fell into Stacy who shoved him back the other direction.

"Get off me, Ray."

"A G a month for twenty years—damn. That's some kind of secret your boy has." Monty smiled at her.

Stacy shook her head and said, "No idea what you're talking about, Monty."

"And I thought you were a cop. A for-real cop."

"I'm more cop than you, you fucking alkie."

"Maybe you are, but it doesn't change the thing that matters—your boy has a secret. And we,"—Monty stood and dipped his head toward Creeley—"we are going to find that secret and put it to the public."

"Most of us already know," Slide said. "It's just the reporters that need to hear it. Put it on the internet, you dig?"

Ray struggled to speak, got out two words. "Fuck you."

Creeley marched toward him. She rolled saliva over her tongue, spit in Ray's lap. He glared at her with pure, animal hatred. "You fucking piece of shit. How dare you put an innocent woman in that place. You fucking—"

"She wasn't innocent," Stacy said. "She fucking did it. And I know she did it. You think she didn't do it? You're more stupid than you look."

Creeley turned to face the woman cop, felt her heart rate burning at some unseen edge. Her lips felt heavy and plump. She wanted to smack Stacy with the back of her hand, but she felt Monty's hand on her shoulder. It surprised her to have his gesture of calm and restraint. With rage flavoring her voice, Creeley said, "How in the fuck do you know?"

Stacy smiled at Creeley, tilted her head in a faux gesture of sweetness. "Because she told me she did it. And she told me while I had my mouth down where the sun doesn't shine."

25/History Lesson: Tiger's Eyes

This is what Creeley called it: flashing tits for tips.

The other girls laughed at her, joked that they got great tips because of the service they provided. *Some service*, Creeley thought, *flashing those tits and smiling about it*. But she did it, too. And didn't give a fuck—she needed rent money and booze money and food money. So what if a creeper got a look at her chi chis? There were worse things to endure in the world—like her boyfriend's rage.

Ronnie was sweet when she first met him, a carpenter in a red trucker's hat sitting at the bar. He nursed his Amstel Light and grinned at her. Talked to her about Green Day and Nirvana, how much he still loved Soundgarden.

A night at the local movie theater and they were making out in the bed of his Toyota. Another night out—a rom-com this time—and they were back at his place, doing more than Creeley thought she wanted. He had a manipulative way about him, like a salesman crossbred with a real estate man.

But handsome.

Chiseled face and day-old facial hair.

Dirty hands from the job site. Always sipping on that Amstel Light and grinning. Until one night they pulled out a bottle of J&B. His hands got bigger then. And stronger.

And it wasn't like he wanted her, but instead wanted to have her. Like he wanted to smash her.

The next day at the bar, Creeley felt a hand in her own—Irma the Tiger. Veteran bartender. Shift leader. All-American tough bitch. It's where the "tiger" part of her name came from.

"I need to talk to you, Creeley."

And Creeley followed her into the muggy back office, sat at the little table where they ate half-price cheeseburgers and sipped gin from Styrofoam cups during breaks.

That look in Irma the Tiger's eyes. "I seen this before. It's always the girl who gets the worst. I can promise you."

"What?"

"I see how you tried to cover it up." Those damn eyes—solid and heavy and immovable.

Creeley put a hand to her cheek, covered the one eye. "It's not what you think, Irma. I just—"

"You just ran into a door. Or you fell off a bike. Or you got drunk and you like it hard like that."

Creeley clamped her mouth shut, sat there staring at the old bartender with her pursed smoker's lips and bushy eyebrows.

Irma said, "It's not like you have to take it."

"I don't."

"You know I don't mean it like that, Creeley." She dug into her purse—rhinestones and tassels—and pulled out a container of tobacco dip. She pinched some and shoved it into her bottom lip. "I mean it's like I say—you don't have to fucking take it."

"I know that."

Irma nodded without blinking. "I get it. First time he done it, huh? You're thinking it's one of a kind, won't happen again. That's what most of us thought. Or think."

Creeley wasn't sure what to say, but shame seemed to add weight to her throat and stomach, hung inside her like a sack of flour. It wasn't shame for hiding what happened—that part of it was natural. It was shame for getting herself involved with Ronnie, for letting him inside her. For kissing him and talking about the future and love. And kids.

Shame, okay.

But maybe she just felt stupid.

Irma spit into a Styrofoam cup. "I was in one like it, you know? My first husband, Gary. He ran the parts department over at the Chevy dealer. Had him a good job. Decent family. He was good in the sack, at least when we first got going. But he used cocaine on the weekends. I did, too."

"What is this," Creeley said, "show and tell?" She watched Irma's unchanged eyes—those solid, straight eyes—and felt stupid again.

"You want the truth, I still like me a line or two. But Gary, he had him a lot of guns. All kinds. Called himself a collector. You know how that is. It's never about the guns, is it?"

"I don't know."

"Nope. You wouldn't. Not yet. But I can tell you: One night Gary comes home from Neptune's—he's tight as a cock in a ear hole. Just zinging back and forth. Talking ten miles a minute about work and guns and me and him. I said one thing to him—I said, 'Maybe you should stop with the crank, dip shit.' Those are my exact words." She spit into the cup again. "He walks back into the bedroom. I hear him turning the combo lock on the gun safe. I hear it, right?" Irma points at one ear. "I hear it and I'm rolling my eyes, thinking Gary's got something to say about some gun or another. German this. Russian that. Old west and new south. Who in the fuck knew? But it was something else. Gary come out with a nine-millimeter and starts pulling the trigger. I saw it happening before it happened. Could see it from the way he come down the hall. I was already up, okay, going for the front door and just about out of there." Irma twisted in her seat, lifted her shirt, and pulled aside the strings of her apron. A flab of white skin revealed itself and Irma pulled down her waistband. A dark spot of skin—misshapen and almost round—showed where she placed a finger. She watched Creeley see it and then covered it, crossed her arms.

Creeley said, "Is that where they took out your appendix?"

"Not quite," Irma said. "But that's a funny one."

"I'm not laughing at it, Irma."

"I know you're not. But if none of this gets through, let me give you one thing: you need any help, I'm your girl."

Creeley didn't need Irma's help. Or didn't want it. At least, that's what she thought while she was sitting in that muggy break room and smelling the tangy scent of chewing tobacco.

I'm all good, Creeley thought. *I got this.*

She told herself that for nine months.

But one day Creeley Nash knocked on Irma the Tiger's

apartment door. And when it opened Creeley said, "I'm looking for your help—that's why I'm here."

26/Tell Somebody

The desert. Out past Dillon Road in Indio—so far out that Creeley had to put the 4Runner in four-wheel drive and gun it through a few sandy washes. Dust tickled her nose, got into her throat. She squinted to see past her headlights as Monty gave her instructions. They reached a forked dirt road and turned north, rattled along for half a mile or so.

Monty said, "Stop here. This is it."

Ray spoke through his busted nose and lips. "The fuck are you doing, Monty?"

"Giving you two what's deserved."

Creeley shut off the engine and heard whimpering. She turned around and saw tears running down Stacy's cheeks. The stone-faced cop was pure mush. Creeley said, "Tough-as-nails, my ass."

"What's that?" Monty stared at her with unblinking eyes.

"Nothing." She hung a limp hand out her window. "What are we doing all the way out here?"

"Right now—we're waiting."

"He's going to kill us," Stacy said, her voice uneven and shaky. "You want to be a part of that? No, no you don't."

"I'm not going to kill anybody. I'm too nice for that—why would I want to get my hands dirty?" He leaned down to stare hard out the windshield. "Here we go—let's get out and meet some old friends, you two."

***

A single-cab Ford Ranger slid to a stop, dust sifting from beneath it. Creeley turned and sneezed into her elbow. The Ranger's headlights dimmed, cut off. Both doors unlatched and two silhouettes got out, walked toward them.

Ray Parks—standing with Stacy in front of Monty and Creeley—spit at their feet and said, "You fucking finks."

One guy, the taller of the two, said, "Fink? What the fuck is a fink?"

The shorter guy said, "It's like a rodent. One of those ones you can't have—it's illegal or whatever."

Creeley said, "That's a ferret." Her comment was volleyed with silence and deadpan stares from the two silhouettes.

Ray said, "You stupid fucking fucks."

"For a long time," the tall guy said. "Yeah. But not anymore. That thousand a month I got? I should have gotten ten times that. Maybe you're right—I am stupid."

Monty said, "You wanted me to bring him to you."

"Yeah. I did."

"What now? Is this all you need?"

The tall guy said, "It'll do, I guess."

Ray started walking toward them and the short guy closed the gap, shot a knee to Ray's stomach. He keeled over, air spewing out of his mouth. The short guy grabbed him by the neck, dragged him around to the back of the truck. Creeley heard blow after blow. Fist after fist. Grunts and yelps. And then, after a minute or so, silence.

The tall guy nodded at Stacy. "Go on and sit back there with your boyfriend."

Monty said, "You're all his now."

Stacy shuffled around to the back of the truck, her head down and her posture crooked. The short guy told her to sit and stood there watching her and Ray, who was slumped on his side.

To Creeley, the air tasted like poppy seeds.

Monty said, "If you can help us somehow." There was a hard stop there.

"It's not much," the tall guy said. "Almost nothing."

Creeley shuffled her feet, tried to understand how all this made sense. How it added up to her brother's death and her mom being innocent. She felt like a child wandering through a sewer system—lost, afraid, and alone. Sloshing through the shit.

Monty nodded and cleared his throat. "People like me can do a lot with nothing." He motioned at Creeley. "I got a feeling she can, too."

The tall guy lit a cigarette. It glowed in his fingers as he puffed and dropped his hand to his waist. "I used to run the front desk at the motel. Night shift."

"What motel?" Creeley took a step, felt Monty's hand on her shoulder.

The tall guy continued without acknowledging her. "I seen her there before—the lady. She was on junk and I knew it. She turned tricks and I knew it." He puffed the glowing red stick. "Never hurt nobody, though. Maybe got hurt a few times."

"Okay," Monty said. "So you knew her."

"I knew a few of the boys came to see her, too. Not for my friends, but from the papers."

"The newspapers," Monty said.

Creeley wiped sweat from her eyes. Still didn't know what this was.

"You got that right." Another puff and exhale. "The lady had a nice look to her. Kind of ratty, but sexy, too. I think it was more than that, though, why he came to see her."

"Why who came to see her?" Creeley felt the words form on her lips, but she had no recollection of pushing them out.

"The mayor, he's the one who came to see her."

"More than once?" Monty was scratching the back of his neck.

"Yeah. About, maybe, twice a week."

"And they scored together—did junk?"

"Yeah, man."

Creeley said, "You're trying to tell me my mother was fucking the mayor of Palm Springs?"

"Unless he got a twin brother," the tall guy said. "This went on for, hell, almost a year. I was only at the motel, like, thirteen months. I quit about a month after the murder. Creeped me the fuck out, man."

"And Ray paid you not to tell," Creeley said.

"A thousand a month off the top. No questions asked."

"Why now? Why decide to tell us now?" That familiar rage was growing inside Creeley, and she struggled to tamp it back down into small embers.

He lifted his chin at Monty. "Man said, I give this to you…He's going to give me Ray. I got somebody needs to see him. Maybe pay Ray back a little something."

"Don't be too hard on them," Monty said.

"It'll be fair."

Creeley licked her bottom lip, shoved her hands into her pockets. She wanted to swing them at the tall guy's face, pummel him as hard as she could. But that wouldn't give her anything. It would do nothing. It was senseless.

Aimless.

She said, "You said it was more than sex—why he came to her."

"That's true."

"What was it, if it wasn't sex?"

"I think he loved her," the tall guy said. "Shit, I'm sure of it."

Up Highway 74, the 4Runner parked at a lookout point. The wind pummeled the cab and Creeley felt funny being there with Monty in the passenger seat—like they were down some secret lovers' lane and wanting to kiss each other. Below, the Coachella Valley was laid out like a flat parachute of yellow lights, the edges fading into the welcome embrace of darkness.

They each popped a can of Corona and sipped. The beers would be warm before they got into a second or third can, but the long day had Creeley craving a buzz. Or more.

Monty said, "I used to bring girls up here."

"You get your first lay up here?"

"Nope. That was in the back seat of my parent's car. In the garage."

"Whoa. In the garage? That's ballsy."

"Not really," he said with his eyes running over the blanket of lights. "My parents were in Mammoth on a ski trip. My brother had a party and me and this girl—Denise was her name—got together in the garage. Kind of one of those teenage moments."

"Good times," Creeley said, not feeling that way at all.

"It was glorious—for me, at least."

Creeley nodded, knew what he meant. But from the girl's side. She flashed on her first—the skinny mohawk hipster with saltine breath and a crooked dick. It made her chuckle and she had to suppress a huge grin. Not the best sexual experience of her life, but it wasn't the worst. And it might have been the most loving— it was a good memory. Mostly scents and sounds. But good.

"I'm sorry about how things went today."

"Would have been nice to know about your kidnapping plan. And your armed robbery plan. And your accessory to murder plan."

"Those two aren't going to kill Ray and Stacy."

"No?"

Monty sucked down more beer, placed an empty can at his feet. He opened another. "Ray's going to get a permanent scar on his face. Stacy—I don't know. They'll probably just try to scare her." He hesitated a moment and then said, "This was me paying Slide what I owe him. And him taking the money but putting me back in his debt. He got us connected to those guys in case he wants to leverage me somehow."

"And will he?"

"Yeah. Of course. I'll try to control it. Get one of his dealers locked up, offer to drop the charges somehow. A thing like that."

Creeley said, "I'm sorry to tell you, but you sound like a corrupt cop."

Monty didn't respond to her. Instead, he breathed deep and leaned his head back in the seat. Closed his eyes.

"I'm not trying to offend you or anything—"

"Of course I'm corrupt. What the fuck did you think? The question isn't about corruption, though."

"It's not?"

"It's about right and wrong."

"Yeah—I know."

Monty grunted. "No, you don't. I learned pretty quick as a cop: I don't make any cases, or arrests for that matter, without some pay-to-play. That's the deal—I give to them, and they give back to me."

Creeley watched the lights, saw an airliner and its white blink at her eye level. She sighed and shook her head. "It's not supposed to be like that."

"Again...No shit, Sherlock."

"God," she said. "This is how the world works."

"Now you're into it, Creeley."

Creeley tossed an empty can into the back seat, popped another. She sipped and said, "This shit about the mayor."

"Yeah, about that."

"I thought this shit would be easy—prove it wasn't her."

"Like I said, you're learning. And fast."

Creeley rolled down her window, propped an elbow on the door. The air—so much colder than the desert below—caught her by surprise. "One thing I can't get out of my mind…That last thing he said." She paused and shook her head, bit the inside of a cheek. "How the fucker was in love with my mom."

Monty groaned an affirmation. "I've been working murders for a long time—let me tell you something: every story is a love story. One way or another, that's what it's about—love."

"Really?"

"Look at you. Even your thing—this mystery you're trying to solve—is about love. You might not like to think it, but it is sure as shit about love. Or some kind of love."

Creeley sniffed hard and drank more beer. It wouldn't take long for her buzz to surface, but she'd want to keep drinking. *Better stop,* she thought, *so I can drive back down the mountain.* She watched the valley lights and searched for more airliners. The half-moon glowed on the horizon. She wondered what Amber was doing, realized she hadn't even called her new friend to let her know what was happening. Another minor Creeley fuck-up—maybe she did need to pick up a cell phone. She finished her beer and started a third.

Monty did the same. "I should have told you my plans."

"No shit, Sherlock."

That made Monty smile and he looked over at her.

Creeley felt his gaze, met his eyes but looked away as fast as they met. "Don't try to romance me, Monty the Detective."

"You're too young for me, sister."

"Am I?"

"You sure are."

"What about that first night—when you took me home?"

"Let's say I was punching above my weight."

Creeley nodded and ran a hand through her hair. "That's a shame. I mean, I was thinking it'd be nice to kiss you. You know?"

"You kiss me, and it won't end there. We both know that's a fact. Am I right?"

"How's it end then?"

"I don't know," Monty said.

"Maybe with love?"

"Like I said, every story is a love story."

Creeley let that run around in her brain for a minute. She did want to kiss him, but it felt weird somehow—like maybe it was a mistake she wanted to make, but couldn't let herself make. Funny. Most things she just jumped into and that came around to bite her in the ass. But with this, she was more cautious—reserved. She bit her bottom lip and said, "I guess something like that—it can wait."

"Sure it can," Monty said. "We got all the time in the world. Until one of us gets strangled in a motel room."

Creeley heard the sound of silverware tapping ceramic. She sniffed hard and groaned, rolled over on the couch and opened her eyes.

Dust moving in sunlight.

Amber said, "Look who decided to join us."

Kimmie chuckled and said, "I hope you got laid, girlfriend."

Creeley smelled burned cheddar cheese and bacon. She put her bare feet on the carpet and pivoted into a sitting position. She squinted through blurred vision at Amber and Kimmie sitting at the round table near the kitchen. "You guys make any for me?"

Amber pointed over her shoulder at the kitchen. "Get it yourself, hot shot."

Okay, whatever. Creeley got up and made herself a plate—burned bacon and eggs smothered in fried cheddar. She slumped into a chair and endured their angry stares while she crunched pig meat. Without looking at them, Creeley said, "I should have called to say where I was."

"You and the detective now—is that what it is?"

Creeley looked up to face Amber's burning gaze, crossed arms, and crooked mouth.

Kimmie chewed with his mouth open and said, "Nice, girlfriend. I bet he's got a decent schlong. Don't think you won't tell us about it."

"That's not what it was—it was part of the case. For my mom."

"I thought we were doing that together." Amber looked back to her plate, dragged a fork through ketchup.

"We are. I didn't know what it was yesterday—I didn't have control over it." She reached across the table and grabbed Amber's wrist, waited until they met gazes. "I'm fucking sorry."

Kimmie made an uh-uh sound in his throat. "You owe us some cocktails, girlfriend."

"And dinner," Creeley said.

"None of this fast-food shit."

"A sit-down place. One of those gay joints on the strip."

"I can dig it," Kimmie said.

Amber shrugged. "It's fine. Did you learn anything we can use?"

Creeley let go of Amber's wrist, dragged her hand back to her lap. She chewed more eggs and thought about what to say and how to say it. *Just come out with it—tell them how it was and what it is.* "My mom was fucking the mayor of Palm Springs. Some guy who worked at the motel said it was more than sex—that the guy loved my mom."

"O-kay," Amber said.

"And Monty is corrupt as fuck. But the cops who caught the homicide of Levi Mackey—my fucking brother, evidently—were worse than he is. We think—Monty and me—that Ray Parks covered for somebody to save the mayor's ass. He pinned the murder on my mom. How, we don't know. But that's what we think, what it looks like." Creeley shoved more food into her mouth, got a sudden fire of hunger in her stomach. She chewed fast, watched Amber and Kimmie look at each other with surprise and irritation.

Kimmie said, "Fucking cops."

Amber said, "Goddamn politicians."

They ate in silence until their plates were empty. Amber stood and took everything to the sink. She rinsed it all and put it in the dishwasher. Kimmie and Creeley watched her until she turned around and leaned on the kitchen counter. At the same time, he and Creeley said, "What now?"

Amber shrugged, tugged at one ear. "I guess we have to talk to the mayor."

"Former mayor."

"Right," Amber said. "Back to the internet then."

✳✳✳

The Smoke Tree neighborhood. Wide streets flanked by tidy mid-century modern homes. The scent of bougainvillea floating through the air like it was sprayed from a bottle. Everything manicured and pristine and grinning old money. Creeley parked along the street, and they stared at the house—Amber in the passenger seat and Kimmie in the back. Creeley said, "Looks pretty swank. These fucking houses are cool."

"Palm Springs style," Kimmie said. "One day I'll have one—umm-hmm."

Amber clicked her tongue. "How do we want to do this, guys?"

"Do what?" Kimmie leaned backward in the seat, disconnected his seat belt.

"Get him to tell us about Blossom, about what was between them."

Creeley squinted at the house with its perfect green lawn and splendid lines, those big floor-to-ceiling windows pointed at the quiet, hot street. A palm tree towered over the house, waving in some breeze high above them. Amber found the mayor's name from the late nineties—Stephen Dorphs—and his current address. Fucking tax records. One thing Creeley had started to realize: no information was safe these days. There were no secrets. Not forever, at least.

Kimmie said, "Maybe you go in and say you were talking to your mom—that she mentioned him. Maybe you want to research her history, help her—"

"Let's pretend it's a community project," Amber said, interrupting Kimmie's train of thought and resulting gibberish.

"Not sure I get it," Creeley said.

"Some community research project. For the city library. I'm interviewing old civic leaders and engaged citizens, trying to talk to them about what once was. And how things have changed."

"But how do we get to the murder?" Kimmie asked in that sing-song sarcastic voice.

"We ask about crime," Creeley said. "And we start with the flagship crime of his tenure."

"The one everybody remembers," Amber said.

"I like it," Kimmie said. "Put that motherfucker on the ropes.

You think he's going to give us anything? Like, you know, really talk?"

Creeley shook her head.

Amber said, "You never know. Sometimes people just want to talk about themselves. They want to say how great they are. Or how good a job they did when everybody was watching."

"Meanwhile," Creeley said, "they're fucking a mistress in a dirtbag motel."

"Sounds like politics to me." Kimmie slid out the passenger side of the back seat, slammed the door. "Let's go, ladies. Time to do this."

Amber and Creeley got out, followed him across the street. They walked up the flower-lined walk—purple and pink tulips nearly dead—and stood ringing the doorbell. They rang for a long time, but nobody answered.

Kimmie said, "Probably out for brunch."

Creeley stepped into the flower bed running along the large window to the left of the front door. She shielded the sunlight with both hands and put her head to the window. "Well, I see why he didn't answer," she said.

Along the wall farthest from the window, Stephen Dorphs's naked body was splayed across a white sofa. Red stains colored the wall above him and the couch near his slumped head and shoulders. There was a shotgun propped between his two knobby knees.

Creeley stepped away from the window, sighed. She shook her head and massaged the bridge of her nose. "Ding-dong," she said. "The motherfucking mayor is dead."

29/Murder, My Friend

Creeley was sweating in the passenger seat of the cop car. She wanted to get out, stand there and wait for the homicide cop to see her, but she also felt nervous about calling any attention to herself. Part of it was the accident that killed Animal's loser friends—she was documented as being at the scene. And now this—she finds a dead body and it happens to be one of the city's premier citizens. Coincidence? No. And that's what Creeley didn't want any cop—except for, maybe, Monty—to put together and ask about. It took twenty minutes for the homicide guy—fit, ten years younger than Monty—to come see her.

He slid into the driver's seat, closed his door. "You okay"—he looked at his notebook—"Miss Nash? I know you just witnessed something traumatic."

"I didn't witness anything."

"Excuse me?"

"I didn't witness anything. All I did was find the body." She knew that irritation with him wouldn't make this faster, but she couldn't help it.

"I didn't mean anything by it. I appreciate you making that point. And, shit, you're right." He tossed his clipboard onto the dash, leaned back in the seat. He gazed at the scene: Yellow crime scene tape around the house. A crowd of neighbors a half block down, held back by patrol officers. Techs in white bodysuits coming in and out of the house—everybody jotting notes on metal clipboards. "This is a fuck stick of a case," he said. "That's me, I get the fuck-stick cases."

"What's a fuck-stick case?"

"Means no matter what you do, whether you solve the fucker or not, you end up looking like a fuck stick. Shit..."

"Looked like he did it himself, from what I saw," Creeley said.

"Could be, but I doubt it."

"Why?" Creeley flashed on Ray Parks—the look he had in his eyes as she drove him into the desert.

The detective looked at her, shook his head. "Nothing I can say right now. But I can tell you, this is a fuck-stick case." He reached his left hand out to her. "I'm Edwin James, detective."

Creeley shook his hand. "Nice to meet you. And just so you know, so you're not surprised, I'm friends with Monty."

"No kidding?"

"Recent friends, but still."

"Hey, no big thing. Monty's a stand-up dude." He grabbed his clipboard, clicked a pen. "You mind telling me what happened, what brought you out here?"

Creeley hesitated—she realized now why she was so nervous. How to explain why she was here? She noticed a tech in a bodysuit taking pictures with a digital camera. He came from inside the house, began taking images of the door and entryway.

"Miss Nash?"

"Sorry—I zoned out for a second."

"It's shocking, I know."

"Huh?"

"Finding somebody like that. It's shocking."

Creeley shook her head, ran a hand along her sweaty forehead. She wiped the sweat on her cutoff shorts, decided the way to do this was the honest way—give it to him. "I was thinking about something else, honestly."

"What else?"

"I'm here—well, me and my friends—because we're trying to solve a murder."

"I'm sorry?"

"My mom is in prison for killing somebody. My brother, in fact. Levi Mackey."

Edwin said, "I heard about that one. Ray Parks, right?"

Creeley nodded, bit the corner of her mouth. "My mom didn't do it. Parks is a corrupt shit head. And the mayor—your dead guy—was fucking my mom way back when. That's what

I'm doing here. I was going to ask this shit bird to tell me the truth, but when I got here he was dead. You think that's a fucking coincidence, Detective James?"

Edwin nodded slowly, his lips and brow tight with thought. "Seems like, maybe, it's not a coincidence."

Creeley said, "Write this down."

✱✱✱

Back in the driver's seat of the 4Runner, Creeley watched Edwin James work the crime scene. In and out of the house, around to the backyard, and back to the squad car where he talked into a cell phone.

Kimmie was asleep in the back seat, tired from the drama and the questions.

Amber, in the passenger seat, had her feet folded underneath her ass. She was shaking her head. "This is some fucked-up shit, Creeley. I wanted to help you when I first met you, but fuck—this is getting crazy."

"You don't have to help me."

"No, it's not that. I want to. I just didn't expect it."

"What?"

"This. A real fucking case."

"A real case?"

"Yes, bitch. A fucking murder. Well, more than one now...And we're right here in it, digging in."

Creeley pinched the bridge of her nose—a headache lurked there between her eyes. "A real case."

"A real case."

"You think Parks did the mayor?"

Amber cracked her knuckles. "Seems likely, that fucking fuck. And now we lost our guy. He was going to give us this shit about your mom, give us the truth."

"I can still get it. No, we can still get it," Creeley said.

"How?"

"Blossom. My mom. I can ask her about it."

Amber shook her head, dangled an arm out the open window.

"What makes you think she'll tell you? I'm not trying to be devil's advocate here, but your mom was a real bitch when you saw her with Monty. Your description, not mine. Plus, it could be that—"

"She'll tell me," Creeley said. "She better fucking tell me. And she's going to tell me about my dad, too. I need her to tell me everything, or this isn't going to work."

"I doubt she'll—"

"She will, for fuck's sake."

"But why? How?"

"If she doesn't, I'm not doing this. She's on her own and she can go fuck a goalpost for all I care."

Amber grunted and said, "You'll just stop?"

"I'll drop the case."

"And you think that'll get her to—"

"I know it will. Because that's what she wants, for me to solve this thing. So it's me and her who did it. Together."

30/Snitches and Stitches

That same sneer on Blossom's face.

There it was, burning through the security glass and imprinting itself on Creeley's retinas.

Creeley put the receiver to her ear and said, "You didn't tell me the truth."

"Oh, whatever." Blossom pressed a finger to a cut on her forehead—it was closed with a dozen stitches, dried blood just visible along the edges of the wound. "You never believed me anyway."

"What happened to you?"

"Oh, you know, a brush up in the showers." The sneer widened.

"Another lovers' quarrel gone wrong?" Creeley watched Blossom's eyes squint with suspicion.

"What are you gabbing about now, daughter?"

"All the people you fuck, from what I'm finding, it can cause some trouble."

"Parks? Fuck you. Never in his wildest nightmare."

"Not Parks, Blossom—I'm talking about somebody else."

Blossom lodged the receiver between shoulder and ear, crossed her arms. She stared at Creeley for a long time before saying, "Who I fuck is none of your business."

"Not true. Matter of fact, it was always my business. Unless you forgot about how it was when we lived together. Did you forget...Mom?" Sarcasm and hatred in her voice.

Something shifted in Blossom's eyes—those memories flickering up from somewhere dark and deep. She bit the inside of her bottom lip, took a few breaths. "I never said I was good for you, but I am your mom. I carried you and put you into this world. You can't get away from that."

Creeley scratched a sunburned cheek, thought about Amber and Kimmie hanging around outside the prison. She was glad they couldn't hear this. It seemed too personal, too rooted in history and disappointment. Our family histories are our own—to be suffered and celebrated in unequal parts. "You've got some kind of fight inside you...Mom. I know that about you. And I love that about you—I always did. But that fight does bad, too. Like between you and me. And this thing, this case. You want to fight me on every slice of truth? I'm gone. And you're fucked. You're totally fucked."

Blossom wrinkled her nose, rubbed at her sliced head again. "I bet you think I'm a lowlife, that I got into the life because I wanted to, right?"

"I don't think anything except what I know, that you—"

"Kept you warm and fed. Since you were a baby, all I did was keep you warm and fed. Telling you now—should have then, but I'm doing it now—that's all I had in me. Yeah, I wanted all the flowers in your hair and the cute pictures down at JCPenney. I did. But it wasn't in me. Did I do drugs with you in the house? Yes. Did I fuck for money? Yes. But all of it—I'm not fucking with you, Creeley—was about keeping you warm and fed. All those dicks in my twat? Because I wanted you warm and fed."

Creeley winced.

"I gave my fair share of blow jobs, too. But I bet you don't want to hear that, do you? Yeah. You want to hear about all the ice cream cones you missed, all the Christmas movies and bicycle rides. All the *Peter Pan* you never got to see."

Creeley sneered and said, "I never knew my grandparents."

"You didn't have none, Creeley. I came up in group homes."

Creeley looked off down the row of booths, noticed the jail guard posted at the door. He was picking at dead skin on his nose, bored and aloof. Not cognizant of the pain happening right in front of him. Creeley wondered how that was possible. How any of this was possible. She looked back at Blossom, her mother, and said, "I saw *Peter Pan* plenty of times. That wasn't even my favorite."

"*The Little Mermaid*," Blossom said. "That was your favorite."

"Yes," Creeley said as her breath caught in her throat. The

word came out short, like an affirmation in a foreign language. "That's right."

"You may not feel like we know each other, Creeley. But we do—me and you are closer than most people ever get."

Creeley bit the inside of her bottom lip. More conversations had started around her, and she caught snippets—complaints about the kids, the mother-in-law, the bills. And through the glass, she saw beaten-to-shit women who had no choice—at the end of the day—but to return to their cells. She glared at Blossom. "Tell me more about your fling with Stacy."

"Yeah—me and her had a thing, like I said. While I was in the jail. Parks wanted it, too, but I never gave it to him. Fucking pencil-prick fucker. It didn't have to do with my case. Me and Stacy liked each other."

"You didn't tell her anything about the murder? Like, that you did it?"

"Fuck, Creeley. Why in the shit would I do that? No. Fuck no. If she said that, she's lying."

Creeley nodded, crossed her arms, and cradled the phone receiver between shoulder and ear. Knew she looked a lot like her mom doing it. "And what about Dorphs, Blossom?"

Those smoker's lips pursed, straightened. Something in those eyes flipped into memory. Blossom struggled to speak, but squeaked out, "How'd you know about that?"

"A witness," Creeley said. "I told you I was taking this shit serious, didn't I? Tell me about the mayor."

"He had a thing for me." Blossom was still hesitant, but her facial expression loosened as the memories churned through her head. "I mean, I had a little thing for him. I liked Stephen. He was nice, but corrupt, too. Like a bad boy who made it somehow. We used to meet at the motel, some other motels, too. He never met me at his place. I didn't blame him. The thing with Stephen, I wanted it to work out...But there was no way."

"And did you see him the night Levi was killed?"

Blossom paused, decided to answer. "That afternoon. In my

room. It was quick because he had somewhere to be. A bullshit city council meeting or something like that. We got each other off—a quickie. Kind of a frantic thing that made it exciting." Blossom gave a fake smile. "Is that enough detail for you, Detective?"

"Did you love him?"

"What?"

"I asked: Did you love him?"

"Love him?" Blossom chuckled. "Is that a joke?"

"So, you didn't love him?"

"God, no."

"Good," Creeley said. "That's good."

"Why?"

"Because he's dead," Creeley said. "Had his face blown through the back of his head with a shotgun."

Before Creeley finished the sentence, Blossom Nash—her mom, a hardened convict imprisoned for life—was weeping like the mother of a lost child.

Amber offered to drive and Creeley let her.

They slogged through slow traffic along I-10, ingested smog and big-rig exhaust. Kimmie wanted an adult hits station and Creeley had to listen to pop stars drone on about fancy cars and club nights. Blossom hadn't given her much after learning about Stephen Dorphs, but she did pass along something of value: the name of Creeley's father. Or who Blossom thought might be Creeley's father. Some mechanic in Blythe—a guy named Ross Mackey.

The name itself somehow flicked Creeley's brain into motion, conjured a memory.

She tried to sift through it—all the dark shadows and muffled voices. How old was she?

Two years old? That was too young to remember anything. Three or four, maybe.

She remembered a mustache tickling the back of her neck. A deep laugh and the clapping of hands. Those muffled voices volleying back and forth. Stiff carpet on her palms and knees— the smell of candy canes and pine. Was it even possible for her to remember that? She didn't know, but Creeley was okay with using her imagination. A lifetime without a father and you earned the right to add some details to any vague, useless memory.

And she saw a Christmas tree, saw herself pushing a silver star across the carpet. Adult hands reaching down to snatch the star. Did she remember her own stifled cries? Feel her own tears?

Maybe.

But she remembered the mustache for certain—that, she knew, couldn't be her imagination. It came up for her a few times over the years. Creeley always felt that tickle there on the back of her neck. And sometimes she woke with her palm clamped to the back of her neck, sweat leaving a handprint on her skin.

It changed her life, not having a dad. It had to. Forget about the two-parent household and the birthday parties and the Christmas stockings. Creeley felt that absence in her soul—as deep as she could feel anything. And it got her thinking about her choices in men, all the dip shits she dated over the years. And the one man who stepped over a line Creeley never wanted to be forced to draw again. She'd only been seriously injured once in her life—it was at the hands of an angry man who promised he loved her. So Creeley stopped seeing men, satisfied herself when it came to sex. Ignored the companionship when she missed it. Read a magazine. Listened to an album. Watched reality TV, for fuck's sake. Anything to avoid another man in her life. And then the tryst with Amber the other night—she saw herself writhing in the bathroom stall, the spasms of climax burning through her like a hurricane. Shit, she even yelped at one point. But that was just sex, wasn't it? Was all this what they called daddy issues? Sure, but it was so much more complex than that.

Absence was the best way to describe it. Or the easiest way.

The more difficult way: an obscure and lingering feeling of abandonment.

The realization that she wasn't wanted or loved by the man who created her.

Maybe she was hated. Loathed. Or worse, forgotten.

Did she want to find her father? Yes and no. There were two stories she told herself. Her yes story: the one about a woman unmoored in a man's world. And her no story: the one about a woman who was so strong she could face down drug dealers and crooks, manipulate cops and detectives. But was it really two stories? Or one story with more nuance than Creeley wanted to admit, or examine, or put to death? She didn't know. But her dad—the bastard—might have something she needed to help Blossom.

He might have the key that unlocked the truth about Levi's murder.

Amber interrupted her thoughts, "Margarita for your thoughts, Creeley."

"I'm thinking about my dad. Forget that I don't know what the fuck he looks like."

"Shit—you having second thoughts about tracking him down?"

"I don't know. Should I?"

Kimmie responded from the back seat, "Fuck fathers. Mine is a complete asshole."

"Mine too," Amber said. "But he did pay for school." Her eyes flitted back and forth from mirror to mirror. She chanced a look at Creeley. "He might give us something we need."

"I know." Creeley watched lights slip past along the highway, centered her gaze on the ribbons of taillights ahead of them. "I guess it's never been in my face like this—my family. My fucked-up family and childhood."

Kimmie said, "Try coming out to a former Marine. Talk about fucked up."

Creeley smiled at that, thought that he was right—everything in life was about perspective. "I mean, the guy never wanted me? Fuck him then. But he might know something that gets Blossom out of jail. And getting this thing turned around, figuring out who really killed Levi...That might be the best thing I do in my life."

Amber drove and said nothing.

Kimmie lay down in the back seat. "Good for you, Creeley. Can we stop somewhere and get a cocktail? I'd love a snort of that white powder, too. This is the last time I let you bitches drag me to jail. I'll go kicking and screaming next time."

They laughed at him and Creeley said, "We're a half hour from town."

"I could use a cocktail," Amber said.

"I owe you two dinner, right?"

"Fucking A right," Kimmie said. "I feel a steak craving coming on."

"Steak? Yeah, right—you'll be lucky to get some tacos."

Amber said, "Can you afford appetizers? Or do we have to spring for that?"

That put Creeley's thoughts on the duffel bag in Amber's

apartment. Animal's shit. The money. The drugs. She needed to solve that problem, and she wondered what the fuck she wanted with his stuff. Why keep it and look over her shoulder at every shady fucker following behind her? *Because you need the money, Creeley. Your bank account is a total shit show—you've got a few thousand, but that's not going to get you to paradise. No,* she thought, *it's not.*

The money, she remembered. *That's why I kept his shit.*

And it's why I'm not going to give it back.

Ever.

"Okay, Kimmie. Steak it is. Let's do it." Creeley felt Amber's surprised look, but it was Kimmie's whoop of joy that got to her. She shook her head and laughed.

The road toward Arizona from Palm Springs was hot, dusty, and—if you asked Creeley—endless. The 4Runner almost overheated climbing Chiriaco Summit, a long, slow climb filled with tractor trailers and recreational boaters. Creeley blasted the heater, stuck her head out the window, and the Toyota cooled down, chugged to the top and settled down once she was on the flat, straight ribbon that burned through the desert. Amber and Kimmie—hungover, both of them—offered to accompany her, but Creeley wanted to meet her dad alone.

If she could find him.

The internet showed a couple old addresses, but Ross Mackey didn't have any property taxes to pay. Creeley wondered if he wasn't dead, though she didn't find any death records. Hell, maybe he was in jail somewhere. Not in Riverside County, though—Amber had checked that already.

Could he be just what Blossom said, a working-class guy wrenching on cars in a sweaty old garage? Could be. But if that was the case, he didn't own the business. There was no record of a Ross Mackey owning anything. At least, not in California or Arizona.

She listened to classic rock until the signal got swallowed by distance and lack of civilization. Then she ran through the desert without music, with only the rush of wind in her ears and the air blowing her hair out the window. She got predatory looks from truckers and smiles from soccer moms riding shotgun on family trips to the Colorado River.

Two long hours and she saw Blythe splayed out before her—like some shimmering mirage. In town, she stopped for tacos at a Mexican joint, wondered how she was going to find Ross Mackey. As she slurped down the last of her horchata, she noticed a bulletin board near the register and soda machine.

Creeley walked over and stood reading business cards and

lost pet printouts. Lots of shade-tree mechanics and childcare providers, but no Ross Mackey. Still, bulletin boards were one place to check—that and local mechanic shops. She started by cruising the streets around the taco place, stopped at an auto body shop and a muffler shop. Both locations the guys gave her plenty of attention, but nobody knew Ross Mackey. As she traversed more streets, expanding outward from the taco shop, she thought about what it must be like to live your working life as a mechanic. Dirty hands and sore knuckles—maybe endless frustration? Or the pure joy of fixing things? Both at the same time, maybe. She imagined her dad's swollen, greasy hands. Saw his dirty face glaring at her with warm gray eyes. Hell, Creeley didn't even know what her dad looked like. She was letting her imagination get out ahead of her.

Blythe had a sleepy desert feel to it—all the people were tan and wrinkled, laboring beneath the obscene weight of oppressive heat. Near 110 degrees. Now and then, Creeley flipped on the 4Runner's heater to cool the engine—that old trick she learned from a hot-rodding boyfriend. Came in handy when she was running drugs back and forth into Nevada, or into northern Utah. As she drove around Blythe looking for mechanics to bother, she thought about her time working for Animal. Falling into that was both lucky and unlucky—how do you explain three years of drug running on a freaking résumé? Hell, you don't. You freaking can't. Animal—as arrogant as he was—wasn't such a bad guy. He'd defended her at times, put the word out to leave her be. He protected her from the typical sexual harassment she encountered day-to-day, and not because he wanted her. But because she worked for him and it was the right thing to do.

Did she feel guilty about ripping him off? Yeah, sure.

But not that guilty.

Creeley saw a transmission shop up ahead—Desert Trans and Diffs—and decided to try there. She parked and walked into a small office with a wooden desk and grease smeared on the walls. The guy behind the desk looked at her and said, "I work on Toyotas, but we got to call out to Riverside or Phoenix for the parts. Takes a day or two longer."

Creeley said, "There's nothing wrong with my tranny."

The guy—short goatee and balding—looked her up and down and said, "No—I don't believe there is." He grinned to reveal lopsided front teeth and a dark tongue. The embroidered name tag on his shirt declared him to be Glenn G. "What can I do you for then?"

"I'm looking for a guy named Ross Mackey."

He leaned back in his creaky chair, cleared his throat. He crossed his arms and played piano on his shoulders. "Ross Mackey, huh? What do you want with this guy?"

Creeley watched him closely, got the feeling he recognized the name. "He's my dad. Never knew him, but I sure as shit started life in his hairy nut sack. Is that reason enough for you?" She took a seat in a folding chair, crossed one leg over the other. She settled her eyes on the chubby mechanic, tried to will him to tell her the truth.

Glenn kept that grin on his face and said, "You just decided to stop in here at random?"

"I need to find Ross Mackey. He was a mechanic, or so I've been told, and last I heard he was here—in beautiful Blythe, California. So, yeah, I stopped in here the same as I stopped in every other shop I've seen."

Glenn nodded and curled his bottom lip beneath his lopsided teeth. He shrugged and said, "Every day you wake up is a hell of a day. That's what I say."

He stood up with a groan and led her out through a swinging door. They walked into a garage with two bays. One bay had a big Ford truck up on a lift, all the tires removed. Creeley smelled grease and motor oil and cigarettes. Creeley followed Glenn and his big round ass out of the bays, through an open-air drive with a few cars in disrepair, and into another shop area. Another truck on a lift—a Toyota full size. Underneath it, a tall guy with a beer belly and plump biceps was wrenching on some random part. He had a cigarette burning in his mouth and wore cowboy boots.

Glenn said, "You got a visitor. And what the hell'd I tell you about smoking on the job?"

Biceps looked at Glenn and rolled his eyes. He pulled the cigarette from his mouth with one hand and, using his other hand, bounced a large silver wrench against his thigh. "Visitor who?" he said with squinted eyes.

Glenn said, "Lady, you wanted Ross Mackey? He's all yours. Don't come crying to me when he screws up your life."

Ross Mackey looked at his full-grown daughter and said, "Who the hell are you, lady?"

33/Daddy's Girl

He smoked American Spirits and cussed under his breath. Said to her, "I never thought I'd see you none." He pulled from a warm can of Miller High Life and squinted at a beat-to-shit Ford F-150.

They sat on stacks of old tires, Creeley uncomfortable there in the sun next to her dad. He handed her a beer, but she didn't bother opening it. Instead, she held it with two hands, tapped the aluminum with her overgrown fingernails.

He said it again to her, "I never thought I'd see you none." He cursed under his breath—a hard "fuck" followed by something unintelligible.

Creeley said, "I never thought so either."

"I been up here and back to Reno lots of times. Been out to New Mexico once or twice. Jobs like this one—had me a gig at a junkyard in Bullhead City. Just me and the junkyard dog. Never did get me out to Palm Springs. Seeing I had to work all the time. And Blossom, shit, she didn't want nothing to do with me." He puffed and coughed. Pulled from the High Life.

"You work on cars, huh?"

He smiled and said, "Huh," mimicking her.

"Well, you do...Don't you?"

"Yeah, I do work on cars. Mostly that's all I done. How I grew up, you learn how to do it. Of course, now they got it so a car got a dozen computers in it and all you do is hook your code reader to it. They flash you a code and, shit, you adjust the timing or whatever. A fucking robot could do it. You know you buy you a new Honda, how many computers that car got in it?"

Creeley did not know. And she shook her head.

"Thirteen computers—no shit. You get you a new Honda and the fucker's got thirteen computers in it. That's like driving a hard drive down Main Street."

"Lot of stuff changes, I guess." Creeley wanted to say something smart. Or funny. But she also felt caught between one breath and the next. She wanted to look at him closer, study his face and ears and neck. Did she look like him somehow? There was no way for her to tell. Not like this. She wiped sweat from her neck, opened the beer. She drank.

"You like that stuff?"

"I like it better cold."

"Don't tell me what I already know." He finished his can, crumpled it, and tossed it into the bed of the F-150. "This buckaroo blew his engine. Tried to pull a six-ton tractor up a twelve percent grade. Dirt road, too. Mud and rocks. Like a Ford could handle something like that. What I say, get you a Chevy if you want to fuck around and get dirty. What you got out there? SR5, I thought I heard. Am I on the money?"

"4Runner. So, yeah—SR5."

"One of them legendary motors. Good on you."

Creeley nodded and drank. "Yeah, I had a boyfriend knew some things about cars."

"Good for him. He didn't try and put a ring on it, huh?"

"Let's say the ring didn't fit."

Ross Mackey laughed so hard he ended up hacking. He brought another American Spirit to his lips and said, "My lungs ain't what they want to be."

"All those cancer sticks."

"Could it might be," he said. Another puff. "I guess you come out to see me about your brother."

Creeley's breath caught in surprise.

"Was it hard to find where I was at?"

She shook her head.

"That's good. I tried to stay where Blossom might have you look. Or around about where she might have you look. But, shit, I never could know."

"She told me you worked on cars. And said I should try out here in Blythe."

"And there you have it."

Creeley finished her beer. She didn't crumple hers but did toss the empty into the Ford's bed. Aluminum rattled at them. "You're right—I want to ask about Levi."

"I'll give you what I can."

"Do you think Blossom killed him?"

"I do not believe that," he said as straight as a churchman in a suit. "No, I do not." He was silent for more than a minute, the cigarette between his lips smoking and burning itself out. "I miss your brother—I miss Levi every single second. That boy did okay in football, but most of all he loved everybody. Lots of boys wanted to fight Levi—he had that fight look to him. But Levi never did it. Always found some way to make them boys laugh. And he had a lot of girls. I'm telling you. Lots of girlfriends. You can bet your last nickel that boy did not die a virgin." Ross chuckled. "No way in hell he was a virgin. That boy had him a time."

"What happened? With you and Blossom?"

He shook his head, puffed more, and groaned. "She run off with you in the Trans-Am. Just took off and never came back. Left Levi with me and when she called—after about two weeks—she said it was a even split. Boys with boys and girls with girls."

"You didn't try to go after her, get her to come back?"

"Shit, that's all I did for around six months. Until I lost my fucking job. Had a good one too—junior mechanic at the transit authority. She just never would come the fuck home. And then it's me and Levi, I mean, shit...You got a little one?"

She shook her head.

"I can tell you the truth—I was scared. All I could do to keep the kid warm and fed."

Creeley flashed on the conversation with Blossom from two days prior. Warm and fed. Seems like that was all that mattered. She wanted to understand it—no, to accept it. But she couldn't.

"You ain't got a little one...I guess you might could never understand it. But that's all you want, all you think about. Keep him warm. Get him food. That's that."

Creeley's anger burned through her body—another crazy parent. And she wanted to slap him. Punch him in his face. Kick him in the balls. Pry his leather-tan skin from his face. Warm and fed is part of it, but it wasn't fucking good enough. She smirked and said, "But you failed at that in the end, didn't you...Ross Mackey?"

Ross Mackey tossed his American Spirit to the ground, snuffed it out with a boot. "Sure did. I failed in the worst way possible. I got my son murdered, and I never did pay for it."

34/Rich Beyond Words

It didn't surprise Creeley that they ended up at a bar. Hawk's it was called. And it was familiar. The sticky bar top and scent of day-old lemon wedges. A fat duck of a biker dude slinging the drinks. Your regular mishmash of sun-drenched alkies, out-of-work tradesman, and barflies with overdue pap smears. Creeley sat across from Ross Mackey in a booth and watched him sip Miller High Life, scratch his right eyebrow again and again with a greasy index finger. He tried hard not to meet her eyes, but Creeley caught his blues once and saw it—endless grief running through him like tainted blood.

She sipped her gin and tonic, dabbed a finger at her lime wedge. "I can't see how it's your fault—what happened with Levi."

Ross nodded as he drank. "Yeah. Maybe I'm just selfish, saying it's on me. But I lost track of Levi once he turned sixteen. It stopped being me and him, and just started being me."

Creeley remembered hopping the train, the red halo of cigarette burning in the darkness of the boxcar. "Teenagers get like that. They drift off into something."

"It wasn't that," Ross said. "I met a woman. Skinny. Pissed off. Pretty damn good in the sack." He met her eyes and blushed. The High Life bottle went to his lips. He put his eyes on the table, stood, and walked to the bar. He came back with another beer and a gin and tonic for her.

Creeley looked at her still-full drink, thought the second one would sit there until the ice melted and liquid spilled all over the table. She wasn't in a drinking mood. "Levi didn't like her?"

Ross crossed his arms. "She mistreated him, lied. Got it into his head that I beat your mother. That I abused you. This lady... She was a tramp. A junkie. I let her into our house and Levi..."

"He believed her?"

Ross shrugged, uncrossed his arms, and drank some more.

"Hell—I don't think he believed her, but she was convincing enough that he had to see what was what."

Hawk's got rowdy as three guys in black biker vests burst inside, commandeered the bar. They carried on about traffic on I-10, started giving shit to the bartender about his bike—a Yamaha parked out front. It sounded good-natured, but the volume itself invaded Creeley's thoughts.

Ross ignored them. "Your brother, he was headed out there—I think—to find you. Blossom he couldn't care less about. He remembered her. I couldn't fucking believe it, but he did. And he remembered her for the fuck-up she was."

Creeley said, "All of us are shit, when you get down to it." She remembered that first drug run, saw herself pulling over in a panic, afraid to see a state trooper pull up behind her. Paranoid. What had she been doing for three years? Slinging junk. Like Animal.

"Maybe we are. But some shit stinks worse than most."

The urge to defend Blossom pushed its way up from inside Creeley, surprised her. What came out was a wedge, but it made sense. "If Levi wanted to find me and got killed doing it, I want to know who did him. And I sure as fuck don't want my mom—no matter what a piece of shit she is—rotting in a cell for it."

The bikers at the bar roared with laughter.

Creeley turned and said, "Will you fat asses shut the fuck up?"

They turned to face her, shook their heads. The leader—all shoulders and tattoos—ambled over, set his Bud on their table. "The fuck did you say to me?"

"I asked you a question—to shut the fuck up." She stared him dead in the face, saw that look in his eyes: all his years of defiance and violence. "And you answered me with a question. How goddamn stupid is that?"

Time slowed in Hawk's. Creeley looked across the table at her father, pursed her lips. Had the thought that she had gotten him into some trouble. No way the bikers would hurt her. But her dad? Yes. Ross Mackey tightened his grip on the High Life bottle, sat back in the booth. He raised his chin at the biker and said, "You ask me, it's the dumbest thing you can do."

The biker's fist—swung bottom first, like a hammer—whipped past Creeley's chin. Ross got his hand up with the bottle in it, but the fist's force was too great. The fist slammed the bottle into Ross's face—glass shattered and rained over his head and shoulders. Ross shimmied up in the booth before the fist could be reloaded and fired. He somehow stood and leaped like a torpedo at the biker, brought them both down onto the ratty carpet. The biker topped Ross and straddled him, brought the fist back over his head. Creeley was out of her seat by then, the gin and tonic launching from her hand to the back of the biker's head. She heard shouting and the movement of bodies. Felt hands grab and toss her as Ross struggled out from between the crumpled biker's tree trunk legs. His greasy hands pinwheeled at the two men clambering for him—the other bikers.

Creeley screamed, scrambled to her feet, and tried to claw for the two men. She was pulled back by the bartender, held tight to his chest. He said, "Let it go, or you're going to get it worse."

The plump sound of fists hitting bone made Creeley cringe. Her dad kicked and punched, sent one biker sprawling. But they had him on his knees and it wasn't long before he was on his back. The uncanny clumsiness of the fight made it seem almost absent of violence, but the sounds were unmistakable. The grunts and yawps and, at some point, the sobs of Ross Mackey.

The bartender said, "Enough, man! You'll get the cops out here!"

The two bikers stopped, stood over Ross Mackey and spit on him. The third biker clambered to his feet, placed a full-strength kick to Ross's ribcage. They glared at Creeley as they stomped past her, left the bar. The sound of well-tuned motorcycle engines started, faded into the night. Creeley kneeled next to her father, swiveled his chin to look him in the eyes. They were open—those steady blues—and the look in them was unmistakable:

I deserved it. I deserved everything I ever got.

35/Nothing Lasts Forever

Small town emergency room.

Pain meds and thirty stitches. A steep bill in the mail —someday.

A twelve-pack of High Life, drank warm in the living room of a rented house in a shitty neighborhood. Pit bulls growling against the chainlink in the backyard, and a monsoon moving toward them from the east. This was Creeley's lone night with her father.

He never mentioned the fight—he wanted to know about her.

"You ever get yourself a man? Or a woman?" He tipped the bottle to his lips, reclined deep in a worn La-Z-Boy. "If you don't mind my asking."

Creeley sat cross-legged on the carpet, her back stiff against a secondhand pleather couch. "I've been with a few guys. Nobody who could fuck worth a shit or hold a job." She hesitated, but came out with it. "One girl—she's sweet."

He raised his eyebrows and nodded at that. "Sweet ain't bad. I can tell you that."

"After I left Blossom…Let's just say I went through some shit."

"I came up in the group homes myself. Out of Phoenix, mostly. Never did meet or find my parents. Always bothered me, right? But you just keep moving forward. All I ever did—keep stepping."

Creeley didn't know how to respond to him. She wasn't here for her family tree, or to have some ecstatic father-daughter moment. No—it wasn't like that. But she did feel bonded to Ross Mackey. She'd never forget the look he had in his eyes as he dove across the table at the fat biker. Pure animal inside him—human cougar. Big teeth and all.

He said, "I know none of it matters. Looks to me like you don't want to know."

Creeley nodded, unsure how to answer. She decided on saying, "It's just that I don't know you. We're like strangers. I'm sorry about the bar, the fight. I—"

"Let that be the one thing I did for you. I didn't ever do nothing else. I can admit it. I accept responsibility for it."

Creeley knew, right as it hit her ears, that this statement was the closest she'd ever get to the universe's humble acknowledgment: You were cheated, Creeley. Somebody, somewhere, did you wrong, but it was nobody's fault. She put her lips between her teeth, thought about what made sense to say. "I get it. You did the best you could."

Ross Mackey groaned as he nodded. His bottle of High Life was half-full.

"Can I use your phone?"

"Still got a landline in the kitchen. All yours. I'm just going to rest my eyes for a second, okay?"

"Sure. Okay." Creeley got up and walked into the kitchen, found the wireless phone blinking on the countertop. She dialed Monty's number and got a groan as he answered. "You're still up, Detective?"

"Nope. Sleeping, but with all the bad dreams I can find."

"You miss me?"

"A little. Where the hell are you?"

Creeley opened the refrigerator. Empty. The open box of High Life was still sitting on the carpet next to her dad. She closed the door without making much noise. "I'm in Blythe. Had to run a little errand."

"What kind of errand?"

"The kind that helps me solve a mystery."

Monty groaned again, made sounds of movement. "I don't know what the shit you can find in Blythe. All it's good for is the Chevron and a place to piss."

"I found Ross Mackey—Levi's dad. My fucking dad."

She could almost hear him nodding. "That's heavy, I bet."

Creeley said, "He tells me Levi went out there to find Blossom. But really, he went out there to find me."

"Catch up with his long-lost sister."

"And I was fucking gone. Hopping trains to Oregon and back

east. A fucking tramp." Again, the rush of feelings and emotions came up in her. Like hot water running over a cup, trailing down a countertop, dripping onto a cold floor. Anger. Hatred. Futile sadness. She felt tears on her cheeks, wiped them away with the back of her hand.

"You didn't strangle Levi Mackey."

The statement hung there between them, like long underwear swinging on a clothesline.

Awkward. Unavoidable. Authentic.

"You didn't strangle Levi Mackey," Monty said again.

Creeley felt herself begin to nod, rock back and forth on her heels. She said, "Uh-huh."

"You didn't strangle Levi Mackey," he said once more.

Creeley cleared her throat and said, "I didn't strangle Levi Mackey. But I'm sure as fuck going to find out who did."

There was a long pause. And then, "That's it. How you have to be."

"How I am."

"Right—how you are."

They listened to each other breathe for a few moments. Creeley broke the spell. "You miss me, Detective?"

"Like a dog."

"Which is what you are."

"Maybe," Monty said. He paused, finished with, "You coming back this way soon?"

"Tonight, I think."

"It's late."

"It's early," she said.

"Tell me you'll be careful."

"I'll be careful."

They hung up and Creeley walked back to the living room, stood watching Ross Mackey, her dad, sleep in a La-Z-Boy recliner. It occurred to her that this was exactly what most people were: tired and beat down and in pain. She was no different. Neither was Blossom. Or Monty. Or Kimmie or Amber. Every one of them—tired and beat down and in pain. You make excuses for the ways in which you fail. You try to blame somebody, put it on some trauma from your past. And maybe it factors in somehow, but it's not the last thing. No—the last thing is you. And if you can't be happy with what you are, and you can't be honest about what you're becoming, that's on you and nobody else. Because the one who has to live with it is you. Alone. All-fucking-alone.

She found a blanket in the hall closet, draped it over Ross Mackey. She grabbed three bottles of High Life from the open box beside the recliner, studied Ross Mackey's face one last time. Those stitches would keep his chin and forehead together. The swelling in his eyes would recede. He was going to be fine. One way or another.

Still handsome.

Still alive.

Creeley Nash locked the door behind her.

She was about to drive through a monsoon.

36/Losing the Way

The 10 was a total shit show.

Creeley had to stuff a hoodie between the driver's side window and the door jamb—the window wouldn't close all the way and rain was pouring in, running across the seat, and pooling under her ass. The hoodie helped, but it was soaked after a few miles and part of it fell out, left an opening for the rain to pour over the seat. Worse, her wipers were a couple years old and they left smears in the center of her windshield. She had to crane her neck to get a clear view through the downpour. The darkness didn't help and Creeley found herself following a pair of taillights. One of those tractor trailers with a thousand running lights on it. She figured the big-rig driver had decent experience. Chances were that he or she had driven in a monsoon like this. As they trotted—maybe forty miles an hour—out of Blythe, the downpour increased and it was impossible to see.

The tick of the Toyota's engine was strong, but Creeley second-guessed everything from her tires to her transmission. Weather had a way of doing that to drivers, she knew.

She wanted to pull off the highway, but that didn't feel safer than driving.

This kept on for more than an hour. With her thoughts focused on the road, Creeley lost all emotion related to her brother's murder. Her brain was centered on survival, on staying on the road. She noticed an ache forming between her shoulders. Tension. Stress.

Be calm, Creeley. Chill the fuck out.

But the rain didn't quit.

Another thirty minutes and Creeley took an exit.

No town.

No gas station.

No lights.

Pure black desert, and all of it soaked with the unending

rain. She made a right-hand turn, saw her headlights sweep an abandoned building. What was it? She throttled forward, felt her tires hit mush—mud. She contemplated putting the 4Runner in four-wheel drive, but decided against it. *I'll be fine,* she thought. Another turn and sweep of the headlights. Looked like an old motor lodge with drive up rooms, a front desk office, and a gate surrounding a pool area. Creeley doubted there was water in the thing, though there would be after tonight.

She circled around back, the 4Runner whip-tailing in the mud.

I'll stay here, sleep out the rain. Get back on the road as soon as possible.

She gunned the engine to race up a slight embankment, aiming to put the 4Runner under an eave. And she felt the rear tires spin, stop. She gunned it again. Nothing but spin and mud slapping the underside of her Toyota. *Fuck me,* Creeley thought. *I'm stuck.*

Just fuck the fuck out of me.

What to do?

Same plan. Wait it out. Figure out recovery after this shitty rain runs dry.

Creeley shut off the Toyota, unlatched her seat belt. She felt the muscles in her back and neck release. God, she was fucking tired. Her ass was wet, and she was shivering.

But she closed her eyes.

And slept.

***

Woke up at full light. The rain gone, replaced by the hot blue sky of open desert. Creeley opened her door and spilled out of it, got a look at her car problem. Her tires were dug halfway into hardening mud, the Toyota's front end cambered oddly against the embankment. She saw now she'd taken a bad line. The shitty thing? In four-wheel drive it would have been no problem. She climbed back in the 4Runner, flipped the ignition, and tried to shift into four-wheel drive. No dice. Probably because she couldn't roll forward at all. She shut the engine off, got out and stood there, thinking. Pissed off. *So fucking stupid.*

And with no cell phone.

She turned in circles, saw nothing but endless desert and the crumbling, white motor lodge.

The highway was only a quarter mile away—that was her main option: flag somebody down or hike to a yellow call box. No water either. Just three empty bottles of High Life on the floorboard. Like last night, a fucking shit show.

She started walking around the motor lodge, thought she'd hike the off-ramp and start there. That way, anybody who wanted to help could exit after they saw her. But she heard voices as she rounded the back side of the motor lodge. A Ford pickup, blue and sitting on beefy tires. There was a tall, skinny guy standing in the bed. He was ripping a pull-start generator as hard as he could, trying to get it started.

"Come on, you fucker!" Yank. Rip. Yank.

Creeley walked toward the truck, saw another guy—no, a teenager—tugging a flexible pool hose through the fence. He hopped over the wrought iron and dragged the hose to the pool, threw it into the center. There was a small splash.

Creeley reached the truck and said, "You don't have a tow strap, do you?"

The guy ripping at the starter cord jumped, almost toppled out of the truck. He caught himself and said, "Holy fuck! You scared the shit out of me." He scratched a lazy beard, smirked. "Who the fuck are you?"

"I got stuck," Creeley said. "Last night. During the monsoon."

The teenager in the pool area said, "Fucking rain fucked up our ride, man."

"Your ride?"

The guy in the pickup—another teenager, but older—held up a skateboard, wiggled it at Creeley. "Best ride between here and Phoenix. Besides the fucking skatepark." He set the skateboard down and said, "Trying to pump the water out of this fucker."

"Like I said—I got stuck last night."

The younger teen said, "We can probably help. We have a couple shovels."

"Worst case," the older one said, "I can bump you out with my truck. Let's go and take a look."

As they walked back around the motor lodge, each guy with a shovel, Creeley had a familiar sense of dread. She flashed on that run to Reno. The gangbanger who wanted to make her his girl. She chanced a look over her shoulder, saw two sweaty teenagers who wanted to skate an abandoned pool. It pained her to think she matched them to the gangbanger, or to the bikers from the bar. All men the same—*no. Not always.* But she also knew that dread was real—it was a learned reaction. *Be careful, Creeley.*

When they saw the 4 Runner, they groaned.

The younger teenager said, "Well, shit. All we can do is dig."

And that's what they did.

37/Hello, Afternoon

Creeley, sitting on the swimming pool steps and rubbing water over her sunburned thighs, sighed and watched the detective. Monty flipped two burgers on the grill, wiped steam from his aviator sunglasses, and sat back down in his lounge chair. She squinted at him from behind her own sunglasses and said, "You need to get more sun." His bare stomach was white as yogurt. His forearms were tan, but his back and neck, too, were white. She could see the white parts of his legs above those knobby older-man knees. "It's gross."

Monty sipped from his red Solo cup—an early afternoon margarita—and shook his head at her. "Everything in moderation, honey. What I wonder, how you can talk to me about my tan when you got lobster skin still."

"Oh, fuck you."

"Don't try to put a desert rat down, sister. This is my winter coat—I'm out here working on my tan. Still plenty of summer left in the calendar. You sure you don't want a burger?"

She shook her head. "I had Mickey D's in Indio. Still sick to my stomach."

"Look," he said, "I don't want to put myself where I don't belong. But I have to ask you about this Blythe trip. I'm wondering what it was that—"

"I'm not hiding anything from you, Monty. I wanted to meet my dad, but it was about my brother. The way I see it, if I can figure out why he was in that room, I can help solve this. That's what it was—and all the other stuff is just noise."

"It's how you have to work a case." He got up, slid the burgers onto a plate waiting with buns. He shut off the grill and sat back down, shoved a burger into his mouth. He chewed with his mouth open, watched her like an insect.

Creeley stood and stepped out of the pool, back into her flip-flops. She walked over to the table, aware of Monty's eyes following her sunburned legs and ass underneath the jean cutoffs. She sat and put her hands behind her head, put her face to the sun. Her skin felt like it was humming.

"Everything helps," Monty said between bites. "It's all information, and it all helps. You don't know how. Maybe not for a long time."

Creeley sighed again and lifted her sunglasses. "It bothers me, why he came."

Monty dropped his half-eaten second burger. He slapped his hands together, leaned back in the chair. "Back to that, huh? Putting a murder on yourself, you didn't even know happened."

Creeley said, "All my life I've been running. But not now. I'm taking all the weight somehow, everything flipped on me when I decided to believe her."

Monty nodded and looked at the sky. He said, "All that weight can't be on you, Creeley. You take what you can, knowing it's hard, but don't take all of it. I told you when you called—"

"I didn't strangle Levi Mackey." She looked at Monty for a long time and decided how she felt about him. Or maybe wanted to feel. "That first night we met...I wanted you, for real."

Monty said, "That was real." A statement from him.

"And it's not this thing we're doing, the case. It can't be that because I've never felt like this. Where I think about somebody. I'm not telling you this because I want—"

"You don't need a reason," Monty said.

He stood and walked around the table, bent at the waist, and put his lips to hers. She met them and it was a short, dry kiss. Not sexual, but loving. Loving and ready to become sexual. But not. Not yet. He walked back and sat in his chair. They stared at each other, and Creeley's cheeks burned hotter in the sun. Or maybe that was the kiss—or both sun and kiss.

She said, "It's been a long time since I kissed a man."

Monty smiled, blushed. "I can tell. You kiss like the inside of a cardboard box."

"Oh, fuck you."

———

MATT PHILLIPS

***

More margaritas in his condo. They sat on the couch and stared at each other for a while. The smells of lime and sour mix made Creeley crinkle her nose. She crossed her legs and said, "I am so tired."

Monty put a hand on her bare knee, squeezed.

"I don't want you to think that I'm—"

"Stop worrying. I don't expect anything from you."

She rested her head on his shoulder. "I know you won't agree, but I'm part of this, what happened to my brother."

"I can see how you feel that."

"And you can tell me whatever you want, but I'll never let that go. I'll never get over it. Because somebody choked the life out of him, and I was far away, but part of it."

"You can find out who did it. And why. That might change how you see it."

"And getting her out of prison. That, too."

"I don't know, Creeley. That's up to so many people...I mean, shit. That's a long order. If it wasn't her—"

"It wasn't."

Monty said, "Then she'll have a chance."

Creeley murmured agreement, closed her eyes. She felt his shoulder beneath her ear. She heard her own heart beating, let the lime scent fill her nostrils. She lifted her cup to her lips, sipped. Swirled the margarita in her mouth and swallowed. *She'll have a chance,* she thought. *If that's all I can do for her, it's enough.* Creeley felt the wall of sleep pushing through her, that heavy feeling of release and comfort. Like a shadow moving through her body. "I am so tired," she said again.

Monty cleared his throat.

She was in a state of quiet so profound that she heard cars passing outside the condo building. A helicopter hovering miles from them. Palm tree fronds brushing against the tile roof. And she heard voices. One she recognized. Paul—the kid who put her on that train. The trashy guy at the stash house in the high desert.

Fucking...Paul?

What the fuck was Paul doing at Monty's condo building?

She popped up and said, "Get your gun, Detective."

"What?"

"Trust me," she said. "Get your fucking gun."

38/Gunplay

"You gentlemen look like you need a drink," Monty said. "Margarita?"

Paul and his white trash buddy locked eyes on Creeley. She was still sitting on the couch, trying to look casual and unafraid. But she saw the bulge beneath Paul's black hoodie, and she knew there was a bulge—not visible, maybe—under the other guy's black hoodie. Pistols. Paul's buddy had shaggy hair and a goatee, some kind of splotchy tattoo on one side of his neck.

Monty closed the door, started for the kitchen.

Paul said, "Sir, can you please stay where I can see you?"

Monty, pointing at the red Solo cup in Creeley's hand, said, "I was just about to make you a drink. That's not okay?"

The white trash guy shook his head.

Monty moved toward the couch, sat beside Creeley.

Creeley said, "I didn't expect to see you again, Paul."

He nodded and cleared his throat. "I got a call from Animal— said I needed to find you. And his shit. Said it was on me if you disappeared."

"How?"

A shrug. "You think any of this has a logic to it?"

The white trash guy said, "You tell us where it is, and we won't toss this place."

"It's not here," Creeley said.

Paul turned and lifted his chin at White Trash. "Find it, Ron-Ron." He centered his eyes back on Creeley, blinked in sporadic flutters. Ron-Ron started pulling out drawers and opening cabinets. There were crashes and cracks in the kitchen as he worked.

Monty said, "Fucking A."

Paul shrugged. He sat down in Monty's recliner, put his hands behind his head. "I'm sorry about this, but it has to be done— unless you just want to tell me where it is. I'm starting here, but your librarian friend's place…That's next."

"Why are you doing this?" Creeley wanted to tell him where it was, but she still hoped to keep it. And giving it to him so easy seemed foolish somehow. But so was hiding it. And lying about it. "The last two guys Animal sent ended up dead."

"I heard about that."

"You think it was an accident?"

Paul smirked and said, "Something like that."

Ron-Ron stomped up the stairs, began to pull drawers from Monty's dresser. Clothes sailed over the banister and landed on the coffee table.

Creeley felt Monty's eyes on her. She avoided looking at him— instead stared at the front door. "I think about you sometimes, Paul. I never told you that, but it's true."

"I'm not stupid, Creeley."

She looked at him as hard as she could. "I think about the kiss. And how you pulled me out of that truck. I think about you lifting me into that boxcar and—"

"I hate fucking perverts."

"I know that, Paul. And you're the one who told me about my mom." She motioned at Monty. "That's what this is—us trying to figure out what happened on the night my brother was killed."

They heard the sound of Ron-Ron tipping the bed against the wall. He cursed and started back down the staircase.

"You're saying he was your brother, the kid who got murdered?"

"Yes."

Ron-Ron said, "The shit isn't here, man. The little bitch put it somewhere, and I'm going to have to slap it out of her."

Paul stood and lifted his hoodie. He pulled a small handgun and pointed it at Ron-Ron. "Stay where you are, asshole."

"What the fuck?"

Paul looked at Creeley and said, "Are you going to tell me where it is?"

Monty stood and Paul put the gun on him.

Paul said, "I'm not some kind of asshole, buddy."

Monty's hands went to his shoulders. "That drink I promised you..."

"I said I didn't want it."

Creeley adjusted her blouse and said, "Paul...Monty. Monty... This is Paul. He's an old pal of mine."

"But no kind of asshole?" Monty lowered his hands, sat back down on the couch.

Ron-Ron watched the three of them and shook his head. "Let's end this shit, Paul. Give me ten minutes and I'll have this motherfucking money. And the product."

Paul looked from Creeley to Ron-Ron to Monty. Did it again.

Ron-Ron said, "You have to think about it, dip shit?"

Creeley saw Paul's body tense, saw ripples in his back show through the thin hoodie. She noticed his face screw to one side. He took two steps toward Ron-Ron and lifted the pistol, brought it down on Ron-Ron's forehead as he raised a hand. The same blow again and Ron-Ron was on his knees. Twice more, and the *thack* of each blow lowered him closer to the floor. When he was all the way down, he lay there whimpering. Paul stood over him and shook his head, wiped his mouth with the back of a sleeve. "You mouthy little rat—shut the fuck up."

When he turned back to face them, Creeley had trouble closing her mouth. She hadn't ever seen—not ever—such an eruption of pure, individual violence. Not at Hawk's back in Blythe. Not from her abusive boyfriends. And not from her mother. The act shook her, and she held a scream deep in the back of her throat.

Monty said, "I take it you mean business, young buck."

Creeley somehow closed her mouth, tasted the dry surface of her top teeth, and gulped.

"Fucking A right," Paul said. "I'll take that drink now. If it's not too much trouble."

✳✳✳

He wanted to know about Levi Mackey.

And Creeley told him.

He finished his drink and asked for another. And another.

He tasted his lips and sighed. He looked at Creeley and said, "Animal is a total asshole."

"Yeah," she said. "So?"

"So, fuck him. I want to help you solve this thing."

"And how are you going to do that?" Creeley was unsure about Paul, but she still had an odd trust in him. It traced back to that night when she hopped the train, but it led to this room and this moment. "You know something we don't?"

"I know how to get word from the inside."

"From the inside? The fuck does that mean?"

"From the joint," Monty said. "He's got an ear in the big house."

Paul nodded, rubbed one arm with his gun. "AB. I'm not in, but I know a guy or three."

"Aryan Brotherhood," Creeley said. "How the fuck does that help?"

Paul looked at Monty. "Can it help?"

Monty said, "It can—if word gets to the right guys. But they don't think this one's on AB. I sure as shit don't. Who's to say they had word about the doer back then? Seems like a waste of effort to me."

Paul shrugged and crossed his arms. "I'm saying I can ask is all."

Creeley felt herself breathing hard, tried to slow it down. "Then do it—ask."

Paul kept nodding, looked down at Ron-Ron, in pain on the floor. He was in a fetal position, recovering from the blows to his head. Paul nudged him with a foot. "You hear that, Ron-Ron? You're going to come in useful. I need you to get up with your cousin Bam, ask if he knows anything about this boy getting killed."

A groan. A shaky voice. "Bam don't know."

"How long's he been locked up?"

"Twenty hard years."

Paul said, "He'll know something. Or he'll find someone who does."

Creeley said, "And what about Animal?"

"Fuck Animal," Paul said. "He can go to hell and die."

Creeley slept at Monty's but she met Amber for breakfast downtown.

Amber stabbed at pancakes with her fork, peered at Creeley over her Coke-bottle hipster glasses. "So, it's you and the detective now?"

Creeley rolled her eyes, forced down a stale English muffin, grape jam spread over it like mud. "I never said you and me—"

"Forget it, Creeley. I like boys, too. I get it."

"He's not quite a boy..."

"Did you two already do it?"

"No," Creeley said. "Shit, no. It's just—he's older, you know?"

"I remember my mom always told me that girls were two years more mature than boys. Like, take our age and add two years. Boys were that far behind."

"I remember my mom used to screw any guy that walked through the door."

Amber nodded and licked syrup off her fork. "You've had a tough life." She frowned and pretended to weep, the back of one hand pressed to her forehead.

"Point taken," Creeley said. "I guess I've been a little dramatic. I'm wrapped up in this."

Amber shrugged, glared out the window at traffic passing on the street.

"But," Creeley said, "I am going to try to talk my way into the motel room."

"The murder scene?"

"Yes." Creeley dumped sugar in her coffee. "I need to borrow your phone. So I can take pictures."

Amber slid it across the table. "You might want to pick up a phone someday."

"Someday."

"I'll be off work around three—you want to meet up

somewhere?"

"How about that tiki joint we went to the other day?"

"Done and done." Amber dropped a twenty on the table and stood. "Take lots of pics."

***

The motel was off South Palm Canyon, tucked on a small street behind a defunct steak house. A motor lodge–style entrance beneath one of the rooms. Creeley pulled in and parked, got out and turned in circles. The San Jacinto mountain range, right up against the city, rose above the building. Amber-colored peaks and sides with tooth-like markings etched in granite. The motel itself was a sun-bleached white with purple accents. It had that vague, duplicative design common to old motor lodge buildings. The lot was almost full—a few luxury sedans mixed with minivans and some beaters. The sun beat down on her and she walked toward the sign that said CHECK IN above a purple door. Creeley opened the door and was met with cool air and pop music. The guy behind the counter—young for Palm Springs and wearing a pink tank top—smiled at her and tossed aside his cell phone.

"Can I help you?"

"Yeah. It's kind of a weird thing, though."

"I'm a motel clerk. I've seen and heard some pretty weird shit. Try me." He scratched one shoulder and tugged at his lip ring.

"My brother was murdered here back in the nineties." *Might as well come out with it and ask.* "I want to see the room where it happened. For, like, closure or something."

"Fuck me. I'm sorry."

"Back then, it was room 23B. Is that still how they're numbered? I mean, I kind of want to see the actual room."

"Give me a second." He dug around in some drawers, found a yellowed map, and laid it on the counter. They both leaned over it and searched for the room. "We keep the map because sometimes people come back for, like, memories."

"Like murders?"

"No. I mean…Like, anniversaries or whatever."

"It's that one," Creeley said. "At the corner."

"Back corner," he said. "Southwest. We call it the sunset room because you get the last light in the summer."

"That one—I want to see it."

"Occupied," he said. "Some old queens from SLO."

Creeley licked her upper lip and said, "Fucking shit."

"But they're out for the moment—brunch at Lulu's."

"And?"

"And I can let you in," he said. "I'm a big believer in closure."

✳✳✳

He let her in and stood at the door, watched the parking lot with the dedication of an armed guard. Creeley snapped an initial pic—the remade bed with purple duvet, the two memory-foam pillows shaped into perfect rectangles, the large flat screen on the wall, and the gray modernist carpet leading to the open bathroom sink and oval mirror. She stepped inside and felt something grip her—a shadow coiling around each of her firing synapses. To know her brother was killed in this room seemed surreal, almost non-essential in its otherworldliness. *A boy died here,* she thought. And then she thought: *he was scared.*

It must be scary to feel the air squeezed out of you. To feel the life pouring out of your own body. Or maybe just vanishing inside you. The way a thought does when you lose it. She wondered what he would have thought—in those final moments. About kissing a girl or hitting a baseball? The tug of a fish at the end of a line? Or maybe just the perfect tang of a taco crunching between his teeth.

She moved deeper into the room, took in the scent of body lotion, bottled incense sprayed by the housekeeping staff. How could this be? That her brother was killed here and it still went on existing? She imagined couples plugging away in naked clumsiness on the bed. No. Couldn't be. Don't they burn a place if somebody is murdered there? Don't they spray it down with kerosene and light a match? Don't they fucking—

"Are you taking your pictures or what?" It was the clerk. "They could be back any second."

Creeley fought tears but started snapping as many angles as she could. She went into the bathroom and made images, took a few of herself reflected in the big oval mirror. The room filled the background like an angry movie set.

"Let's go. You're making me nervous."

"Okay, fine," Creeley said. She walked out but turned around and examined the room once more. Shook her head. Nothing seemed real. Or solid. As they walked down the stairs at the end of the open corridor, the motel clerk asked if she felt it at all. "What?" Creeley said.

"The closure."

"Fuck no," she said. "I feel what I've felt from the beginning—fucking rage."

40/History Lesson: Stick Shift

She learned to drive in a Hyundai—a manual with tinted windows and a silver-gray paint job. Not an ex-boyfriend's car, but an ex-boyfriend's sister's car. Tricia King.

Badass, white trash, Tricia King.

She tipped back Coronas like they were hard cocks, knew all the dirty ironworkers and construction guys were watching her. Nice rack under her wifebeater tank. Red bra straps poking out—white-trash chic, she called it. Cutoff jeans and a backyard tan. Teddy bears tatted on the inside of her wrists. She liked Creeley. And Creeley liked her.

"Let me ask you, Creeley, my teeny-dick brother taught you how to drive yet?"

Creeley was eighteen—hot as any girl in the small Oregon town, and she knew it. Her boyfriend, an auto body tech named Ryan, kept saying he was going to teach her to drive. She popped another Corona for Tricia. "No—he's busy working all the time. And me, too. You know how it is."

"When you get off, Creeley?"

"Half hour. At six."

Tricia gave her the sexy look, that dark eye shadow giving a mysterious shade to her brown eyes. "I think we need to make this happen. You're my project today."

Creeley popped the clutch and stalled the Hyundai six times before they left the parking lot, got onto one of the bumpy neighborhood surface streets near the bar.

"Keep it smooth with the left leg. When you do get on the gas with your right, don't baby it. Otherwise, you'll stall or make the engine hesitate. It's like burping a baby, be rougher than you think you should." Tricia didn't wear a seat belt. Crossed one bare leg over the other and smoked a menthol with her window cracked. "You drive a car like you drive a man—harder than he expects."

Creeley laughed as she shifted into third and then fourth. "I guess I've never driven a guy."

Tricia looked Creeley up and down, shook her head. "Baby, you've been driving men since your titties sprouted. Don't think otherwise. It's about the only power we got." She pointed with her cigarette. "Make a U-turn at the stop sign, cruise back the way we came. We'll get you on a main street in some traffic."

Creeley hit the brakes too hard, and they both lurched forward in their seats.

"Easy, Creeley. Go hard, but stop easy."

She made the U-turn with the little Hyundai stuttering under her unsure clutch operation, somehow got up to speed and headed back toward the bar.

"Pisses me off," Tricia said. "You not knowing how to drive. It's like what they do over there in the Middle East."

"What?"

"You don't know?"

Creeley shook her head, checked the mirrors. Nobody behind them and the dusk coming down like a dark cloud before a storm. She put her eyes on the road, shifted into third. She was starting to feel comfortable, surprised at how easy it came to her.

"I think it's Saudi Arabia, they have it so girls can't drive."

"Are you fucking with me?"

Tricia rolled down her window halfway, tossed her cigarette out, closed the window again. "Why would I lie about something like that?"

Good question. Creeley came to another stop sign, followed Tricia's directions to get onto a busier surface street. She stalled while making a right-hand turn, had to restart the car while Tricia talked her through it. They rolled through town. Passed 7-Eleven and Fred Meyer. Made an unprotected left at the Boys & Girls Club, Creeley excited that she didn't fuck it up. "I feel like I'm getting it," she said.

"You already got it. Let's head back to the bar."

While Creeley pulled into the parking lot, Tricia lit another menthol and filled the car with smoke. They parked and Creeley rolled down her window, felt the cool night put goose bumps on her skin.

"You need a car, Creeley."

"I wish."

"And you need to dump my shit-for-brains brother."

"Why? I like him."

Tricia rolled her eyes. "He's a fuck-up, girl. And he's bad to people. He's bad to himself. You and me both know it."

Creeley watched the door of the bar open—an older couple stumbled out, pawed each other as they made their way to an old Toyota pickup. They crawled into the front seat together, slammed the door. She thought about her boyfriend—saw him sitting on the couch watching football. Cussing at the TV and telling her about his coworkers. She heard the anger in his voice, how he loathed other people. But he was handsome and took her out and liked to dance.

Creeley said, "He's not a bad person."

Tricia laughed and said, "Okay, Creeley. I can tell you something from experience: you hang around with trash and that's what you are yourself. Trash. Fake it until you make it, okay?"

"I don't know what that means."

"You're going to save up. Two, three grand. Get you a beater car and drive the fuck out of here. Wherever you end up, don't call him. Promise to never see him—or me—again." More couples tumbled out of the bar, stood smoking cigarettes out front. Tricia tossed her menthol again. "Just drive away, Creeley."

"This is the first time I, like, really got behind the wheel."

"I'm going to give you lessons, girl. What time you work tomorrow?"

"Three."

"I'll pick you up at two. We'll drive around and listen to Guns N' Roses."

Creeley giggled. "Why G N' R?"

"They make good driving music, that's why." Tricia tapped

Creeley on the knee. "You're going to need lots of good driving music."

"I still don't get why you'd say that about your own brother."

"If you learn nothing from me—besides how to drive—learn this: if it's true, you better fucking say it. Otherwise, everybody's walking around not saying a goddamn thing."

Creeley watched the smokers, shrugged, and looked at Tricia glaring at her with dark eye shadow and those sexy wrist tattoos. "Okay."

"I'm serious."

"I know," Creeley said. "I get it—fake it until you make it."

Two slices of cheese pizza with jalapeños and Creeley's lips were burning. She killed a glass of Coke and shook her head at Amber. "What a weird combo. Are you nuts?"

"Pretty fucking great, right? It's my favorite."

Monty, sitting on Amber's couch and flipping through a manila folder, cleared his throat and said, "Best pizza I ever ate was at a Greek restaurant."

Kimmie chuckled. He was sitting at the kitchen table with Amber and Creeley, slicing his pizza with a butter knife and eating it with a fork. "Because cops know all the best places to eat, right?"

Monty shrugged and said, "Something like that. But we know all the shitty places to eat, too."

Amber took Creeley's plate to the sink. She was standoffish with Creeley this afternoon. She sensed the friction with Monty in the room, and Creeley attracted to him. But she hadn't said anything to Creeley. Instead, she wanted to know how Monty got the box of case files.

Levi Mackey's murder—it was all in front of them.

Monty sat down on the couch as he looked at a few photos.

Creeley stared at the manila file folder in front of her. It was labeled with a date and Levi's name. On the front, beneath a printed label that said 'contents,' four words were scrawled in black ink: 'Parks's Diagrams and Notes.' Drawings and notes by Ray Parks, the corrupt detective.

Creeley took a deep breath and opened the file.

The first drawing—like all of them—was somewhat crude, but it depicted the motel room from above with a stick-figure dead man lying upside down on the bed. The top of Levi's head was depicted as pointing at the bathroom. There were a few notes next to the body—Parks noted Levi as face up on the bed, scratches on his belly, and a black bruise on one side of his face.

Creeley felt a lump form in her throat. She said, "What should I be looking for in all this shit?"

Monty said, "Something that's inconsistent. Evidence that Parks manipulated something. Or that he somehow fucked up really bad."

Amber sat down and opened her file. Kimmie pushed his plate aside and did the same. He got a mean look from Amber but ignored it.

Creeley found it creepy to read all the notes from Parks. He had lots of phone numbers written down next to various names. He'd jotted down general impressions, too: 'Snarky,' 'old as dirt,' and 'decent rack but a liar.' He had detailed notes of his interaction with a prostitute named Leesa:

'Said she saw the other pros enter the room with the vic. They were laughing and drinking beer. Door locked and she heard the TV and laughing. Twenty minutes later heard sounds of struggle but thought intercourse. Never saw anybody leave room. Next thing she heard cops from inside her room. Bad wit, but saw suspect and vic together.'

His drawings were bad but oddly helpful. He even laid out the motel and drew a grid with the cars parked in the lot. A Toyota pickup, a Ford pickup, two Toyota Corollas, and a Harley.

Creeley said, "Would they interview everybody in the motel?"

Monty nodded. "That's why case files get so big—you send patrol officers and detectives to interview everybody you can find. I'm certain the motel employees were interviewed, most of the occupants, too. But that doesn't mean they didn't miss somebody. People have a way of scurrying off when the homicide squad shows up—it's understandable. And it complicates things. Well—not a damn thing here." He tossed his file in the box on the coffee table, fished out a new one. "We also can't believe what people tell us more generally. Once you start seeing and hearing some consensus...That's probably closer to what happened."

"What about vehicles? Do they hunt down every owner, try to interview them?"

Monty sucked on his lower lip, moved his head from one shoulder to the other. He squinted at his open file. "Doubtful, but possible. Depends on whether the car could be involved. But they'd make a list of every car—license plate number, make, model. You just start interviewing and pretty quick you get a car. You go to the list."

Creeley started shuffling through her file, found more diagrams, notes on another interview with a hooker. And then she found it—the list of every vehicle in the lot. And there it was: Harley-Davidson, black, license plate number 23X4142. "Can we look up one of the license plate numbers, see who owned the vehicle at the time?"

Monty tilted his head. "We can try."

She stood and handed him the sheet, pointed to the Harley and the license plate number.

"Why that one?"

Creeley said, "I have a feeling." She sat back down while Monty made a call to a cop buddy, listened for a while, and started jotting things on his yellow legal pad. When he hung up and sat back down, he looked flustered. "Well," Creeley said. "Who is it?"

"Been registered to the same guy for almost forty freaking years."

"And?"

"And we have a current address. Some guy named Regan P. Alma. Lives in Palm Springs—the north end. He's got a decent record, too. Lots of assault and battery, but nothing that sticks, puts him in the joint for a long stint. I'm guessing he's a small-time crook, makes a living at it. Or he's an MC guy."

Amber opened her laptop, started typing. She said, "Wow—if this is him, he looks like fucking Elvis. I mean, like, a super-ugly Elvis."

Creeley gulped, became aware of the hanging smell of pizza in the air. The bitter taste of warm Coke still on her tongue. She walked to the table and bent to peer over Amber's shoulder. It was him—the guy her mom was fucking for money. When she was a kid. Before she ran away.

"Odd," Creeley said.

"Why?" Amber looked up at her.

"My mom used to fuck that guy—for money."

They dropped Kimmie downtown—he said he didn't want anything to do with their law enforcement "hijinks"—and headed toward the north end in Creeley's 4Runner. Dusk was coming down on the desert and Creeley loved how the mountains flushed purple and black. As she drove north, she saw the texture of sand dunes and, beyond that, the 10 freeway. She knew the area—she'd hopped a train this side of the 10, and never looked back.

Now, it seemed she was bound to this place with steel chains.

Maybe she'd never escaped.

Maybe she'd always been bound to here, but without knowing.

Amber leaned over the front seat and said, "You do a lot of police work on the north end?"

Monty sighed and said, "What do you think?"

Amber leaned back in her seat, crossed her arms.

Creeley squinted at her through the rearview mirror. Amber was getting at something and Creeley knew what it was. She said, "The fact that we're calling it the north end tells me something. That should tell me something, right?"

Amber had some irritation in her voice. "It's a racist name for the north end of Palm Springs, where mostly black Americans live."

"How is the name racist?" Monty seemed sickened to ask.

"Because we all know what it means—that's why."

"We all know what it means. Sure, we do. How can we not all know the same thing about such a vague characterization? You know, I'll never understand this wack-job liberal stuff."

Creeley said, "What wack-job liberal stuff?"

"Calling me racist because I use a nickname that everybody else fucking uses—that liberal wack-job—"

"Most cops are racist, Detective." Amber's sarcasm was thick now. Like frosting on a shit cake. She still had her arms crossed, her black fingernails digging into her bare biceps.

Monty said, "Turn left over here and go down to the end of the block."

Creeley made the turn, an unprotected left, and caught a last glimpse of the dunes darkening into night.

Amber said, "Do you disagree with that, Detective?"

Monty appeared to think about it. As they cruised the street—dumpy bungalows interspaced with vacant lots—he scratched the back of his neck and sighed again. Deeper this time. "You know, I think most people are racist. Every single one of us. Some of us, like you, go around and try to blame shit on everybody else. Like it's our fucking problem. And maybe it is, but you don't ever look back at yourself. That's what I found. Everybody crying 'racist this' and 'racist that'? Take a look in the mirror and you'll find one goddamn thing—a racist staring back at you. You work in the library, right?"

Amber didn't answer.

Creeley said, "Yes—she works at the fucking library."

"Park right here," Monty said. "It's that pink stucco house up there on the right."

Creeley pulled to the curb and shut the 4Runner off. They were three houses short, looking at the pink stucco house from maybe fifty yards down the street.

"A library is one of the most racist places in America."

"How the fuck do you figure that, Detective?" Amber's repetition of the word was, of course, meant to piss him off more. Like a lot of things Amber did, it was working as intended. "That's the one place everyone is welcome."

"With a couple goddamn caveats." He chuckled. "One: African American literature is in its own section. Separate, but equal... Isn't that right? Two: there is a vast chasm between the number of white librarians and librarians of color. I never looked up the stats, but I can goddamn guarantee there's more white—"

"I can't fucking control that, Detective."

Monty turned in his seat. "You don't fucking say? But aren't you then complicit in the institutional oppression of potential librarians amongst people of color?"

"You're so far off the mark."

"Am I though? You're saying all cops are racist, and maybe they are, but then it serves to reason that all librarians are racist. I mean, look, you've benefited from your skin color to get where you are. You think there's some people of color on the wrong end of your privilege?"

"But I don't carry a gun and shoot people."

"You're right. And you don't have to wear a bulletproof vest when you clock in for work."

Creeley cleared her throat and said, "I'm not sure what you two assholes are talking about, but I kind of want to have a word or two with Elvis."

"First, let's watch for a bit." Monty leaned back on the headrest and closed his eyes. "Well, you two watch. I'm going to rest for a little bit."

"Forcing the girls to do all the work, huh?"

Monty chuckled. "Empowering you to do the work. Isn't that what you want...to be empowered?"

"Asshole."

Creeley glared at Amber through the mirror, shook her head. She unlatched her seat belt. "Why watch?"

Monty reached out and put a hand on her knee. "Might be better to catch him in public. Wait till he leaves the house for a while." Monty still had his eyes closed. "You never know what a fucker like this is up to."

Creeley pushed his hand away, put a foot on the dashboard beside the steering wheel.

Amber wouldn't let the conversation with Monty die. "How many black people have you arrested? How many have you shot?"

"Christ," Monty said. "I wish you'd leave me alone. I'm a detective. Most of what I do is paperwork. When I was a patrol officer, yeah, I gave some people headaches with my baton. Pepper sprayed some punk motherfuckers. But I never shot anybody. Had no reason to shoot anybody. Most of the people I ran into, they were drunk. You let them get wound up, next thing you know they're puking in the gutter. I'm not saying there aren't shitty cops out there. I'm not even saying you're wrong about any of this shit. All I'm saying is take a fucking look in the mirror."

"So what do you think about black people being killed by cops? As smart as you are, Detective, you should have an opinion. Or are you so racist that it's obvious?"

"Again, I'm a fucking homicide detective. My opinion—no person on this earth should kill any other person." He paused and thought for a second. "Not without a good reason, at least. I think cops should stop killing people. Keep your gun in your holster and give a motherfucker a headache. If, and only if, that's what he needs."

"You never shot anybody?"

Monty opened his eyes and looked at Creeley. "Will you tell your smart-ass friend I never fucking shot anybody?"

Creeley said, "He says he never shot anybody."

"That's what he says," Amber said.

"It's the goddamn truth!" Monty whipped around in his seat, stuck his face into Amber's. "Stop asking me about this shit. You don't know a fucking thing about what I do."

Amber put her hands up and said, "Don't fucking shoot."

"Fuck me," Creeley said.

Monty turned around shaking his head, closed his eyes again and tried to slow his breathing.

"Maybe we should leave this conversation for a pleasant happy hour on some distant sunny morning." As she spoke, the Elvis impersonator came out of his house in a red motorcycle jacket. He walked around the side of his house, and they heard a roar. A moment later, he emerged on the black Harley.

Creeley said, "Same bike."

"Yes, sir," Monty said. "Wait until he makes the stop sign, and then let's follow him."

Creeley flipped the 4Runner on, shifted into drive. The

motorcycle reached the stop sign, rolled through it into a left turn. Creeley got on the gas.

Amber said, "Just for the record, you don't know anything about what I do either."

"No," Monty said. "I don't. And I don't want to. Librarians are fucking wimps—and that includes you."

***

They followed Elvis—how Creeley thought of him now—to an auto body shop in Cathedral City, off Perez Road. It was an easy tail down Highway 111 and green lights the whole way. Palm Springs traffic was almost nonexistent at this time during the summer, and Creeley was starting to enjoy it. Monty told her to drive past the shop and she followed his instructions, made a U-turn at a Toyota dealership.

"Make the right," Monty said. "But drive past the place and we'll park somewhere he can't see us."

Creeley saw the black Harley parked out front as they passed—a one-story building with a wall of glass looking in on the waiting area. Next to that an auto yard surrounded by chainlink topped with razor wire. And then two vehicle bays with their sliding doors closed, though yellow light came through the small windows in the second door.

Amber said, "Somebody's home tonight."

Creeley found a spot in the parking lot for an adult video store. She locked the 4Runner and the three of them walked back toward the auto body shop. It was dark and the night air was hot and muggy. For some reason it made Creeley think of wet summer in Oregon—and that hot yoga shit she tried once.

As they approached the building, Monty started to trot, and Amber and Creeley followed. They crossed behind the shop, alongside the far section of the building where they saw lights. As they reached the rear of the building, Monty stepped around the corner, cautious with one hand on his holstered gun. Creeley looked at Amber who rolled her eyes and made a gagging motion with one hand.

The rear of the shop was protected by a chainlink box. It was filled with piles of smashed bumpers and dented fenders, hoods creased to useless shapes. Monty tried the gate, and it was locked with a huge chain and padlock. He nodded at them to follow, and they reached the auto yard. It, too, was surrounded by fencing and filled with cars in various stages of repair. They stopped to listen but heard nothing.

Monty motioned at them to go back, and Amber and Creeley led the way back around the building and onto the sidewalk. As the three of them reached the sidewalk, a voice called out with a precise, mixed tone of surprise and anger.

"The fuck are you shit heads doing back there?"

Creeley turned and saw Monty marching toward the voice. It was Elvis—he was sitting on the Harley with his helmet in one hand and a cell phone in the other. He said, "I'm a call you back." He brought the phone down and put it in his jacket pocket, squinted at Monty moving toward him. "Hey, man—the fuck were you doing back there?"

Monty kept moving—he started to jog.

"What the fuck?"

Monty laid out like a linebacker, caught Elvis square in the chest and they both went over the bike, landed on the pavement. Elvis cried out as Monty flipped him over, pressed a knee into the center of his back.

"Shut the goddamn hell up," Monty said.

"The fuck—"

Flush hand to the back of the head. "I said, be fucking quiet."

Creeley and Amber jogged toward the men and, when they reached them, Amber said, "That's fucking police brutality, dude."

Creeley said, "What the fuck, Monty?"

"I bet ten Gs this motherfucker has a gun on him." He patted Elvis down, started with one foot and moved all the way up. Then the other foot—he stopped halfway up Elvis's left leg. "There it is." He rolled up the leg of Elvis's jeans and pulled a small black handgun from an ankle holster. "Compact Glock, what we got here." Monty removed the magazine and examined it. He slid the magazine back into place and shoved the gun into his own waistband. "Why you need a baby gun like that?"

"Why the fuck do you think? I just got attacked by a cop."

"Detective, you stupid fuck."

"Detective of what?"

"Homicide, buddy. I'm murder police."

"The fuck do you want with me?"

Creeley said, "We want to ask you what the fuck you were doing on the night my brother was killed."

"Who the fuck are you, bitch?"

"I'm Blossom's daughter, you fucking trash."

"Who?"

"Blossom Nash—don't tell me you forgot about her."

He grinned with his face in the pavement. "Never. She was nice and tight, that one. But I'm betting she's loose as a goose by now."

Creeley bent to one knee, cocked her fist, and punched Elvis straight in the eye.

***

Monty, one hand resting snug on his hip holster, had Elvis propped against the wall outside the auto body shop. Creeley stood beside Monty, glared at Elvis with his scraped cheeks and deadpan eyes, one plump as a peach from Creeley's knuckles. Amber leaned against the wall, arms crossed, her angry gaze centered on Monty.

Monty said, "Fucking fuck head. I bet you wanted to pull that gun on me, huh?"

"I hate cops. Detectives, too."

Creeley moved a step closer, glared at him. "You were there that night, weren't you?"

"What night?"

"When my brother was killed."

"Look, I guess me and your mom had a thing, but I never saw any kid around besides you." He looked her up and down and said, "And what a specimen you turned out to be."

Creeley lifted a hand, swung it up and sideways, slapped Elvis's cheek—a *crack* like a gunshot smacking the air. "I wouldn't let you fuck me with Matt McConaughey's cock."

Amber said, "Shit—that's good."

Elvis shook his head, smirked at Creeley.

"You were there," Monty said. "And we can prove it."

"I told you I don't know nothing about a kid."

"Levi Mackey. Tall and strong. Fucking handsome. Seventeen going on forty, or so I've heard. He was there to see my mom, to see me."

"Oh, shit. You're talking about the thing back in the nineties. What was it, like..."

"Ninety-six," Amber said.

He shook his head. He ran a hand through his hair, shuffled from one foot to the other.

"You remember now," Monty said.

"Yeah, shit. I remember I left my bike at the joint. I knew one of the front desk guys. I was headed with some buddies over to the Roadhouse on 111, and I couldn't take the bike. Planned to drink my way through the night. My guy said I could leave my bike and pick it up in the morning. I left it there because they had a clerk on duty all night. Figured it'd be safe."

"You didn't stay at the motel?" Creeley wanted so bad to find Levi's killer, she felt herself generating rage at Elvis. But it felt off, like she was lip-synching a Madonna song in a country western bar. She wiped sweat from her forehead, shook her head at Amber.

"No—fuck, no. I know Blossom was there, though. And that's what I told the cops. They called me, oh, about a week after that boy got killed."

"You told them you saw Blossom at the motel?" Monty pulled his hand from the gun, produced a small notebook from a pocket. He started jotting notes.

"Yeah. Shit, I did see her. She was on the second-floor balcony when I rode in. Gave me a smile and asked me did I want a turn before her date." He glanced at Creeley but spoke to Monty. "I didn't have time because my buddies were headed over. I joked around with her for a second, and then I walked out into the street."

"You picked up your bike the next day?"

"Day after, I think. Maybe two days after. I remember they had the place sealed up the first morning. Some cop told me to come back later."

Amber said, "They didn't question you when you showed up?"

He turned to face her, settled his plump eye on her notable cleavage.

Amber said, "Up here, dip shit."

He met her eyes and said, "They got my number, said to expect a call. Like I said, few days later I get a ring from some detective."

"What detective?" Monty's pen hovered over his notepad.

"Real gruff dude. The fuck was his name? Shit...Raymond, I think."

"Ray Parks," Creeley said.

Elvis snapped his fingers. "Yeah. That was him."

"And you," Amber said, "told him about Blossom?"

Elvis looked down at his boots, shook his head. "Funny you ask it that way. I mean, yeah. I told him she was there." He paused.

Monty said, "But?"

"He asked me first, did I know a Blossom Nash? When I said I did, he comes out and asks did I see her at the motel on the night that boy got murdered?"

"And you said—"

"I said, hell, yes."

Creeley said, "But you didn't testify at the trial."

"Fuck, no. You think I'd be a good witness? Shit. I been in the joint more times than I remember. I think it was Parks called me a month or so later. Said they didn't need me. Had them some DNA proof. You know how that is. Last thing I want is to sit in front of a judge. Even when I ain't done nothing wrong."

"The guy at the front desk. The one you say you knew—what was his name?"

Elvis hesitated, but said, "Old buddy of mine named Rickles. Cary Rickles. Tall as a motherfucker."

Creeley looked at Monty. "Do we know this guy?"

Monty squinted at Elvis and said, "I believe we do. Matter of fact, I believe you met him two days ago. And we gave him Ray Parks."

Amber said, "You're shitting me?"

Monty lifted his chin at the auto body shop. "What are you doing out here tonight?"

"I forgot to turn off the shop lights this afternoon. Came out to check on things and turn everything off. I'm sick of my boss being up my ass about shit." Elvis smiled at Creeley. "I know something else you don't. That mom of yours—she was fucking the mayor of Palm Springs. Fucking A. Believe that, right? Me and the mayor, fucking the same pale whore twice a week. Goddamn, that's a riot."

Creeley pulled back her fist, aimed for Elvis's other eye.

To make it match.

43/Sunburns

Kimmie said, "You need this, girl." He sipped his piña colada and pulled his sunglasses over his eyes. He put his hands behind his head and his face to the sky. His bronze stomach shined with tanning oil. "You know you need it."

Creeley lay beside him in her own lounge chair. She wore jean shorts and a halter top, so much sunscreen that her shoulders were caked with white smears. "I guess so," she said as she watched the pool. Deep blue and shallow. Filled with L.A. types in Wayfarers and butt floss. The pool deck was packed with lawn chairs, too. Everybody tanning and sipping blended cocktails. Waiters in flower-print shirts carried oval trays of food and cocktails, smiled at her beneath straw hats. A band on a stage—two older dudes on bongos and a keyboard—played Jimmy Buffett and UB40 tunes. It was an odd scene to Creeley. So far removed from an Oregon reality that she wanted to vomit. It wasn't the heat or the alcohol, but the stench of faux resort vanity. Or maybe it was being here when she shouldn't be. When instead she should be hunting down more leads. But after their encounter with Elvis—when Creeley found her penchant for a mean right hand—Kimmie insisted she take a day to rest what he called her "fireball storm of woman-rage."

Kimmie said, "Do you always have so much trouble relaxing?"

"I'm not used to scenes like this, that's all." Creeley watched a smug-looking guy, late fifties in her mind, shuffle toward them in flip-flops. He was shirtless and hairy—black stringy stuff running up his chest and shoulders. She expected to see it on his back as he walked past them. He had a smear of sunscreen on his fat nose, and a pair of those big-ass Vegas-style sunglasses on his head.

The guy stopped before he reached Kimmie, tossed his blue resort towel onto an empty lounge chair. He looked at Creeley and said, "You mind I lay next to your guy here, babe?"

Creeley smirked and lifted her sunglasses. "He's not my guy, and I'm not your babe. But you can lay wherever the fuck you want. It's a free country."

The guy smirked at her, spread his towel on the chair, and lay back with his hands folded behind his head. "Not a bad scene, babe. Lots of tits and A. Not a bad way to spend an afternoon."

"Christ," Creeley said. "You must be the CEO of a Fortune 500 company. A mouth like that."

Kimmie said, "But he's wearing cheap cologne. Drugstore scent. I know a con artist when I smell one."

"Do you now?" The guy scratched his chest hair, sneezed into an elbow. He went back to the relaxed position.

"I can guess," Kimmie said. "My eyes are closed."

"Guess what?" Creeley was interested now, almost captivated by this odd California scene.

"No watch on his wrist, but pale skin because he wears one. It's a fake Rolex, probably. He's got a ring on a pinkie finger— gold inlaid with small diamonds."

The guy said, "They're real." He held up the pinkie finger on his right hand, showed Creeley the ring.

Kimmie said, "They're cubics. Like what you buy for all your sugar mommas."

"And daddies," the guy said. "Boys like diamonds, too."

"That's for real," Kimmie said.

"I know it is."

Creeley swung her feet off the chair, sat up to face the hairy guy over Kimmie's gleaming stomach. "Do you two know each other?" The pool deck was hot and Creeley scrunched her toes to protect the bottoms of her feet. She reached for her flip-flops, slipped them on, and laid a towel over her bare knees. So much sunscreen, but she already felt her skin tingling.

"Our friend here isn't hard to know," Kimmie said.

"I guess I picked the wrong seat."

"You did. Unless you're paying for the drinks."

"I never pay for anything. You should know that." The hairy

guy raised his hand and flagged a waiter who jogged toward them.

"What can I get for you, sir?"

"We'll take three summer hummers."

"What room, sir?"

"Forty-two twenty-seven. Registered to Perry."

"Back in a flash, Mr. Perry."

"Call me Ace," the hairy guy said. "It's a nickname."

The waiter jogged away with his tray under an arm.

Creeley said, "So, what's your deal, Ace?"

"He's a con man," Kimmie said. "A crook. A fink. A flimflam man. A cheater. A fleecer. He's a flipster and a trickster, bunco as a car made in North Korea."

Ace said, "I prefer to be called a con *artist*, but I take no offense."

"So what is it out here? You find some old hag to finger and she hands you some dough?"

"God, no. I never resort to sexual favors. And I prefer"—he lifted his sunglasses and admired Kimmie's bare stomach—"those of another persuasion."

Kimmie lifted his own shades, opened his eyes, and examined Ace from big toe to unibrow. "You're one hairy son of a bitch, aren't you?"

Ace ignored Kimmie and said, "The game, sister, is to build relationships. That's all this business is, and all it's ever been. It's a game of relationships. Like with any other profession. What is it, pray tell, that you do?"

"She's a drug runner," Kimmie said.

"Kimmie!"

"What? You are."

"Ah," Ace said, "the darker arts."

"God, where am I?"

Kimmie said, "You're at the Marriott."

The waiter showed up, sweat running off his forearms and chin. "Here we are. Three summer hummers." He handed each of them a plastic cup with a pink straw and pink plastic flamingo for a stir stick. "And here you are, Mr. Perry." He held out his tray with a paper check and a pen.

Ace signed with a dainty flourish and grinned. "I hope twenty for you is okay? My portfolio isn't doing so well in this market. You understand?"

The waiter chuckled. "Twenty is beyond generous, Mr. Perry."

"See you in ten."

The waiter jogged toward a group of young women—bachelorette party just getting started—as they waved and shouted at him from the pool.

Ace sipped from his drink.

Creeley looked into hers and said, "Are you really Ace Perry?"

Kimmie said, "Am I really Al Capone?"

Not Ace Perry said, "Let's go for lunch after we finish our drinks. I'm enjoying your company. And I could use some accomplices. Trust me, you'll thank me later."

✳✳✳

"The way I play it," Ace said, "is I like to make it so they give it to me as a gift."

Kimmie was swirling a glass of white and chewing celery and hummus.

Creeley had a margarita—too tart—and she was thinking about ordering a thirty-dollar cheeseburger. "Like, how do you make it a gift?" She met eyes with a waitress across the dining room—modern decor and that echo sound of fine silver on porcelain—and lifted her chin.

Ace said, "You become friends with people. Not friendly, okay? I'm talking you actually become a friend. And people will do anything for their friends."

The waitress said, "Another drink for anybody?"

Kimmie gulped his wine, slid the glass across the table. "Too kind. I'd love one."

"And for me as well," Ace said.

Creeley grunted and pointed at the menu. "I'll take the thirty-dollar cheeseburger. I'm feeling frosty today."

"Cheddar or Gruyère?"

"Grew-fucking-year," Creeley said with a wry smile. "Of course." How could she not smile about choices in high-quality cheese? Talk about the fats of freedom—her mom likely hadn't tasted Gruyère before she got locked away. And here Creeley was, dining like a queen. The waitress trotted off, swinging her tight little ass for Creeley and the gay men sitting with her.

"Sweet little thing," Ace said. "But poor as shit."

"How do you know?"

"Desperate to please, Creeley. Have I told you? I love your name. Familiar, but unique. A perfect name for a con artist." He lifted his whiskey tumbler to his mouth and slurped. "Like I say, desperate to please. You have to read people, Creeley. People with money are desperate for nothing—everything belongs to them. And they know it. Take that couple, for instance." He lifted his unibrow toward the front entrance that looked out on the pool and, beyond that, a curvaceous, green golf course.

Creeley followed his gaze and settled her eyes on a midfifties couple in well-fitting resort wear. The guy in mid-thigh khaki shorts and a Tommy Bahama flower-print shirt. The woman—fit, prim—in a clingy white dress. She wore understated gold pieces in her ears and around her neck. Done nails. Done hair. Face-lift and botox easy to see from more than twenty yards.

But sexy, Creeley had to admit.

Pretty damn sexy.

"And now she'll point at the table she wants," Ace said.

The woman tapped the hostess on the shoulder, pointed at a table near a window. The hostess gave a worried look into a file folder, marked something with a pen, and guided the couple to the table. The man kept his arm around the woman as they walked. Intimate enough to draw looks, but shy of creepy or possessive. They sat and the woman appeared to order a drink from the hostess.

Ace said, "And she can't wait to get those lips around a bottle of Chardonnay."

Kimmie chuckled. "You are one bad mother, Ace."

"Except to you. You can call me daddy."

"You two are gross." Creeley watched the hostess run off and whisper in a waiter's ear. He nodded and began trudging toward the service well at the bar. "I guess she'll get what she wants."

Their waitress came back with the drinks and Creeley smiled at her.

Ace said, "You see the couple that just came in, darling?" He motioned at the couple—they were watching the dining room like vultures, ignoring their menus stacked on the table. "I remember the gentleman from my last visit. We had drinks at the Gnocchi Room." He snapped his fingers twice. "I can't remember his—"

"That's Mr. And Mrs. Weiss," the waitress said. "Weiss Foods of the Valley—the grocer."

"Right. Weiss. Now I remember. Thanks, darling."

The waitress looked at Creeley and said, "The chef is at work on your cheeseburger." She curtsied—an actual fucking curtsy— and wagged that tight little ass to another table.

Creeley said, "I don't think it takes a chef to grill a burger."

"I served tables. All I ever saw a chef do was yell at people and try to get it on with teenage hostesses." Kimmie swirled his new glass of white.

"Watch and learn, shiny new friends." Ace stood, straightened his white button-up—one of those light fabric beach shirts—and strode across the dining room. He stopped at the couple's table, bowed, and put two fingers on their table—like he was balancing himself. They were laughing within ten seconds, making room for him within thirty, and waving at Creeley and Kimmie to join them before a minute had passed.

Kimmie said, "This motherfucker knows what he's doing."

Creeley nodded, stood in her jean shorts and midriff blouse. "He sure does—and I think we're in for a long night."

Kimmie licked his bottom lip and said, "I'm in for a long night, girl. You're just first-string arm candy. You'll be home before eight—if I have anything to say about it."

The man fixed his gaze on Creeley the second she sat next to him.

His wife didn't seem to care—she flirted back and forth with Ace and Kimmie, seemed to enjoy their candor and willingness to talk smack about other restaurant diners.

And that left Creeley with Morris Weiss.

He smelled of aftershave and nicotine. A closet smoker, she guessed. Hiding it from his wife. Like he hid a lot of things. But not his attraction to Creeley.

"You are completely gorgeous, Creeley. Let me pay for your next drink. For all your drinks."

"That's generous of you, Morris. But, I mean, I'm kind of taken." She smirked. "Same as you?"

Morris slid toward her by an inch or two. "My wife and I are in a certain phase of life—call it a tour of pleasures. We have an understanding about these sorts of things." He touched her hand with a pinkie finger, raised an eyebrow.

Creeped Creeley the fuck out. She pulled her hand away—just short of snatching it.

She said, "Are you hitting on me?"

"Something like that. Would you like a martini?"

"White wine," Creeley said. "Something nice."

Morris waved the waiter over—a surfer-looking kid with long curly hair and a decent tan. "The nicest bottle of white, please."

Morris's wife turned from Kimmie and Ace and said, "Your nicest Chardonnay." She laid a hand on Morris's forearm and slowly pulled it away and clasped the stem of her wine glass.

Thanks for ignoring me, Creeley thought.

"Tell me about yourself—what do you do?"

Creeley said, "I'm in logistics."

"A field I know all too well. We used to bring cases of wine in from Chile—a stellar blend that was hard to find. I knew a few wholesalers in South America, but they couldn't keep this blend in stock—popular with the locals and chefs in Los Angeles, you see. I made an arrangement with a distributor out of Long Beach and—"

"Nobody gives a shit about your exploits in the world of middle-grade wine, Morris. Least of all me. I'm a gorgeous woman with too much shit to worry about. I don't need some heroic story of how you helped a few dozen housewives imbibe some imbecile's idea of a decent wine." She smiled at him and said, "And where the fuck is *my* wine?"

Morris stood and motioned at a busboy. "Wine, please. Find our waiter."

The busboy scampered off with a crazed expression on his face.

"There you go, Morris. Help them remember how much money you spend here."

Morris chuckled and shook his head. "Another one of the victims, am I right?"

"I'm sorry?"

"You're a victim, I know—everything that ever happened in your life is somebody else's fault."

"Oh, fuck you...Morris."

The waiter arrived and showed Morris the Chardonnay. He nodded and they both watched the waiter open the wine, pour a bit for Morris to try. He slid the sample to Creeley, and she tasted it, smirked at the waiter.

"I guess it'll do."

He poured for each of them and pivoted to another table.

"I know your kind, Creeley."

"My kind?"

"That's right. Reckless, assuming, torn between square life and other bullshit."

She turned to study Morris as he raised a glass to his lips. He churned the wine in his mouth, ran air over his tongue, and swallowed.

"Big oak," he said.

"You don't know a fucking thing about my life."

"I'm guessing you come from a broken home. Maybe you've been assaulted in your past. Sexually, I—"

"Do you think I won't slap you in front of your wife?" Creeley was aware of some dull conversation between the wife, Kimmie, and Ace. She couldn't follow it.

"I think you'd kill me if you had to."

"You're goddamn right, you creepy old fucker."

Morris laughed. "I can't say things haven't been unfair for you. I imagine you've had your knocks, but does that give you an excuse to live in the gutter? Not in my book—no."

"Your book? How much money did Daddy put in your bank account, Morris? That's what I'd like to know. Really—how-fucking-much?"

"My daddy sucked tailpipe when I was ten. Couldn't face getting laid off from the meatpacking plant downtown. He was a sucker and loser."

The way he said it made Creeley's throat catch. She saw the rage in his face—knew he felt cheated by the death of his father. She was used to that, how it felt to be cheated. Even in cheating herself—it was her supreme talent.

"I saw that and decided it was all going to be on my own terms. Whatever I did. Wherever I worked. Whoever I served. On me. And me alone."

"So, you think you have my number because—"

"I'm just like you."

Creeley sipped her wine and blinked. She cleared her throat.

"Except for one thing," Morris said. "I never let it make me into a piece of shit."

"I'm no piece of shit." *Except I am. Drinking fine wine and expecting high-grade meat while Blossom rots in a cinder-block hell.*

"Sure you are—won't even let yourself be happy."

"*Let* myself?"

"You heard me." Morris sighed and finished his glass, reached for the bottle. He filled up and offered to fill hers.

"Yes—why not?"

"That's it," Morris said. "You deserve wine, to be drunk, to be loved, to be respected..."

"What else?"

"What do you want?"

Creeley thought about it for a moment. She shrugged and said, "I want to be heard."

Morris bit his bottom lip, nodded. "I'm listening to you. I hear you."

"It's about time somebody did—Jesus."

They sat there and drank the bottle of wine, listened to the other three at the table chat in meaningless syllables. The waiter delivered Creeley's thirty-dollar cheeseburger, and she ate it, ravenous as a dog. Morris passed her a napkin, and she wiped her lips and chin. The white fabric came away red with ketchup. If you didn't know better—and hadn't seen Creeley eat—it'd be easy to think the napkin was soaked in blood. Creeley crumpled it into a ball and pushed her plate to the edge of the table. A busboy appeared and removed the plate.

Creeley said, "Are we happy yet?"

Morris looked at her and poked a cheek with his tongue. "That's the trick, you know. Some of us don't need to ask. The answer is obvious."

Some answer, Creeley thought. *Some kind of asshole fucking answer.*

Kimmie said, "Ace is a little boy in a man's body." He sucked on a vanilla milkshake from McDonald's and scratched the back of his head. "Last night was cute, but I ain't got no time for games. The last thing I want is—"

"Did you actually fuck him?" Creeley crumpled the wrapper from her crappy McDonald's cheeseburger into a ball and tossed it over her shoulder. The wrapper landed in the 4Runner's back seat. Funny, it was somehow better than the thirty-dollar burger she had the night before. She picked up the coffee from between her legs and sipped. Late afternoon and they were sitting in the parking lot outside a McDonald's in Desert Hot Springs. A group of homeless people shook out blankets and jawed at each other alongside the restaurant. A police black-and-white rolled up, rolled down its window. The officer shot the shit with the group for a minute or two, squealed out of the parking lot with a thumbs up out the window. A few homeless people flipped the bird.

"God no. I never fuck anybody," Kimmie said.

"Did he fuck you?" Creeley leveled her eyes at him.

"A fairy never tells."

"God, I can't believe you. You're such a slut."

"Me? You're the cop fucker, little miss thing." He sucked harder and got a big gob of vanilla, chewed it like Bubble Yum.

"I have not yet fucked the cop, Kimmie."

"Yet, baby. Not yet. Speaking of that handsome, corrupt son of a gun...Why didn't you bring him to meet this—what did you call him—fat black guy with a temper?"

Creeley started the 4Runner, balanced her coffee in one hand and steered out of the parking lot with the other. She put them on a surface street headed north. "That's what he was when I met him. I can't imagine I need to be politically correct with you, of all people."

"I prefer you call him a big-boned black American with an

anger management complication."

Creeley chuckled, sipped bitter coffee.

"No—you don't have to be politically correct with me. But I do hope you'll be honest."

"About what?"

"You think this guy will help us find the guy you need, Cary Rickles?"

Creeley turned them west for a block, took the next right. She was trying to get back to the drug dealer's house by vague memory. She got there before by following Monty's instructions—realized she'd blanked out while driving. But she'd know the place when she saw it. They crossed into a neighborhood of tract homes, familiar to Creeley now as she cruised past beige stucco and red Mexican tile. All the brown lawns too sad in the oppressive heat to go green.

Creeley said, "I think this is where we start. For some reason, I think Cary Rickles is going to be a real bitch to find."

"Yeah? What tells you that, girl?"

"The other night, after I punched out Elvis, Amber did the computer research thing she does. Nothing turned up." Creeley circled once and slowed the 4Runner, decided to make a left. A hundred feet later she saw it: a black Escalade on big-ass rims. She slowed and pulled to the curb. "This is it," she said. "Let's go have a little talk with a big-ass black man."

✱✱✱

That endless loop of *SportsCenter* still played on the flat screen.

Slide collapsed onto the sofa like a sack of potatoes rolling down a staircase. He put his hands behind his head and said, "Skinny white girls always come back to me. I guess it's my charming personality." He tasted the underside of his top lip, motioned at Creeley and Kimmie to take a seat on the sectional. "You brought a fairy with you, huh? I ain't got nothing against it. Ask me, they got the same rights to shitty jobs and divorce settlements as the rest of us. Fuck it."

Creeley sank into the sectional, but Kimmie perched on the

edge of the seat. He propped his chin on a bent hand and said, "I feel so thankful to have your support."

"Kumbay-fucking-yah," Creeley said. "I didn't come here to verify your membership in the Liberal Corps of America. I'm here because I want you to give up your guy."

"My guy?" Slide didn't turn his head, but he did let his eyes shoot toward Creeley. "Who the fuck is 'my guy'?"

"Cary Rickles, big boy." Kimmie grinned as he said the name.

Slide started paying greater attention to *SportsCenter*.

"Your drug dealer pal, right?" Creeley watched for a reaction from him—big fat zero. She said, "I know you arranged it with Monty to give Parks to Rickles. And Parks paid Rickles hush money for...decades, I guess?"

Slide chuckled, his throat cracking as the sound passed over his lips. "You think all this is about your momma, I bet."

"What else would it be about?"

Slide rolled his eyes and they landed on Creeley. "It's about what everything is about, white girl. It's about money. You that confused you can't see it?"

"Maybe she is confused," Kimmie said.

"Yeah," Creeley said. "Maybe I am confused."

Slide sighed and shook his head. "Cary Rickles isn't 'my guy,' okay? You can't believe what you hear, what people say. Comes down to it—if I can admit it to myself—I'm his guy. You ever wonder why money got passed from Parks to him? Like, ask yourself that question. You think it's Parks trying to shut him up about some working girl in the joint?" He watched Creeley for a reaction, but she gave him nothing. "All this"—he tilted his head back and forth between Creeley and Kimmie—"is about Parks keeping shit quiet. But you think he'd pay the man for all those years, something that far in the past? Come the fuck on."

"I'm still not seeing it, Slide."

"No motherfucking kidding. Man, look at this shit from up top. Like, look down on it. Who the fuck does Ray Parks work for?"

"Palm Springs PD."

Another chuckle. "Palm Springs PD? Okay. Then tell me this: Who does Palm Springs PD work for? Can you riddle me that, dumb fucks?"

Kimmie, sarcastic as hell, said, "They don't work for the greater good of the community?"

"Man," Slide said, "you two are the real deal. Sherlock and Holmes just sitting here in front of me. They work for The Vandals. The MC is tied all up and down that department."

Creeley flashed on Monty's face. Saw his lips mouthing the words: The Vandals.

Kimmie said, "I feel like I'm in a network TV series."

Creeley stood up and put her hands on her head. "Fucking shit. Fuck the fuck out of me."

"Now she got it," Slide said.

Creeley shook her head and scratched her cheeks before saying, "Monty—you fucking asshole."

46/Open Eyes

Flat black road across blue sand dunes—wind turbines spinning above it all like shadows in a dream. She saw Monty smiling at her, felt his hand on her thigh, heard his voice whispering in her ear. And that laugh—certain and seductive and melodic. And where was he back in 1996? Working patrol and headed nowhere fast. Look ahead three, four years and he's working homicide.

A detective.

Possible? Sure. Likely? Creeley didn't know, but hearing Slide say it—The Vandals—shook something loose in her head. And in her heart. It wasn't right, the thing with Monty. He wasn't right. Oncoming headlights yanked Creeley from her thoughts.

"Creeley!" Kimmie slapped her shoulder with the back of his hand.

She swerved back into her lane. "Fuck. I'm sorry." The headlights zoomed past them, a horn sounding and receding. "My bad, Kimmie."

"Where were you, sister?"

"Thinking about Monty."

Kimmie stared out the window. They were on the road back into Palm Springs, San Jacinto Mountain now towering over them like God's profile. Kimmie sighed and sucked air through his teeth. "When I saw you at the pool the other day, I just—"

"Wanted a partner in crime."

Kimmie made a kissing sound and said, "Something like that, Creeley."

"I'm sorry I dragged you into this shit. And Amber, too. It's a total cluster fuck."

"I'm not asking you to be sorry. I'm telling you that—fuck, how do I say it—you are making me feel like I fucking matter. Like, you know, I'm alive." He turned to her and wagged his shoulders. "I'm in with you all the way, sister. It doesn't even matter what the fuck happens."

Creeley grinned, the expression spreading over her face like a mask poured from wax. "So, you're going to stick with me when I go cuss out this fucking cop?"

"Isn't he a detective?" Kimmie said in his smart-ass voice.

"Yes, you're right. I'm going to cuss out a detective."

"Maybe we should beat his ass?"

Creeley laughed, but the laugh faded to silence. She drove for a mile before saying, "We might have to torture him for information."

"I'm sorry...You are one sick, twisted little white girl."

"What? I think he knows something, and he never told me."

"And you think it's tied to some motorcycle gang?"

"The guy I run drugs for...Animal, he said—"

"Animal?"

"Yes. Animal. It's a nickname."

Kimmie shook his head, "You don't say?"

Creeley rolled her eyes, changed lanes as the road expanded. She passed a car in the slow lane, and they sped past the north-end neighborhood where she and Monty and Amber had started following Elvis the night before. "Animal said that Monty had something to do with The Vandals."

"How'd he know you were hooked up to the detective?"

Creeley thought about the skinny guy in the fancy house, about taking the money from him after she set Monty up that night. And she thought of Kimmie pepper spraying the skinny guy—Hero—when he tried to hunt down Animal's package at her motel. "I told him about what I did for Hero, and somehow he knew shit about Monty."

"Hero?"

"That guy you pepper sprayed."

Kimmie nodded and said, "He was trying to get that bag from you."

"Animal's shit."

"Sure. Animal's shit." Kimmie sighed again and said, "But how the fuck are Animal, Monty, and Hero tied together?"

"I don't know," Creeley said. "But we need to find out."

"Torture the detective?"

"No," Creeley said as she made a left-hand turn into Hero's neighborhood. "Let's torture the guy who calls himself Hero."

***

Same house.

Same manicured landscape.

Same shiny, expensive cars in driveways.

And that same brush of lawn sprinklers and tint from solar lights against the palm trees.

Kimmie said, "That scumbag lives *here?*"

Creeley pulled to the curb, killed the 4Runner's engine, and said, "This is where I met the fuck." They watched the quiet street for a moment, all the solar landscape lights casting palm tree shadows against stucco walls and slick sidewalk. "I wonder if we can find a way to surprise him." It didn't come out of her mouth as a question.

"But, like, how?"

"Around back, I guess."

"Like the movies then," Kimmie said as he opened his door and stepped into the night.

Creeley got out and they both closed their doors with subtle clicks. She said, "We don't have any weapons. That might be a problem."

"Pepper spray. We have pepper spray."

That reminded Creeley. She opened her door, reached across the driver's seat to open the glove box. She pulled out a small pepper spray canister, slipped it into a pocket. She clicked her door shut again. "You're right," she said, "we have plenty of pepper spray."

They walked side by side down the sidewalk, past the house and the jet-black Audi sitting in the driveway. Creeley wanted to find the gated backyard entrance. If it was locked, they'd scale the fence. She said, "There's a camera right there," and pointed at a small wireless camera above the garage.

"You think somebody monitors?"

"I don't know."

"Keep walking."

They passed the house and stopped in front of the next home, turned to look again. A low flowering hedge separated both yards, but it was small enough to step over and cross. Creeley saw a white metal gate beyond it that entered the rear of Hero's yard.

"If we go in through this yard, step over the hedge, I'm thinking we won't trip the camera."

"You don't think they have more in the back?" Kimmie scratched the back of his neck and sighed. "I guess we can try it, though."

"We're not getting in the front."

"Okay, sister." He stepped onto the pad of wet grass and moved toward the hedge. He stopped when Creeley didn't follow. "Are you coming or what?" His face was yellow against the night, and he wore a small, simple grin.

Creeley said, "This is turning you on."

"I love danger—let's go, you wimp."

Creeley shook her head and followed. They both hopped over the hedge and Kimmie reached over the gate and popped it open. He said, "Not locked." He pushed it open, and they both entered the backyard and its darkness.

✳✳✳

Creeley bumped a blue recycling tub and bottles clinked and cans rattled.

Kimmie turned to squint at her and said, "You're not much of a crook."

She gave him a sarcastic smile. "You don't know jack shit about me, Kimmie." She followed him through the dark side yard— the high stucco wall of the house on one side and a high green hedge on the other. The blue light of the pool became visible as they reached the back corner of the house. They both studied the backyard for a minute. Empty patio furniture and the pool empty, too. Blue light illuminated the pool deck and yellow solar lights revealed pygmy palms splayed like broken fingers. They came out of the side yard and onto the covered patio. A curtain was closed behind the ten-foot-high sliding glass door. The flashing light of a television showed through the translucent curtain. Creeley noticed another sliding glass door to their right, set back a bit from the patio. No curtain, but a dark room beyond the glass. "Over here," she said and felt Kimmie follow as she hopped paver stones across wet grass and reached the slider. She shielded her eyes and put her head to the glass—the round shape of Hero's pimp bed, but it was made and empty. Creeley gripped the pepper spray canister in one hand and wiped sweat from the back of her neck with the other. She smelled oleander and pool chlorine, wondered if now was the time to turn back and step into her old life. Back to Creeley the drug runner.

Back to Creeley the runaway.

Kimmie said, "What are we waiting for?"

"Do you know how to break in through a sliding glass door?"

"Maybe just, you know, see if it's unlocked?"

It was.

They stepped out of the heat and into the cold air-conditioned room where Hero did...whatever it was he did. Kimmie slid past her as she pulled the slider closed. He began searching the dresser across from the bed. "What are you looking for?"

"A gun, girl—the fuck do you think?"

Creeley shook her head but had a thought. She slid the pepper spray canister back into a pocket and went to her knees. She slid her hands between the round mattress and the wood frame beneath it. She worked her way to the left and it didn't take long before she felt a solid object. It was cold to the touch of her fingertips. She placed both palms on the object and closed her hands—some kind of pistol. "I found one," she said and pulled it out.

"Let me see." Kimmie took it from her as she stood. He held it at arm's length and said, "It's a Glock. Nine-millimeter." He pushed a button and the magazine fell into his hand. He examined it and clicked it back into place. He smiled. "It's loaded and I'll hold on to it for us."

"Don't shoot anybody, okay?"

Kimmie rolled his eyes at her, twirled on a heel.

She followed him to the bedroom door, and they opened it and peered both directions down the hallway. Darkness except for the flashing television lights from the living room. They looked at each other and Creeley nodded.

Kimmie led the way down the hallway—Creeley crouched behind him, aware of the gun pointed out in front of him. Their footsteps were soundless on the tile floor. The air conditioner clicked off and the low mumble of the television reached Creeley's ears. There were no voices.

She wondered what the fuck her and Kimmie were doing.

Finding Hero? Yes, but like this?

What was she going to do, put a gun to his head and spit in his face?

Shoot him in the knee like they did in those mafia movies?

Maybe cut a finger off with a kitchen knife like she saw in a horror movie?

No. Nope. None of that.

The light from the television got brighter and she squinted as they reached the foyer, where the girl with the pink hair had let Creeley in the week prior.

Kimmie paused and Creeley bumped into him. His hands shook with the gun extended out from his chest, but he took a deep breath—she saw his shoulders lift and drop—and strode into the sunken living room. "Don't move, you motherfucking assholes! Don't you fucking—"

Creeley hopped after him, was surprised when he gulped and ran back toward her, past her, down the hall. She heard him slam a door open and begin to vomit.

She took two more steps, turned to face the sofa.

The girl with the pink hair caught Creeley's acute attention.

The stab wounds appeared to be grouped on the right side of

her body. From her rib cage, into her breast, and upward into the red mess of her throat. Both her eyes were open and staring at the ceiling. Her own blood was dried on her abdomen and her bare legs. She was in cutoff jeans and a halter top. Like Creeley. Her pink hair was tossed to one side of her head, tufts of it somehow caked to the beige sofa pillows with dried blood. Hero was sprawled beside her, shirtless. His wounds directly to his breastbone—to his heart. Less brutal a killing, from what Creeley could see, but more immediate.

Creeley said, "Holy fuck."

She didn't feel nauseated or afraid. It was clear the girl and Hero had been dead for some hours—the dried blood and smell told her that. The killer was long gone. Got away with it.

The same as the one who killed her brother got away with it.

Creeley stood there and watched two dead bodies for far too long.

Two thoughts turned again and again inside her head: *Who in the fuck is killing people in Palm Springs? And why?*

47/Chain of Evidence

"**I**'m looking at something that doesn't have an explanation." Creeley gulped and closed her eyes. Kimmie was still in the bathroom. He came out once to give her his cell phone, but he was back there now. Hugging the toilet, Creeley figured. She propped the cell phone between her shoulder and ear, scratched her face with one hand.

Monty said, "I don't know what that means, Creeley."

She opened her eyes and focused on the gashes that lined the pink-haired girl's abdomen and throat. "It means I'm looking at murder. I don't know who. And I don't know why." A nauseous thread pulled at her stomach, rose through her chest, and into her throat. She tried to swallow, but her throat closed and she choked.

"Are you okay?"

"Fuck no."

"What's going on, Creeley?"

"You tell me, Detective. You're the one working with The Vandals."

He hissed, "The fuck is coming out of your mouth?" All that sweetness and care gone from his voice. "You don't know jack shit about me—remember that."

Creeley nodded although he couldn't see it. "That might be the one real thing you've said to me. And now I'm looking at this and, I swear to God, I'm wondering if this is your handiwork. If the mayor—I mean, shit, he had the—"

"I've got no idea what you're talking about."

"What are you capable of?"

"Oh, go fuck yourself." He hung up on her.

Creeley lowered the phone as Kimmie stumbled into the foyer, looked at her from across the living room. "Are you okay?"

He ran a hand over his pale, sweaty face. "I just threw up a fucking lung. What the fuck are we dealing with here? I swear, I saw you and I thought you were trouble. But never this, this kind of trouble."

Creeley punched a button on Kimmie's cell phone and put it to her ear. "I'm calling Amber."

"Right—that seems like something you shouldn't do. But what the fuck do I know?" He crossed to the couch and stood there staring at the dead bodies.

Amber's voice answered the ring, "Where are you guys?"

"I'm going to text you an address. It's not far from your place."

"Okay." She said it like it was twice as long a word.

Creeley hung up and texted the address. Amber responded with a question mark but said she was on the way. "Amber will be here in a few minutes."

"And what the fuck is she going to do?"

"I don't know." Creeley walked toward the sofa, stood next to Kimmie. "It looks like she put up a fight."

"Most definitely."

"Him, not so much."

"Caught him asleep, maybe?"

Creeley squinted at Hero's lifeless frame. "Yeah. Him first and then she wakes up. She tries to fight it off, but he's strong and it just..."

"Something like that," Kimmie said. "Or that exactly."

"I need a drink."

"I need a goddamn tranquilizer."

✳✳✳

Amber stood there and shook when she saw the bodies.

Like it was colder than hell in the house.

Creeley took her hand and guided her to the kitchen, poured her a shot of Belvedere vodka. Amber took the shot and pointed for another. She took that one, too, and nearly coughed it up, but the liquid stayed down and she shook her head like a maniac in a padded room.

Creeley said, "It wasn't us—me and Kimmie."

Kimmie said, "No shit, Creeley." He had a tumbler of vodka in his hand, a dash of cranberry juice making it tint red. A bad color given the situation.

"I thought you wanted to talk to me about something. Or maybe you found out something. But this is just a fucking shit show of a way to—"

"I'm sorry, Amber." Creeley met her eyes and tried to beam a thought into Amber's head: *I'm sorry about how I've treated you. Not just this shit you're involved in right now. But that, too. Yes, I'm sorry for that, too.*

Amber said, "Why the fuck haven't you called the police?"

Creeley looked at Kimmie. No answer. She licked her lips and said, "Me and Kimmie broke in. I'm afraid, like, how it might look."

"You didn't fucking do it, though. What the fuck, Creeley?"

"My mom didn't fucking do it either. Look at her." Creeley cut herself off, tried to take a deep, long breath. Kimmie and Amber were silent. Amber stared down at her empty glass. Kimmie refilled it. Added some to his own. Creeley reached across the counter, yanked the bottle away from him. She lifted it and poured vodka down her throat.

"Point taken," Amber said. "I understand you. But we need to call the police. At this point, we've all been here, and who the fuck knows what kind of evidence there is of our presence."

"I christened the latrine."

"What?" Amber stared at him, wild-eyed and sneering.

"Kimmie lost his lunch when he saw...the bodies."

"This is my fucking point, you guys."

Creeley cleared her throat. She didn't want to call the cops. She didn't want to be here. She didn't want to be wrapped up in this mystery that—somehow—had taken hold of every aspect of her life. She wanted to be back home in Portland, sipping huckleberry wine and watching shitty reality TV. Anything to be a simple fucking drug runner again. She swallowed and said, "I don't think Monty is somebody I should call."

Amber said, "Are you fucking kidding? The cop you're fucking can't—"

"I never fucked him," Creeley said while staring straight into Amber's eyes. "I promise."

"Let's just dial 9-1-1." Kimmie gulped and swallowed some of his drink. He burped and covered his eyes with a shaking hand.

"I don't think we should do that," Creeley said.

"What then?"

"The detective from when we found the mayor."

"Oh, right," Amber said. "That other fucking murder scene you discovered."

"There's something about him. He's..."

"What?"

"Honest?"

"Great," Kimmie said. "Let's call the honest detective and try to explain what the fuck we're doing here."

Creeley shook her head. "We can't be here. I don't want to be here." She turned and walked through the kitchen, out into and across the living room. She entered the foyer and opened the front door. She turned and looked at Amber and Kimmie standing at the kitchen island. "Let's go. We'll call him from the road. Or from a dive bar. I need more to drink."

"Can we at least go out the back?" Kimmie said. "So we aren't, like, advertising the fact we were here."

Amber pressed her palms to the sides of her head. "I came in the front, you assholes."

Creeley closed the door and locked it. "Yeah," she said. "Let's go out the back."

***

A pay phone outside a 7-Eleven on Ramon Road. Across from the airport.

Creeley watched an airliner take off and circle west toward the mountains, disappear into a crushing wave of white, early-morning cloud cover. Amber and Kimmie stared at her from the 4Runner, parked across the small parking lot.

Creeley put the phone to her ear, shoved a couple quarters into the machine. She looked at the card in her hand and dialed the cell number for Edwin James, homicide detective.

It rang once and Edwin picked up the line. "This is Detective James."

Creeley tried to speak, but words wouldn't cross her lips.

"Hello?" A pause. "Who is this? Angie, that you? What kind of trouble you—"

"This is Creeley Nash, Detective." She watched another airliner take flight, veer north toward endless sky. "I'm the girl who—"

"I remember who you are, Miss Nash. It is Miss, isn't it?"

"Yeah—probably always will be." Creeley sighed and started chewing on an index finger.

"Don't sell yourself short, Miss Nash. Everybody deserves love."

"Thanks, Dr. Love. Too bad that's not why I called." He didn't respond but instead waited for her to fill the silence. She hugged herself and bounced on one foot. "So, what's up with the case?"

"What case?"

"The mayor, for fuck's sake." She shook her head and sighed. Kimmie and Amber were still in the truck staring at her. No movement there.

"You don't watch the local news, Miss Nash?"

"Fuck no."

"The show at eleven every evening? You watch that?"

"What the fuck do you think?"

Edwin chuckled. "I think, like a lot of motherfuckers, you're ill-informed."

Creeley, bored now and thinking about how to tell Edwin about the bodies in the house, came out and said, "You cops are such arrogant assholes. You know that?"

"It's what you get when you mix testosterone with righteous indignation. The reason I ask—about the news—is that we arrested somebody. We got our man."

Creeley's jaw dropped, and she blinked twice. Another airliner taxied and started engine thrust, but she closed her eyes and said, "It wasn't a suicide."

"No, Miss Nash. It was not."

Creeley flashed on her mom—she saw Blossom's yellow teeth smiling at her through the prison glass, those black gums gleaming with spit and blood. She thought about steel bars and locks clicking, the sounds of a cage banging around inside her. Why? She didn't know. She should be thinking about the mayor dead on his couch, the back of his head blown onto the cream-colored wall. She felt Edwin's hand in her own, the firm shake and feel of his sweaty fingers.

"Matter of fact," Edwin said, "it was straight-up pre-meditated murder. A capital offense. And you might want to take a look at the news. Reason being, the guy we picked up just as the news aired last night—he's a cop. Man, they got a live shot and everything."

"A cop?"

"A detective. Just like me, Miss Nash. Call it ironic if you want, but he's a homicide detective."

Now her memory flashed on Ray Parks. She saw his bulky frame, that smudged fuck pie of a face. She heard his voice and saw the vague shadows of him being beaten out in the desert. Monty pushed him—and this is what they got in return. "Ray Parks," she said. "Shit."

"It ain't Ray Parks, Miss Nash. Not him at all."

"Then who?"

"Emeril. Monty Emeril. You remember Monty, right? He's the guy helping you to—"

"Jesus. Fucking. Christ. I talked to him last night...I *called* him."

"You should of heard what they said down at the station."

Creeley felt Monty's lips on her neck, felt his hands moving along her hips, her bare thighs. She saw him sitting in front of her mom, those squinting eyes prying into the distant past and near future. She smelled the fucking guy—cheap cologne, gin, and mint aftershave. "This has got to be wrong. This is wrong, right? A fucking mistake?"

"No, I'm afraid not. It's a fuck stick of a case, but it's my fuck stick. And I know my fuck stick better than anybody. He did it. Monty Emeril killed the former mayor of Palm Springs."

Creeley said, "This ugly world."

"You got that right, sister. Hey—you called *me*, though. You wanted to give me some information or something? What can I do for you, Miss Nash?"

She hesitated, but then said, "I think I got another fuck stick for you."

"Is that right?"

Creeley Nash sighed and said, "Write this down."

48/Interrogations

"The way we do this," Detective Edwin James said, "is we sit down together, and you tell me everything that happened. Whatever you can remember. Shoot, all of what you remember."

Creeley lifted her head from the steel table. The interrogation room smelled like cat piss and snide comments—she imagined most police headquarters carried the same stench.

Edwin sat down across from her, laid a legal pad and two pens on the table. He motioned for the woman to sit next to him—the other detective. She was younger than Creeley. And better looking. "This is my partner, Detective Hicks. She'll be joining us for the moment."

The lady detective nodded at Creeley and said, "Hello, Miss Nash." She sat and pulled out her own small notebook and pen.

"Everything I told you on the phone," Creeley said. "That's how it was."

"We understand that, Miss Nash. But right now? We got two dead people in a house here in Palm Springs. And this shit don't look good—let me just say that right out. It don't look good."

"I know how it looks. I was there." Creeley crossed her arms, sat back in her chair, and smirked.

"For the event?"

Creeley rolled her eyes at the lady detective—fucking Hicks—and said, "What fucking event?"

"The homicides," Edwin said. "Plural. And let me just say, if you want to get something off your back, some heavy weight..." He cleared his throat. "That's what we're here for, okay? You understand that, Miss Nash?"

"A weight? Like, you want me to say I did it?"

"I never said that."

"You're working to it, though."

"No," Edwin said. "I'm not."

Hicks said, "We know it wasn't you alone—there were two of you in that house."

"And how do you know that?"

"They're called witnesses," Hicks said. "They see shit and they say shit."

Creeley laughed at her and said, "Can I have a cup of coffee?" She glanced at Edwin, and he shrugged, stood up, and left the room. Creeley stared at Hicks in silence. Edwin opened the door, set a paper cup of coffee in front of Creeley, and sat back down. "I was hoping for some cream," Creeley said.

"You can want in one hand and shit in the other."

Hicks said, "Some of us like it black."

Creeley looked from Edwin to Hicks and said, "I bet some of us do." Creeley stirred the black coffee with an index finger, slurped it off with the side of her mouth. "You were saying?"

"It was more than just you," Edwin said. "We know that for a fact."

"No—you were talking about weight."

"What about it?" Hicks grinned, popped a pink bubble of gum from between her teeth.

"Like, I was wondering, is that what you tell everybody? You know, when you lock them up in this shit hole? Does it actually work?"

"Sometimes," Edwin said. "People are human."

"Duh," Creeley said with disdain.

"What I mean is, people find their humanity in letting something go. They do something horrible, something terrible, bad, disfiguring to their souls. And it eats at them, just burns away at everything inside. They let it go, spit it out, and that thing, it stops eating them."

"Maybe," Creeley said. "But then it's the world that eats them. All this"—she raised her eyes at the ceiling—"and the two of you. People just like you all over the world. Justified by a tin shape pressed into your hands...This eating of disfigured souls."

"Look at you, Miss Nash—little smarty pants." That grin and

the pink entrails of gum moving behind her teeth. "What we do is enforce the law. In law school, we called it justice."

"So you're an educated bitch, huh?"

Edwin slapped the table. "Not like that, Miss Nash—I won't fuck with that." His face was sweaty and crunched, wrinkled past his age. "Maybe you want to be a smart-ass? Okay. But don't forget you're in some serious shit and that involves putting yourself at a brutal murder scene—"

"You know I didn't do that."

They sat there and stared at her.

Creeley said, "You're not that fucking dumb—you've been doing this shit too long." She looked at the lady detective for an instant before pivoting to Edwin. "At least, you have."

"Let's walk through what happened, what you know."

Hicks put her elbows on the table. "None of this has to be about who did what—just take us through it. How'd you start the evening? Where were you?"

Creeley nodded for a long minute, almost unable to stop her head from bobbing back and forth. "And you want to know who I was with, right?"

"We'll find out," Hicks said. "I promise."

Creeley laughed. "I believe you, but it doesn't change one fact."

"Yeah—what?"

"My mom—my fucking mother—is in prison for some shit she didn't do."

"So?" Hicks said as she shook her head.

"So, what makes you think I'd say fat dick to a homicide detective?"

"What happened with your mom," Edwin said, leaning forward and putting his elbows on the table alongside Hicks, "has nothing to do with tonight. It's got nothing to do with the phone call you made, why you called me. This is us in here and nobody else."

Creeley remembered her drive down to Palm Springs, stopping outside Monterey in that little bar. She remembered that glass of wine, the sound of the bartender's voice. You'd think that moment was a big nothing, a minor stop on a short trip. But no—it was the first moment of this confusing, confounding, oddly epic transformation. For the first time in her life, Creeley Nash had something to fight for. She wanted to fight and search for the truth. She wanted to fight for her mom, for the woman and mother she could have been—that best version of Blossom Nash that existed in some far-off dimension. Because that's what she deserved, a chance to be seen—only seen—as the best possible version of herself.

She deserved to be seen as innocent, and Creeley wanted that for her.

And for the first time in her life, Creeley Nash wanted to fight for somebody else—herself.

Hicks sneered at her and said, "Are you going to come clean, or what?"

Creeley giggled into a hand, shook her head. She felt free, that weight of the years falling off her like a warped skin. "I don't think so," she said. "In fact, I want a fucking lawyer."

49/Changing Directions

She didn't need the lawyer.

They let her go and asked that she not leave town.

Creeley thought: *Where the fuck would I go?*

She got into her 4Runner—parallel parked outside the station—and closed her eyes. Creeley needed a fucking minute. Two fucking minutes. Ten fucking motherfucking minutes. Because the last two weeks—Creeley had to admit—felt like a fucking decade. She tried breathing through her mouth, held it in and put a hand on top of her belly. She breathed out through pursed lips and licked her bottom lip. She had to take stock of the shit show that was now her life:

A brother she'd never met was dead—murdered.

Her mom was in prison for life—for a murder she didn't commit.

Creeley's drug kingpin boss (sort of) was still after her.

She'd had her first sexual experience with a woman (not sort of).

She'd found two murder scenes.

And she'd almost fallen for a homicide detective who, according to his own colleagues, murdered a retired politician and—if Creeley could read between the lines—maybe even two low-level Palm Springs drug people.

Shit show times ten. Or twenty.

And Creeley didn't know what to do now. Or how to do it.

Should she find a way to see Monty? Ask him what the living fuck he was doing? Or go back to Amber and Kimmie, try to talk all of this out? She was no closer to finding out who killed her brother, and wasn't that the whole fucking point? Getting her mom out of prison—she was so far from that it was insanity to consider.

But she had to move forward and keep fighting. She had to keep feeling like she felt in that interrogation room. She had to keep being at least half a badass—she owed that to her brother, to herself, and to her mom. It was time to open her eyes and keep them open.

When she did open her eyes, she almost shrieked at the face staring at her through the window.

✳✳✳

Paul lit up and smoked in the passenger seat, tapped his ash out the open window.

Creeley said, "Did you have to creep me out like that? Good God."

Paul shrugged and blew smoke out the window. "I thought you were asleep."

"I was concentrating."

"On what?"

"On the shit show that is my life."

He nodded as if he understood. Probably, he did.

"I don't know what to do next."

Another nod and long drag with the requisite exhalation.

"I'm guessing you heard about Monty?"

One corner of Paul's mouth twitched. "I knew it before, but yeah—I heard."

"You knew he killed the—"

"That, no. I just knew he was a bad cop. A bent cop."

"And you didn't fucking tell me." Creeley crossed her arms, looked away from him and stared at the police station across the street. A beige building with mid-century modern leanings, but kind of half-assed in execution. "When I think I know something, or I think I understand it, I really know jack shit. But I guess that's how it's always been."

"I knew from Animal—him sending me to find you. And he knew the detective, like knew exactly who the fuck he was. And where to talk to him, for that matter."

Creeley nodded without meeting his eyes.

"So, I don't know. Somehow he was into the drug game. My guess? He tipped Hero off to anything that might touch him—wiretaps or undercover narcs, shit like that." He sniffed hard through his nose. "Your regular badge, if you ask me. Straight up pig."

Creeley turned to watch him as he threw his cigarette out the window.

"And you found me to tell me that? Thanks, but you're too fucking late. Apparently, he also kills people for reasons I'll never know."

"The mayor."

"Former mayor."

"And Hero," Paul said. "Plus, his girl."

"That's what the cops think."

He nodded. "They're probably right. I told you I'd get word to the inside, see what I could find out. See if anybody knew anything about your brother, about what happened."

"And you found dick, I bet."

Paul grinned, picked at a molar with a dirty fingernail. "You'd be surprised what dudes doing time can remember. Call it institutional knowledge or whatever."

Creeley got a lump in her throat, felt her chin wrinkle.

"Word—if it's true—is that a cop killed your brother. The street always knew it was a cop. And it was probably the cops who knew—it's why they found a way to make it stick to your mom."

"Ray Parks," Creeley said. "The fat fucking asshole."

"Nope," Paul said. "Not him."

Creeley felt her jaw drop. Her mouth was dry and she ran her tongue across her bottom teeth. She tugged at a lock of hair beside her ear. "*Not* Ray Parks? What the fuck? It had to be him. Why—"

"Your pal Monty," Paul said as he turned to stare at her. "He's the one who did it."

Creeley's stomach churned and she felt vomit touch the back of her throat. She tried to speak, but no sound came from her throat and her lips felt numb.

"There's a guy who works for AB around here, does stuff for The Vandals, too. Everybody calls him Skinny. Word is that Skinny had Monty in his pocket from the time he was a street cop. These two dudes knew each other from school or something."

"Skinny?"

"Yeah—he goes by Skinny."

"That's it? Skinny?" Creeley said.

"I mean, I'm sure that's not on his birth certificate."

Creeley closed her eyes and then she saw him in her head—the tall skinny guy with black hair. His weasel voice as he met them in the desert. What did Ray Parks call him—a fink? Yeah, that was it. A fink. And the skinny guy didn't like it. But he didn't know what it was, a fink. His pal had to clarify it for him. Creeley remembered that about him. None of it made sense to her. She could see the skinny guy and that almost fit, but how did he add up to running Monty?

"I don't understand—when I first got into this with Monty, we took a couple detectives to a tall, skinny guy. Like, as a payment for some information."

"What information?"

"He told us about the night my brother was murdered. Said he was a clerk at the motel. He's the one who gave us the mayor, said my mom was fucking the mayor and that he loved her. And then we tracked down a guy—he looks like Elvis—who used to visit my mom back at the hotel, when me and you were kids."

"I think I remember him," Paul said.

"And Elvis mentions Cary Rickles," Creeley said. "Amber couldn't find anything online about him. Me and Kimmie tried to track Rickles down, but...Now, I'm more confused than before."

Paul sighed and scratched his head. "What in the fuck?"

"If Monty was lying to me, whatever he said about Rickles was a lie."

"I could ask around, see if—"

"No," Creeley said. "You said they were in school together. We need to go to the library."

"What the fuck? Why?"

"Yearbooks," Creeley said. "We need to look at high school yearbooks."

50/Mug shots

Amber didn't look happy to see Paul, but she smiled at Creeley and gave her a hug when she came around the librarian's desk. "You okay?"

Creeley shrugged but didn't know how to answer.

Paul said, "We need yearbooks."

"Yearbooks?"

"For Palm Springs High. Do you guys archive those? I feel like that's a thing."

Amber led them into the stacks, down a dark hallway, into an anteroom filled with dusty shelves and—at its center—a large wooden cabinet with pull-out drawers. She touched three drawers and said, "Local yearbooks here, here, and here. Any idea what year you need?"

Creeley shook her head, looked at Paul.

He said, "I'm thinking mid through late eighties. Maybe 1990, but I kind of doubt it."

Amber slid one drawer open and tilted her head at Creeley. "They're all yours—need my help?"

Creeley reached out and grabbed Amber's hand. "No. We're good. I'll find you if we come up with something."

"When," Amber said. "*When* you come up with something." She brushed past Creeley and left them alone.

Paul said, "I never been in a library before."

"Not even on the inside?"

"Right..." He nodded. "I guess that does count."

"Okay then." Creeley started pulling books from the drawer, identifying the books by the years on their spines. "I'll take eighty-eight and nine. Here's eighty-five, six, and seven." She handed him three books and opened her first one on top of the cabinet. "Let's look for Monty and try to find his senior year—we'll look for the skinny guy in that book. If we don't find him, we'll move backwards through each class year."

They both went to work searching for Monty in the mug shot pictures for each class level. Paul found him first. "Got him. Looks like he's a sophomore in eighty-six."

Creeley flipped to the senior class in eighty-eight and found him. "Here he is. Alright, let's start from the front, see if we can find this skinny, dirty fuck." Paul peered over her shoulder as she scanned each face. All these pimply kids with big fake grins. A few grungy-looking kids and—there he was, the skinny guy. Younger and gaunter, but with the same greasy complexion and brown-eyed gaze. Kind of a fractured look to him, like an egg cracked and glued back together. Creeley put her finger on his face. "That's him. I know his fucking face."

"Reed Gant," Paul said.

Creeley ran her finger over the name and repeated it, "Reed Gant. Fuck me. Cary Rickles is Reed Gant. So even his name was a lie."

"So, what now? I can put the word out, see if somebody knows where to find the guy."

Creeley said, "Follow me," and walked out of the room into the stacks.

***

Reed Gant paid property taxes on a house in Desert Hot Springs.

It took Amber about ten seconds to find the address online. Creeley thanked her with a soft kiss on the cheek, left her standing in the library lobby with a red tint coloring her cheeks.

Creeley drove while Paul punched the address into his cell phone.

He said, "Around twenty minutes. Looks like he lives in the boonies."

"There's a gun under the seat," Creeley said.

Paul looked at her for a long moment and then he reached under the seat. "Nice—"

"A Glock," Creeley interrupted him. "A nine-millimeter. I think it was Hero's gun."

"No shit?" Paul studied it and gave a surprised nod.

"It's loaded."

"No shit."

"No shit, Paul." She merged as the four-lane road became two lanes and they crossed the sandy desert beneath towering windmills. The 4Runner groaned as she passed the fifty-five limit and a slow-moving sedan.

"Hey—watch out now. We don't want to get pulled over."

Creeley slowed, prided herself on knowing what he meant. All those runs to pick up Animal's shit had taught her how to avoid trouble, how to be so quiet as to be unnoticeable. She was letting her anger and confusion bleed into her actions—she needed to stay calm. "What do you think it was with Monty? I mean, why the fuck..."

Paul rubbed at an itch inside his left ear, smirked. "I can't tell you what bends a cop, but killing people—had to be he was into something bad. Political shit, maybe. I don't fucking know. Did the cops say how they put it on him?"

Creeley shook her head. "They didn't give me shit. The only thing I can think is he left some evidence at the crime scene. I mean, more obvious than, like, DNA or whatever."

"Did the fucker drop his badge?"

"Maybe." She still couldn't believe it. "I almost fucked the guy, you know. I wanted to fuck the guy. Like, I seriously wanted to fuck him."

"Way TMI, Creeley. Please don't lay that on me right now."

She glanced at him. He was staring out his window, clutching the gun against his rib cage.

"You always did have a crush on me."

"For the two nights I knew you? Yeah. Some big fucking crush."

"You thought about me when I ran away."

"I did more than that," Paul said.

"I knew it. You jacked off to me, huh?"

"You're so gross."

"Just admit it, Paul. You pulled your little teenage pud after I kissed you that—"

"Before that, too."

"Before!"

He laughed. "What? You're the one who asked if I ever—"

"Okay, dude. Let's not go there."

Paul slid the Glock back under the seat. "You won't need it."

"Are you sure about that?"

Paul shrugged and said, "Trust me."

They drove in silence for a few miles. The phone told her to turn left at the next four-way stop. She followed the instructions and—still listening to the phone—turned into a rundown neighborhood of cheap tract homes. The street had homes on each side, and it meandered in a loose, figure-eight way for about a mile. The phone told them the address was two hundred feet away, another stucco home with a red tile roof. Creeley parked before they reached it. She noticed a dead lawn in front and two Harley-Davidson cruisers parked in the driveway. She also saw the pickup, a Ford Ranger. Same truck from the night in the desert when they handed over Ray Parks and Stacy Brewster. "That's his truck—he fucking lives here."

She looked over when Paul pulled a different gun from his waistband, one she'd seen before—he'd aimed it at Monty. He winked before saying, "Surprise. I guess I get to impress you again, huh?"

51/History Lesson: Love Sick

Creeley liked the skinny kid—Rooster with the mohawk—most of the time.

Hell, she almost loved him.

But she knew what a risk it was to love anybody—and for some damn reason she always thought of her mom when she thought of love. Always thought of those fake moans and dramatic squeals, the creaking of the motel room bed frame. Creeley saw tattoos and rotten teeth, heard *fuck* and *shit* and *cunt* in her head every time she thought of love. To her, thinking about love was like slicing her wrist with a razor—*fucking kill me now*.

But he always said it to her. When they were sitting at the table near the window drinking cheap beer and wine. When they turned off the light at night, stoned to hell and trying to sleep in their lumpy motel-room bed. When he called her from the restaurant pay phone, all the laughter and strong voices coming at her—reminding her of what she didn't have. Stability and—more important—fucking *money*. Rooster had the dishwashing job, and she was working the morning shift at a Portland coffee shop. She loved the job, but three six-hour shifts wasn't cutting it. And tips barely got her enough for lunch at the sandwich joint across the street.

All this.

And one more thing—he always told her he loved her when she was fucking him in the shower. Rooster with the sideways dick and crooked-eye O-face. But he was kind of hot and—when she wasn't too tired—she enjoyed the sex. But still...*Love?*

It came tonight when he let himself into the motel room. He had a paper bag from Fred Meyer, red pasta sauce stains down the front of his apron, and he smelled like chopped onions. He sat down next to her on the bed and kissed the side of her head. "I love you."

She tapped at the TV remote, deadpan staring at the flipping channels.

"What are you watching?"

She ignored the question and said, "Did you get any booze?"

He got up and shoved his hands into the bag, came out with two forty-ounce Miller High Life bottles. He twisted the cap off one and handed it to her. "It's the Champagne of Beers."

She took it and stopped the TV on an episode of *Cops*. She took a sip of the beer, grimaced as it sloshed in her mouth and went down her throat.

Rooster said, "This is the episode when that white trash dude spits on the old lady."

"Oh, yeah."

"Hey, Creeley. I was wondering if—"

"You're not going to ask me to marry you." She stared at him with the beer bottle near her lips, dared him to fall to one knee while she sipped her shitty beer.

"No, I mean, I told you how I don't believe in marriage. Like, I don't even think it matters."

"Good. Me either."

"I was just going to ask, like, what's up with you?"

She stared at a fat farm-boy cop as he tried to chase down a black kid somewhere in Kansas. "I think I want to be alone, Rooster. I know that isn't going to feel good to you." She looked away from the TV and watched him process the statement. He scratched one cheek with a dirty fingernail, tried not to let his chin wrinkle. His mohawk was tilted over, grown too long to take instruction from hair gel. Though he still shaved the sides of his head with one of her pink Bic razors.

"It's not you—it's me."

"Like I haven't heard that before."

"Don't get bitter, Rooster." She stared at him without blinking. A good, solid look that meant she was serious. Meant that she was being honest with him. "I like being with you. It's just...there's something wrong with me."

"There's nothing wrong with you—you keep telling me that."

"But there is. And you can't see it."

"What am I supposed to see, Creeley?" He swigged from his forty, gulped at her.

"How fucked up the world is. And how fucked up we are."

He shook his head and said, "We're not—"

"We live in a dumpy motel by the airport. You wash dishes at a chain restaurant. I'm a barista at a smelly coffee shop for hippies and—"

"We're just starting out!"

"This," she said after taking a long swig. "This is what you call starting out?"

"How the fuck else are we supposed to start?"

She shook her head like a dog, so much so that her whole body began to move back and forth on the bed. She lifted the beer to her lips and tried to drink, spilled it all over her hands and forearms and lap. She stood and poked him in the chest. "We don't start, Rooster. And if we don't start, we never have to end. That's the whole fucking point."

His eyelids lowered and he poked at one cheek with his tongue. She could see him coming to terms with what was happening, what she was telling him. That they were done. That this thing—*this* thing—was over and they had to go in different directions. He shook his head once, twice. "Well, what the fuck do you want me to do then? Since we're so fucking over..."

Creeley set her beer on the carpet beside the bed. She pulled her hoodie up over her head, dropped it. She unbuckled her jeans, stepped out of them. She unsnapped her bra and lowered her panties. She sat down on the bed again and slowly slid backward to lean against the headboard.

"What do you want me to do?"

She cleared her throat and said, "I want you to fuck me one last time."

And that's what they did. They fucked. And Creeley groaned as Rooster shuddered into her and wept. She turned him over and brought him back into her, plunged against him while he watched her with hateful eyes. When she finished for a second time he was crying still, almost comatose in his movements. She slid off him and jumped in the shower, stood there crying herself in the hot water and steam. When she got out, a crispy white towel wrapped tight around her slim body, Rooster was gone.

And so was all his shit.

52/Skinny Guys and Gunshots

They decided to bang on Gant's door.

Play it straight.

It took him a minute, but he opened it—he was shirtless and wearing baggy jeans. His chest was covered with tattoos of smudged green ink, the images impossible for Creeley to make sense of. A smell like fish sticks and beer hit them from inside the house. The sound of some sporting event—baseball, Creeley thought—filtered out from some deep recess of the place.

Gant smirked at Creeley and said, "What do you want now?"

Paul pulled the gun from behind his back and wiggled it like a magic wand.

Creeley said, "You lied to me about who you are. I want to know why."

Gant tried to slam the door in their faces, but Creeley stepped across the threshold. She pressed one hand into the door, slammed it back against the wall. Her other hand went to Gant's chest. She shoved him hard enough that he stumbled backward, caught himself against the wall.

"What the fuck?"

Paul moved past Creeley like a good rush of blood. He stopped Gant's mouth by putting the gun to his head. "We got some questions for you, you skinny stupid fuck."

"Hey, man—fuck." Gant slowly straightened, kept his eyes on the gun pressed to the center of his head. "You got questions…I got answers, brother." His eyes swiveled to Creeley. "And sister. I got your answers, okay? Just don't plug me full of lead. Okay? Are we cool?"

Creeley tasted something bitter inside her mouth. She said, "Let's go somewhere we can talk."

✳✳✳

Gant's dirty kitchen. Overflowing trash can and dishes piled in the sink. Old pizza boxes on the counter. Six boxes of Natural

Light, all filled with empty cans. They sat at his kitchen table—a glass top and uneven legs. Creeley sat across from him, her face burning with anger and hatred.

Paul sat at the head of the table. He had the gun resting on the table, his right hand covering it.

Gant kept his hands flat on the table and said, "Whatever you want to know, sis."

"Blossom Nash. Start with her."

Gant's eyes showed recognition. "I told you what I knew. That first time with Monty—"

"We'll discuss the detective after we talk about my mom."

Gant shut up for a moment, licked his upper lip. "I told you what I know: she was fucking the mayor. That fuck, Parks, paid me to shut up about it."

"He paid for more than twenty years?" She leaned toward him. "Add that up and it doesn't make sense."

Gant stared at her.

The kitchen air tasted like burnt bread. Somewhere, Creeley heard a clock ticking. A loud truck passed on the street outside the house.

Paul cleared his throat and Gant's eyes shot to him, back to Creeley. "All I can tell you," he said, "is that Parks didn't want it out there—that the mayor was fucking your mom."

Paul slammed the gun into the side of Gant's head. It was a nasty blow with the force of his whole body behind it. Gant toppled over in his chair, a sharp whimper coming out of him as he hit the floor. Creeley pushed back in her chair and stood up as Paul moved around the table. He set the gun on the glass table and punched Gant twice in the nose—blood sprayed onto Gant's bare chest and started pooling on the floor. He moaned with the pain and Paul kicked him in the ribs—that drew an elongated *oomph*. It was another sudden thrash of violence that surprised Creeley. Worse, it scared her. It was nothing like the bikers and her father back in Blythe. That was drawn out and provoked. Inefficient in its mayhem. This moment of violence was targeted, precise, and so aggressive as to be carnal. It ended when Paul said, "Don't lie to her again."

Gant pushed himself up, didn't bother to stem the bleeding. He scooted backward to rest against the wall and smiled at Creeley through his blood. "Point taken. Ask away, sis." He coughed hard and blinked at her.

"He didn't pay you to—"

"He wasn't paying me."

Paul started toward him.

"Wait, man—shit! He was passing money through me, and I took my G off the top."

"Passing money to who?" Creeley guessed The Vandals but needed to make certain.

"The Vandals MC. A guy named Skin Abrams. He's the chapter president out here."

"Where'd Parks get the money and what was it for?"

Gant laughed. He coughed again and said, "You know...None of this is about your mom."

"Answer her questions," Paul said through clenched teeth.

"Fuck if I know where he got it, but it was from the city."

Creeley didn't understand his answer. *The city? What the fuck?* "I don't get it," she said. "And I want you to explain it to me."

"Fuck—the two of you have no goddamn idea." He cleared his throat, wiped some blood from his nose and smeared it on his ribs. "The city pays off The Vandals. Regular payments to keep their bullshit out of sight of tourists. They do their drops and drug deals, murders, whatever the fuck, out in the desert. No eyes on it, you know? Got to keep the L.A. people coming in for the weekend trips. Got to keep all the retirees feeling nice and safe in their gated fucking communities. The cops collect off the bigger hotels, the golf courses...whoever. They take some off the top, but they keep The Vandals paid in full. It's been that way for damn near twenty-five years. Since your mom's fuck buddy—the mayor—made a deal with Skin Abrams. And you and me don't have a say in it, sis. Never did."

"So, Monty and me—when we took Parks to you..."

"The Vandals wanted Parks to get a beat down. He skimmed for a few months to buy himself a Cadillac. Turned out your detective—if that's what you want to call him—called Slide and asked about him. Slide had word from the street about what The Vandals wanted. Shit worked out, you know?"

"And Stacy? The lady detective?"

Gant shrugged. "Skin's little cousin. She was along for the ride and played it cool. Said she even gave you some tears to make it look right."

Creeley looked over at Paul. He had his hand on the gun again and he was staring like an animal at Gant. His jaw was clenched, and his nose was pointed at Gant like the point of a sword. She looked back to Gant. "What the fuck does this have to do with my mom? Or my brother being killed? What does any of this have to do with that?"

Gant shook his head. "I swear to God, I don't know. She was fucking the mayor, and maybe she knew Skin. But your brother? I don't fucking know."

"What's with the Cary Rickles identity? Tell me that."

Gant shrugged and said, "I'm a crook. A name for this, and a name for that. Wasn't easy for you to find me, was it? That's why."

Paul said, "They used to call you Skinny."

"Monty did. When we were in school. But that was a long time ago, man."

"He was in your pocket all these years? As a cop?"

Gant shook his head. "We did some things way back, but Monty got crazy a long time ago. You couldn't talk sense to the man. I don't know him now, except to say his name."

Creeley said, "No matter who I see, no matter what I ask, nobody knows a fucking thing."

Gant chuckled and said, "The fuck did you expect, sis? Enlightenment?"

Paul leaned down and punched Gant until he slept.

✹✹✹

MATT PHILLIPS

Driving back through the desert, Creeley's sense of how dangerous Paul was grew. When she heard his voice, she saw that small kid with the surprised look on his face as she kissed him. But Paul was—beyond all doubt—a violent man with a criminal past. "Thanks for what you did back there. I appreciate everything you've done for me."

"What I've done for you, that's about all I've done right in my life." She looked over at him, and his gaze was centered on the two-lane road. Immovable. Like the stare of a ghost.

"I can't imagine that."

"You don't have to—it's a bone-dry fact."

Creeley powered the 4Runner through a yellow light and across a freeway overpass.

Paul said, "What are you going to do now?"

"I need to talk to Monty. I guess I need to call the other detective, James. What about you?"

He cleared his throat and said, "I'm going to find Skin Abrams. And then I'm going to bring you to him. He owes you a motherfucking apology."

"At the least."

"The very-fucking-least."

53/The Bullshit Maze

"This is Detective James."

"It's me, Detective." Creeley cringed as she sipped black coffee at Amber's kitchen table. Kimmie was snoring on the couch behind her, and she imagined Amber was still curled up in bed—maybe naked. A thought that made Creeley's stomach flip. Little by little, she was coming around to the idea that her one-night stand with Amber wasn't a one-night stand. That maybe it was her way of seizing something she always wanted—true connection and love from another woman.

Edwin James snapped the thought from her when he said, "What do you want now?"

The audacity of this motherfucker, Creeley thought. *Maybe he isn't corrupt like the rest of them.*

"Well—what do you want?"

She said, "I want to talk to Monty."

Edwin laughed at her. "Maybe he'll give you a call."

"I doubt that."

"I get the impression you were falling for him. That what this is about?"

She cleared her throat. "It's about information. He lied to me about what he knows."

"When it comes to your brother's murder?"

"Yes."

There was silence over the line as Edwin thought about how to respond to her.

From the bedroom, Amber said, "Creeley? Is that you?"

Edwin James said, "Let's meet up, me and you."

"Where?"

"The parking lot at the bottom of the tramway—you know it? I can be there in half an hour."

"Okay," Creeley said and ended the call. She centered her gaze on the slightly open bedroom door. "It's me."

"Get in here," Amber said.

Creeley got in there.

***

The parking lot at the bottom of the aerial tramway served a small mid-century modern structure with an arrow-like ceiling design. Creeley parked facing the building and studied it. "What is this place? What a weird freaking building."

Amber said, "It's a visitors' center now. Used to be a gas station, I think."

Creeley looked past the building at the rugged peak of San Jacinto Mountain. The tramway road stretched and ambled upward in a snake-like pattern. It disappeared into a pass. Creeley squinted and thought she could see a tram car gliding up the cable to the top of the mountain. "You ever been up there, or what?"

"Once—last winter."

"That ex-boyfriend of yours?"

"Yeah," Amber said. "Him."

"You made me smile this morning," Creeley said.

"I made you do more than that." Amber reached out and laid a hand on Creeley's bare thigh.

"There he is." Creeley watched Edwin's battered police-issue Crown Vic pull into the parking lot and turn toward them. He pulled alongside Creeley's 4Runner so they could talk to each other without leaving their cars. The Crown Vic's brakes squealed as Creeley rolled down her window.

Edwin lowered his own window and said, "You told me Monty lied to you. I figured we could take it offline, talk in person."

"Are you corrupt, Detective?"

Edwin squinted at her. "I beg your goddamn pardon?"

"Are you corrupt?"

"You offend me, Miss Nash. I'm as straight as it gets, being a cop." He shook his head and sighed. "And here I was thinking you had—"

"I believe you," Creeley said. "I need you to get me in touch with Monty."

"And why should I do that, Miss Nash?"

"Because Monty is dirty. Ray Parks is dirty. I'm guessing half the Palm Springs Police Department is dirty, and it goes all the way up to the mayor and city council."

"That's it, huh?" Edwin scratched an ear.

"No—that's not it. My brother—Levi Mackey—was murdered, and it was a cop who did it."

"Is that a fact?"

"That's a fact, Detective James. A cop killed my brother and then a bunch of other cops put my mom in the joint for that murder. I can't tell you exactly who. And I can't—for the fucking life of me—tell you why. But that's what happened, and Monty Emeril has something to do with it."

Edwin James nodded. Kept nodding as he said, "I'll get you in a room with Monty, but I got to be there. That's my only thing—I have to be there."

Creeley looked at Amber. They met eyes for an instant before Creeley swung her head back and grinned at Edwin James. "Okay, Detective. Have it your way."

***

Monty no longer smelled of aftershave or martinis.

He smelled of sweat and prison disinfectant. A pitiful scent of cleanliness and hopelessness. He looked bad as the corrections officer sat him in a chair and clicked his cuffs into a metal latch on the table. He didn't look at Creeley sitting across from him—not right away. Instead, he stared at Edwin James and sneered.

Edwin said, "Good morning, Monty. You look well."

"Well as a fucking pile of dog shit." He swung his eyes to Creeley and there was nothing of love or warmth in them. Only hatred. A burning hatred so profound and certain that it scared her. He smirked at her and leaned down to scratch one eyelid. "You still thinking I'm the one to help you solve your brother's murder? After seeing me like this?"

"That's right, Monty. I still think you're the one to help me solve my brother's murder."

"And how's that?"

"I think you know what happened. I think you know who killed my brother."

Monty leaned back in his chair and it creaked beneath his weight. His ankle chains rattled under the table. He repositioned his hands and the metal clip scraped against his cuffs. "I had a thought that you were nuts, Creeley. But I didn't take it serious. Now, I wonder if—"

"You're in here for murder, Monty."

He chewed on the inside of his lip, sighed.

"That means you have it in you," Creeley said. "And I know that Slide told you The Vandals wanted Parks. You were just the method—I was part of that method."

"The Vandals didn't have shit to do with—"

"What'd you do? Did you rip them off? Is that why you had to kill Hero and his girlfriend? You ripped off The Vandals and you're cleaning house?"

"Don't act like you know what you're talking about."

"Oh, she's not acting like she knows," Edwin said. "The lady knows—you can wager your ass."

Creeley said, "And the mayor, too. You did him. He knew everything there was to know. I bet he knows who killed my brother."

"Knew," Monty said.

Creeley snapped her fingers. "Right—he knew. What did you do with the rest of that money, Monty? What you took from Parks that day?" She figured he wouldn't tell, and she was right. "What I don't get is why you got into this with me. I think maybe you wanted to keep track of me, or maybe you got turned on by it somehow. I want you to tell me why."

Monty sighed again and glared at Edwin. "This is done. Unless you have my lawyer on the way." He looked back at Creeley and shrugged.

"I let you touch me."

Monty chuckled and shook his head. "That's your problem,

you know that? You think it's all you—that you do all this shit to yourself. Grow the fuck up, Creeley."

"What the fuck are you saying?"

"Did you ask for this? For any of it?"

"No."

"Well," Monty said, "there you fucking go. Think about that for a long while. And maybe me and you, we'll see each other in another life."

"Like hell we will," Creeley said. "Like burning hell."

54/Muckraking

As Creeley sipped her Pinot Gris in a bar downtown, a thought crossed her mind: If the Palm Springs Police Department was as corrupt as she thought, who else would know about it but a hot-shot, tough-as-shit reporter? She needed to go see Dawn Griffin again. And she needed answers.

Edwin James slid onto his stool after five minutes in the little boy's room. He took a long swig of his light beer and said, "I feel like I'm letting you down."

"I don't even know you."

"But I'm a murder cop, and your brother's murder—I don't know—feels like we got it wrong."

"You fucking think?" Creeley appreciated Edwin starting to see things from her perspective, but it wasn't going to help get her mom out of the joint. That much, after all this, was something Creeley was certain about. It was going to be nearly impossible to get her mom off, but solving her brother's murder...It was possible. And now, for Creeley, that was the gold standard. But she still wouldn't trust a cop. Not after what happened with Monty. She finished her glass of wine and said, "I hope you don't expect me to trust you. Not after all the shit cops have put me through in this shit-fucking-hole of a resort town."

"I think it's a decent place."

"Sure it is. If you don't mind getting strangled, put in prison for a murder you didn't commit, or getting fucked over by the so-called cops."

Edwin nodded. Drank without responding.

"You know it wasn't me who did Hero and his girlfriend, right?"

"I wouldn't be here if I thought you did."

"Then I'm going to ask you for a future favor. And it's the last thing I'm going to ask for—I promise you that."

He tasted the insides of his mouth, coughed, and wiped his sweaty forehead with a cocktail napkin. "I'm always afraid of favors."

"If I find out who killed my brother, will you—"

"I'll call the DA for you and I will ask him to look into it."

Creeley watched him while he said it. Hard cheeks and wrinkled brow. Eyelids slim, and that glare as focused as a snake. She believed him. "Thank you."

"There's nothing to thank me for. It's called doing my motherfucking job."

***

Back in the Movie Colony neighborhood.

Almost dusk, and the yellow landscape lights were starting to flash on and illuminate palm and mesquite trees. A scent of bougainvillea tickled Creeley's nose as she knocked on Dawn Griffin's door. She had the Glock shoved in-between her ass and her G-string. Not sure why she took it, but it felt somehow right to have the gun as she approached Dawn's house. On the way over from the bar, she'd been thinking about her encounter with Dawn. To Creeley, it felt as if Dawn had given her and Amber valuable information and insight. But did she give them everything she knew? Or was she trying to protect somebody? Dawn herself had mentioned having an affair with a cop. Did that make her corrupt, too? Creeley didn't know. But she wanted everything Dawn knew.

And she was going to get it tonight. All of it.

The door opened and that stench of cigarettes filled the air. Dawn poked her head out and said, "You forget your purse or something, chick?"

"No," Creeley said. "But I did forget to tell you how it is."

***

Dawn poured Creeley a gin with two shaking hands holding the bottle.

She brought the glass to Creeley and sank into the couch next to a stack of yellowed newspapers. Creeley stood in the living room, sipped her gin while spinning in circles and taking it all in—Dawn's framed newspaper clippings and pictures with celebrities. A testament to life in the news, that safeguard of truth. After working her way around the room, she planted her eyes on Dawn and grinned.

"Did you lie to me? Or did you just neglect to give me all the information you have?"

Dawn said, "I know what's in the papers. And that's about it."

"You knew Levi Mackey was my brother. That wasn't in the papers. Not even the one you wrote for." Creeley sipped more gin, chewed a sliver of ice.

"A small fact I picked up. It's what you get when you have your ear to the ground, chick."

"What else do you know? What other facts?"

"You got all of them, babe." Dawn gulped from her glass of gin, showed clenched teeth behind her wrinkled lips. "The facts are the facts."

"Which cop were you fucking?"

"When?"

"Back when my brother was murdered."

Dawn chuckled, coughed a smoker's elongated cough. "I think, at that time, I might have been fucking Parks. But that was only for information and good times. Not for love."

Creeley nodded, somewhat amused. "Could have figured that, you old hag."

"So rude. And after I helped you."

Creeley finished her gin, set the tumbler on the glass-topped coffee table. She reached around behind her back and came out with the Glock. She took two steps toward Dawn Griffin before stopping to examine the gun. "I've been around people who use guns, Dawn. For a few years now, I have. But I never thought that little old me would have to use one of these. I really didn't."

"There's nothing you can do with that to make me—"

Creeley cut her off by firing the gun. She did it all in one smooth motion—brought her eyes up at the same time as she pointed the gun and squeezed the trigger. Her ears rang for a moment before she realized she was hearing Dawn's high-pitched wail. The old reporter's hands were pressed against her face, but the wail was coming through her fingers like vomit through a sewer grate. The shot had plunged through the sofa just to the left of her head. A near miss by any account. And Creeley imagined the pain in Dawn's ears was significant.

Creeley screamed at her to shut up.

The wailing stopped.

"Do I need to tell you that a bullet in your knee will be painful?"

Dawn shook her head.

"Who was it?"

"Parks," Dawn said. "It was Ray."

"I know Parks is a corrupt piece of shit. I plan to pay him a visit. But what else do I need to know? And don't fucking try to—"

"Not what," Dawn said. "But who."

Creeley waited.

"Jimmy Goffs. An old pal of mine."

"Where do I find Goffs?"

Dawn gulped and said, "You'll find him at a bar called Colors—it's in Cat City."

***

Creeley ran two red lights as she drove across town. And there was a thought she couldn't get out of her head. When it came to her brother's murder, she knew the what, the when, and she was on the verge of knowing the who. But she sure as fuck didn't know the why.

That was the biggest question still: *Why?*

55/Gay Bar

Creeley stormed past a fat bouncer who was dressed as a sailor. He tried to stop her, but she slipped into the crowd of half-naked male bodies. All dancing and slicked with sweat, the whole bar moving to the pumping bass of electronic dance music and pure jets of testosterone. She pushed her way through the men, screaming at them to move the fuck out of her way as she kept her eyes on the bar. According to Dawn Griffin, her old pal Jimmy Goffs was gay as silver tinsel and spent ninety percent of his time at Colors. All of it sitting at the bar and ogling buff bartenders in pantyhose. This proved to be true.

Creeley saw him—a bear in khakis and a too-tight purple tank—leaning into a bartender's ear about twenty feet from the dance floor. The song hit a rare bass-less moment and she thought she could hear his voice—a weasel wrapped inside a smelly white sock, from the sound of him. She squeezed through two over-sexed senior citizens and darted toward Jimmy Goffs. But she caught his eye. And Goffs hopped off his bar stool and sprinted past the bar into a dark hallway. The bartender stared open-mouthed as Creeley gave chase, screaming for Goffs to stop running if he didn't want his ass beat to a pulp.

She lost sight of him as she entered the hallway—smelly and filled with couples in numerous compromising positions. The bass started pumping as Creeley turned a corner. When she did, a shadow seemed to move toward her face. At the last second, she somehow ducked and raised an arm. A wet two-by-four glanced off her forearm and she yelped. The fucker was running again.

He slammed into an employee exit and sprinted into the parking lot.

Creeley ignored the pain in her arm and followed.

They sprinted through the parking lot and across a side street.

Goffs—with Creeley about twenty feet behind him—tried a few doors in a battered strip mall.

Nothing opened.

As he reached the end of the strip mall, he turned toward her and put his hands on his knees. His shoulders heaved up and down and his breathing was audible. He looked up at her with his chubby red face. "I never thought I'd see you," he said.

Creeley had stopped sprinting, and she slowed her jog to a stomping walk. She pulled the Glock and pointed it ahead of her like a spotlight.

He straightened and lifted his hands out to her, backed against the door to a nail salon. "No. God. Please. Don't shoot me."

Creeley stopped with the barrel of the gun planted against the round tip of his nose. "Why'd you run from me, you fat old dirty fuck?"

His eyes were wide and wild. "I just—I just—I—"

Creeley moved the barrel of the gun to the plump space between his eyes. "Spit it out, fucker."

"I—I know who you are."

"Tell me who I am."

"You're her daughter. Blossom's daughter."

"And why the fuck," Creeley said, "would I want to talk to you?"

"Because you think I got your brother killed."

Creeley put the gun down, shoved her face into his. Their noses almost touched. "Why the fuck would I think that? Just why in the fuck would I think that?"

"My story about the mayor. The one from ninety-six."

Creeley stared at him, but she didn't say a word.

It took a long time, but Jimmy Goffs did at some point say, "You don't know about my story, do you? Jesus. You don't actually know about my story."

***

Jimmy Goffs lived in a shitty apartment building in Cathedral City.

Bottom floor.

The place smelled like cat piss and dollar store incense. He had gay pornography papering the walls, all of it cut from magazines. His apartment had the charm of a torture chamber.

Creeley looked for a place to sit while he dug into a file cabinet. She settled on standing.

He said, "This is it," and came out with a yellowed copy of the *Desert Sun*. "Before I hand it to you, will you promise not to hurt me?"

"Sure, but I don't always keep my promises."

Jimmy gulped, but he handed her the newspaper. "Left column. Above the fold."

Creeley licked her upper lip as she read the headline: 'Mayor Tangles with Motorcycle Gang.' She looked up once at Jimmy Goffs before reading the story. He was biting the nails on his right hand and watching her with unblinking eyes. The story was a political hit job:

Mayor Tangles with Motorcycle Club

By Jimmy Goffs

Mayor Stephen Dorphs is in bed with a local motorcycle club, according to law enforcement sources in the Inland Empire. Last October, city hall sources, including sitting members of the city council, raised concerns about Dorphs taking an armed escort to meet a member of the motorcycle club at a local motel. While no sources have agreed to go on record, the *Desert Sun* has significant proof of these actions. The proof includes images and sound recordings.

The meetings, according to two sources, began after a bar fight in Palm Springs last December. Three members of The Vandals motorcycle club were arrested after inciting violence at the Dune Bar on Tahquitz Canyon Way. "They came in here and tried to have a good time," said Dan Owens, the bar's owner. "Thing is—there were some cops around and things didn't go well."

Police reports document significant facial trauma to

two Palm Springs police officers, both rookie patrolmen. Palm Springs PD refuses to comment on the matter but did initially release a statement claiming the officers were assault victims.

The alleged assaults followed a series of rapes and assaults during the previous few months.

All perpetrated, according to eyewitnesses, by members of The Vandals.

Law enforcement sources tell the *Desert Sun* that Dorphs made a deal with the club president to limit their presence in the Palm Springs area. The terms of the deal include right-of-way for drug smuggling both into and through the city of Palm Springs and the nearby I-10 corridor.

The mayor's office denies these claims but refused to release an official statement.

Nor would Dorphs respond to interview questions.

The rest of the article detailed Palm Springs's organized crime history and gave an account of Dorphs and his questionable political rise. But none of it seemed important. Creeley squinted as she looked up at Goffs and studied him. She folded the paper and crossed her arms. She knew her face was a portrait of confusion. "So, Dorphs was a corrupt piece of shit. And The Vandals had the drug game locked down. But why the fuck would this get my brother killed?"

Goffs bit the nail off his pinkie finger and chewed on it. He swallowed and said, "Your brother was at the meeting between Dorphs and The Vandals," he said. "He saw and heard everything."

***

She sat in the 4Runner outside Amber's apartment. The radio played Pink Floyd and Aerosmith and AC/DC. Music that didn't quite match the soft thump of Creeley's heart as she considered her brother's murder. Sounded like he got snared in some odd tryst. And Blossom—her mom—had the same problem. When you work the streets, you take whoever comes at you. So long as they pay. There is no distinction between married man and single hustler, between cop and crook, between politician and crime boss. They're semi-hard cocks and dollar bills.

That's about the measure of most shit in this world.

The radio went to a commercial and Creeley climbed out of the truck, moped across the parking lot. She walked through the courtyard and turned the corner to climb Amber's stairs.

Animal said, "Took you long enough."

She stopped and stared. The Glock was back in the 4Runner, hidden beneath her seat. Animal was sitting on the second step. His crazy smile on, a sideways grin with one eye victim to an unnamed palsy. He wore a Trailblazer cap twisted sideways and a bulky Nike sweatsuit. A gold chain swung from his skinny neck. "You're the one who took his time," Creeley said.

"I got me some people who I thought, you know, could do the job."

"Not true."

He rocked back and forth. "You right on that. Seems like I lost another one."

"Paul and me go way back," she said.

"So, that's what it is?"

She grinned herself and said, "It's something like that."

"This girl turning my own boys against me."

"All I asked was for your patience," she said.

"You think it's me, but it ain't. I mean, what the fuck do I care about your mom in the joint?"

Creeley sighed and nodded. "That's a pretty popular opinion around here."

Animal closed his mouth and lifted his chin at her. "I know you got what I came for. What I wanted to do, was to go up there and tie up your little girlfriend and her fairy BFF. But I figure that's, like, a crime. You know, going up there all violent and shit. But if I get you to hand over my shit—that's just me and you doing business." He held his hands out like he was getting a gift. "Here I am, baby. Just like you never wanted."

A GOOD RUSH OF BLOOD

"I'll give it to you, Animal. But I'm asking you not to hurt my friends. They've got nothing to do with this shit. All of it, I brought it to them."

"It ain't them, huh?"

"Not a single bit. All the shit—it's me. I tried to fuck you over. Promise that you won't hurt my friends. You can do whatever to me—I don't give a fuck anymore."

"I promise, baby." He stepped forward and moved to the side of the staircase, gestured to her as if opening a door. "I'll wait right outside. If you aren't back in three minutes, this joint becomes a murder scene. And you're coming with me, too." There was that loopy grin on his face, the sideways cap tilted so it shadowed his crazy eye.

Creeley walked past him and climbed the stairs without looking back, let herself into the apartment after fumbling with her key ring.

Kimmie was sleeping on the couch, that light snore coming from under his blanket. Amber was reading at the kitchen table and looked up at Creeley. She smiled and said, "Who's that punk waiting outside my door?"

"The guy I used to run drugs for. In other words, my fucking boss."

"And you gave me shit about my ex the other day? Who has a fucked-up history now?"

Creeley shrugged and said, "You know I'm a total asshole, right?"

"Does he want that bag of yours?"

"Yeah. He does." As Creeley said it, there was a cough from somewhere down the hallway. The bathroom door opened, and light reflected off the beige walls. Paul's head poked out of the bathroom, and he nodded at Creeley.

He said, "I found Skin Abrams and he's in town."

"Animal is downstairs and he's asking for his shit. If I'm not down in three minutes he's going to come up here and kill us."

Amber said, "Jesus-fucking-shit."

Paul came down the hallway and pulled his gun from under his flannel shirt. "Good. Let's get this over with right now." He blurred past Creeley without glancing at her.

Creeley said, "Paul, just wait a fucking minute."

But he was out the door and moving down the stairs.

Creeley turned and heard Animal say, "Yo, look who it is."

And then she heard three gunshots. Something told her Animal had just been put to sleep.

The duffel bag hung from her right hand.

She followed Paul into the bar. Hard rock on the jukebox. That dingy smell of mold and body odor. A few girls sitting in a booth gave her the evil mascara eye. Six bikers in leather vests surrounded a pool table, bottles of Bud sweating in their hands. Paul nodded at the bartender—sexy in a low-cut blouse—and headed for the back of the bar. The bartender batted her eyelashes at Creeley.

They crossed through a patch of darkness. Emerged into a halogen-lit area with booths lining the back wall.

The music was lower in volume back here, but there was a mood of general violence and fear. Creeley counted nine more bikers, most of them standing around one of the booths. They nodded as a fat man with a razor-shaven head rattled off commands at them—no doubt the fat man was Skin Abrams. Two of the bikers stood off to the side, motioned for Paul and Creeley to approach.

They patted Paul down and he passed inspection, his gun tossed into a dumpster behind a local Mickey D's. They took their time with Creeley. The prying hands discovered nothing but tits and ass. As she and Paul were ushered toward the fat man, he grew silent and motioned for her to sit. Creeley set the duffel in the center of the table and slid into the booth across from him.

He said, "You look like your momma."

She didn't respond.

"I look in the bag, it's all gonna be there?" He sniffed hard and scratched one brown eyebrow with his thumb. "Not that I'm accusing you of anything."

"Hero took his portion, and that's it."

"I guess he don't need that no more." He shifted in the booth and his leather vest squeaked over his bulky shoulders and arms. "Pal of yours made certain of that."

"Monty is not my fucking pal."

Skin grinned with his lopsided teeth and shrugged. "Yeah—I guess that dude has a way of surprising people." He looked away from her and studied Paul for a moment. Looked back to Creeley and said, "How's your momma doing up there in the joint?"

"Not good. Considering she didn't kill my brother."

"I can see how it's a difficult thing." He motioned to one of his men and a skinny guy with a beard to the center of his chest took the bag, drifted off into another part of the bar. "I can see how it eats you, and maybe even understand what it does to her."

"You aren't locked up."

"No, that's true—I'm not."

"And you know who did it."

Skin sighed, drank from a bottle of Bud. "But it doesn't make a difference."

"A sworn affidavit would make a difference."

"From an ex-con, a known member of a violent motorcycle club? You don't think a prosecutor would toast my ass by telling folks who I am and what I done?"

"It might help her."

"It ain't gonna help her."

Creeley looked at Paul. He was standing beside the booth with his chin on his chest.

"Me and you both know it ain't gonna help her," Skin said.

"There's a chance."

He shook his head.

Creeley's anger started in her heart—a rapid thump that spread up her neck and into her forehead. She almost went blind for an instant, Skin's fat body blurring into a lump of white-and-black mass. She leaned forward over the table, blinked as hard as she could, and groaned.

Skin said, "You hating me doesn't change anything."

Creeley took a long, deep breath. Felt the air fill her belly and chest. She spit it out at Skin, her lips rattling against each other. "There's a few people I want to kill in this world."

"How about this room?"

She narrowed her eyes and said, "Only one."

Skin nodded at her and leaned back in the booth. "Monty Emeril killed your brother. He was a patrol cop at the time, detailed to the mayor's office. He hung around with Dorphs, went with him everywhere—especially to meet me. At the time, Emeril wasn't jack shit. He was just a guy who knew what was happening in the city, slowly getting up to speed on everything. Dorphs wasn't corrupt like people think—how they painted it in the papers. His thing was that he didn't want the boys scaring the hell out of tourists and old people. I would have told them to get their shit together anyhow—I don't like heat—but Dorphs asked to meet me. I used him to get safe passage for my packages. Used him to secure my hold on a lot of the drug and flesh trade. The papers had that right—especially the fairy reporter."

"Jimmy Goffs."

"Yeah. Goffs. Just so happened he got the story when Parks convinced your mom to confess. But he wrote it so—I don't know—you could guess it was something weird with it."

"But it didn't matter," Creeley said as she crossed her arms.

"How's it gonna matter when all the cops are corrupt as turds in a urinal? Whatever they wanted to happen, it was gonna happen."

"Like your cousin is corrupt?"

Skin said, "Like her—yeah."

"So they framed my mom to protect Monty."

"And every other cop in the city, but yeah..."

"Parks and Monty, though—they hate each other."

Skin shrugged and shook his head. "Parks—and I'm just guessing—never knew exactly who murdered your little bro. He just knew it was a cop. You got to protect a fellow cop, you get a confession from the working girl. Easy play. Makes sense to everybody."

"But what was she doing there?"

"Your mom? Working. A few of my guys got up with her back in the day. Shit, I did myself." He scratched his eyebrow again.

"I don't mean anything by telling you this—it's just how it was."

"The guy who looks like Elvis. Rides a bike. Is he one of yours?"

"He does some shit for me. But he's no Vandal. Didn't make it past prospect."

Creeley puzzled over this information. She saw her mother working at the motel that day, maybe her brother showing up to see her. And then, what, Dorphs shows up and so does Skin? She needed more than the result—she needed the narrative. "Tell me how it happened."

Skin grunted and drank more beer. "Your mom had a room at the motel. Dorphs and me talked about meeting there and he gave me the room number. Me and some of my boys, we got there about a half hour early. I go up to the room and knock— your mom answered. Me and her exchanged services for twenty minutes or so before Dorphs walked in with Emeril, the patrol cop." He finished his beer and motioned at one of his boys. A second later, a new beer hit the table and Skin drank. "Dorphs is batshit because I got there early, had some fun. Surprised the hell out of me when he starts screaming at your mom. After a while, Dorphs gives up on her and we talk. It didn't take long—he just wanted assurance my boys wouldn't run wild in Palm Springs. Both of us are sitting at the little table there by the window. Your mom is sitting on the bed, and Emeril is by the door. Me and Dorphs shake hands and that's it—I walk out of the room."

"You walk out?"

"All the way down the stairs and into the parking lot. We're about to fire up the bikes and I hear Dorphs yelling again. Something about 'Who the fuck is this? What's this fucker doing here?' On like that for a minute or two, and then I hear your mom scream. And then all the shit goes quiet. We fire up the bikes and get the fuck out of there. And that's the way it went down."

Creeley dropped her eyes to the table, studied her pale hands. She felt cheated by her mom. By Blossom. She never told Creeley the truth—not about her own shit, and not about Levi's murder. He had been hiding in the room and heard it all.

"I can see that even your mom's been lying."

Creeley looked up at him and met his brown eyes. Not hard eyes, but knowing eyes. "She didn't ever tell me what happened, how it was."

"I'm sorry about that, but you know that a momma—"

"Don't make excuses for her."

Skin drank from his beer. "As it goes, your mom's had it set up okay in the joint."

Creeley studied him and frowned. "You?"

"People I know."

Creeley said, "Thank you."

"They try to make us think life is cut and dry—good and bad, right? You and me know that's a lot of bullshit. There's people who got power. Like them. Like me. And there's people like your mom."

"People like my brother."

"That's right."

Creeley said, "I'm trying to take some of it from them. From you."

"Good goddamn luck."

Paul said, "I need to tell you something, Skin."

Creeley and Skin looked at Paul.

He said, "I killed Animal."

Skin chuckled and looked at Creeley. "Talk about power, huh? You want a job, Creeley Nash?"

57/The Liar and the Killer

When Ray Parks pulled up in his sleek black car, he hesitated opening the driver's side door. Creeley, sitting on the steps of his mobile home in the warm desert night, gave him a slight wave. She tried to look as harmless as possible—the truth was, she felt harmless. She was convinced that Ray Parks was nothing more than a shitty detective. He wasn't a killer. No. Monty Emeril was the killer.

He finally climbed out and leaned against the front fender. One side of his face was discolored, bruised, and swollen. Creeley said, "I know you didn't do it on purpose, Ray. I know you didn't have anything to do with it—not like I thought."

"Christ. You must be crazy, lady. I got no idea what the fuck I have to do with any of your shit. The way it happened is the way it happened. Your mother confessed to killing a young man."

Creeley ruffled her hair and took a deep breath. While she didn't believe Parks was responsible for her brother's death, he might have some information she needed. So she wanted him to trust her. "It was Monty Emeril who killed my brother. And I know it for a fact."

Parks looked down the ratty trailer park dirt lane and shrugged. "What I heard he did this week, I can believe he had something to do with it. But it don't change what happened—I heard Blossom Nash confess to that murder. I was in the room with her."

"And you believed her?"

He didn't respond.

"But you put her in for it. Some kind of justice, huh?"

He shook his head and shoved his hands into his pockets. He didn't look like a tough cop anymore. He looked more like a kid grown too old for his body. He looked bored and inconsiderate. Useless and worn. "Nothing I've ever done as a cop has been about justice."

"Tell me about it."

Ray Parks chuckled and said, "Is there something I can do for you?"

"Help me get my mom out of there. A sworn affidavit from you would help. Something that helps me prove it was wrongful—"

"I hear what you're saying, but I'm not going to do that."

She stood and crossed her arms. Cold now, though the air was warm and still. "Why not?"

"I just can't do it. I followed the facts, and we got the confession. There was evidence that tied Blossom Nash to the murder. And I didn't fabricate or place any of that—it's real. There's other reasons, too. People who would hurt me in ways you never will."

"But I know that Monty killed my brother."

"I just can't do it—that's all."

Creeley watched him stand there in his still, uncaring demeanor. She narrowed her eyes at him, knew what it was. "You're scared. Of Monty. Of the department. Of The Vandals. You're scared to do the right thing. What a fucking joke. Some guy who pretends he's tough is scared to do the right thing."

"You're wrong," Parks said. "It's not about right or wrong. I'm scared to do something stupid. Me helping get your mom out of prison—that qualifies as stupid."

What a world, Creeley thought. But his response didn't surprise her. Self-preservation and pride have always outweighed justice. *And they always will,* Creeley knew. *They always fucking will.*

***

Edwin James had himself a Gibson martini and a decent bucket of buffalo wings. He was digging in at the casino bar while slot machines rang all around him. Creeley called him after she met Parks, and he asked to meet her at the casino. She slid onto a bar stool beside him and ordered a vodka tonic. After her chat with Parks, she was nauseated and needed something that—maybe, hopefully—would settle her stomach. Or calm her growing anxiety.

As he licked buffalo sauce off his fingers, Edwin said, "I know Parks ain't trying to help you."

"Why would he?" Creeley chugged her drink.

"Exactly what I'm saying."

The casino hummed and clinked around them. There were some cheers around a craps table and Creeley shook her head at the chubby cocktail waitresses in their nylons and short, frumpy skirts. The bartender was an old man with a crazy eye. He cleaned glassware and counted tokens.

"You think you can get me another sit down with Monty?"

Edwin sucked meat off a chicken bone before dropping it onto his plate. He licked his fingers again. "Monty got himself a criminal defense attorney. I doubt he's willing to say jack shit to anybody, anywhere. It's mum over there, far as I can tell. Guy like him, he's no dummy. The attorney gets ahold of him and, shit, his IQ goes up twenty, thirty ticks."

"But you can question him?"

Edwin sighed. "I can, I guess. But that ain't going to do much."

"My mom did not kill my brother. She just didn't. My brother— Levi Mackey—was killed by a sick fuck cop who was working for the mayor."

"You don't know it for a fact."

"Yes. I fucking do. And so do you."

Edwin nodded, chewed three more wings before saying, "I don't think there's anything I can do. Not from my end. You get one of these lawyers who knows what's what...That could maybe—"

"I can't afford a motherfucking lawyer."

"I hear you."

"I thought you were a real detective. Like, somebody who solves crimes. You said you'd get in touch with the DA and—"

"He'd laugh at this. It's outlandish."

Creeley said, "But it's true."

Edwin wiped his runny nose with a wet nap. "Lots of whodunits out there, Creeley. I get to the ones that matter right now. Today."

"So, this is how it is?"

"How else is it going to be?" Edwin chewed on his bottom

lip before he said, "I got to homicide, called up, and I had a few years on the street behind me. I still believed, you know, generally, there's good people out there. Had a guy take me out to lunch after I'd been in homicide a week. He says to me, 'Everybody you see and talk to, they're lying. People lie so damn good, they lie to themselves...and got no trouble believing it.' That right there is the last true thing I ever heard doing this job."

Creeley said, "That lines up."

He turned to her with curious eyes. "Looks like there was a shooting over at them apartments."

"What apartments?"

He chuckled at her. "Where your pal lives—the cute librarian."

She said, "It doesn't have jack shit to do with me."

"Oh, I bet it doesn't." He went back to his wings, finished one. He wiped his fingers clean and said, "You know who it was, told me about the lies?"

"Don't say it."

"A bent cop named Monty Emeril," Edwin said.

"I never did like cops," Creeley said.

"And how about now?"

It was her turn to chuckle, but she couldn't even do that. All she could do was clench her teeth and fume somewhere deep inside herself. She finished her drink and left Edwin licking buffalo sauce off his fat fingers.

58/Yesterday and Tomorrow

Creeley went to the prison alone.

It smelled of sanitizer and cigarette smoke. Felt like a hospital from a horror film.

When her mom came out and took a seat behind the foggy glass, the lines on her face told Creeley everything—she was giving up. Or giving in. Or whatever you wanted to call it.

They each picked up the phone receiver and Creeley tried to smile. It felt more like a twisted sneer, what you'd draw onto a killer's cartoon face. She said, "It's good to see you."

Blossom grunted in response.

"I came here to talk to you about Levi."

Blossom swallowed and perched her head on a hand. "I'm listening."

"You didn't tell me the truth. You didn't tell me what happened." Creeley saw her mom's thoughts turn inward, then rebound somehow and focus on the present. "Why didn't you tell me? I don't understand it. You knew that—"

"You were right to run off, Creeley."

Creeley found it her turn to gulp. Tears formed at the corners of her eyes.

"It only got worse. I only got worse. The men—they got worse, if there is such a thing."

"I know it hurt you."

Blossom shook her head, leaned back in her chair. She held the phone to her ear with a shoulder and crossed her arms. "No, it didn't. It didn't hurt me at all, Creeley. I was proud of you. I was proud of you for doing what you needed to do to survive. That's all this life is—survival."

Now the tears came and ran down Creeley's cheeks. She didn't bother wiping them away.

"I didn't tell you what happened because..." She sighed and thought for an instant, gathered the phrases welling in her throat.

"I didn't tell you because I'm selfish. I wanted you to do something for me because you love me. I wanted to feel that love—after all I put you through. And I was afraid of what happened, but I knew you'd find it. What was true. What was real. And if you could do that, you'd know the truth about me. I'm bad for you, Creeley. I always have been. And this thing, your brother's murder, was the last thing I could give you."

"But you gave me to the world."

"You and me both know it should have been somebody else."

"I still love you. I mean, I hate you...but I love you."

Blossom's eyes were clear and still—sober as cold running water. "Monty Emeril strangled my son—your brother—until he turned blue and stopped breathing. Until his heart stopped. And I didn't do one damn thing to stop him."

"You couldn't have. How could you—"

"I didn't even try," Blossom said. "And you did. Twenty-five years later, you tried to do something." She pointed at Creeley through the glass. "That's who *you* are." She put her finger to her own nose. "And this is who I am."

"Mom, I'm going to try to get you out. You didn't kill Levi. I can get you out." Frantic now, almost pleading with her mom who was becoming a shadow in front of her. A shadow beneath the bright halogen of the prison lights.

"Did you get in touch with my PD?"

Creeley said, "Jenny Frost doesn't want anything to do with this. And the prosecutor—"

"Hector Alonso," Blossom said.

"—is a prick without a conscience. I talked to both of them on the phone. Fucking pointless."

"I'm never getting out of this place, Creeley. You and me know it—I'm going to die here."

Creeley did not want to argue about lawyers or evidence. She didn't want to mention sworn affidavits or corrupt cops. She didn't want to puzzle over motives and actions. No. She wanted to memorize the lines of her mom's face. She wanted to study the architecture of her bone structure. The texture of her skin. She wanted to see herself there in the steady, sober eyes of her mother.

She wanted to be her mother's daughter—a hooker's lone surviving child.

And she did see herself—she saw her life unfolded at the cruel intersection of bad luck and poor choices. But there was nothing irrefutably bad in that. Or wrong. Instead, there was understanding.

And there was the way forward. Into the rest of this uncontrollable existence.

***

Creeley got the call two weeks later.

She was sitting on the floor of her apartment, watching Amber drill holes to hang a curtain rod.

Creeley was saying how it was going to be a dark Oregon winter. All the rain on the way and now these gaudy curtains draped across her windows.

Amber said, "We can make this place cute, Creeley Nash. Just give me a couple weeks."

"What for? Why do we need to make it cute? That's the freaking question."

"Because Kimmie and his new boy toy will be here next week. And I'll be damned if I host two gay men in this apartment without window dressings."

"That is such a stereotypical assumption."

"What assumption?" Amber said.

"That they'll judge us."

"Of course they'll judge us. I'm just hoping they'll judge us less."

And then the vibrating cell phone between the couch cushions.

"Hello?"

"Is this Creeley Nash?"

"Maybe. Who the hell is this?"

"I'm calling from the California Department of Corrections

and Rehabilitation, Miss Nash. Are you Blossom Nash's daughter? I was told to contact the next of kin about—"

"The next of kin?"

"Yes, Miss Nash."

Silence while Creeley prepared herself. After a moment, she said, "How'd she do it?"

The voice cleared its throat. "Are you sure—"

"Yes."

"Shoelaces, Miss Nash. I'm sorry."

One word, Creeley thought. *One fucking word?* Shoelaces. *Fucking hell.*

There it was—just like that. One lonely word: shoelaces.

* * *

Skin Abrams said he liked the sound of Creeley's voice. "It's the voice of a badass—a new, badass boss. I was wondering when you'd call. Hey, look—I heard about Blossom. I'm sorry."

Creeley said, "Everyone ends."

"Shit—that's true."

"I'll do it," Creeley said. "Move your product." She scratched her chin and watched Amber stirring a pot of boiling pasta. "But I use my own people. That's the only way I do it."

"Who does the driving?"

Creeley said, "Paul does. Or whoever he wants."

"I trust Paul," Skin said. "He doesn't fuck around."

The sound of gunfire echoed in Creeley's brain. The Palm Springs Police Department didn't solve Animal's murder. Creeley thought Skin Abrams and The Vandals had something to do with that. They had to have something to do with it. "No," Creeley said. "Paul does not fuck around."

"Okay," Skin said. "Tell your boy Paul to come see me. Let's get to work."

Creeley hung up and set her cell phone on the counter.

"You're going to do it?" Amber wanted to know.

"I don't know anything else," Creeley said.

"I don't want you to get in trouble."

MATT PHILLIPS

"I'll be fine," Creeley said. "I always am."

She sat there and watched her girlfriend make pasta and drink cheap red wine. A live recording of Peter Frampton played in the living room. The sound of thirty thousand stoners listening to a guitar talk. The water boiled over and Amber cussed, poured it into the sink. She started the sauce and hummed along with the guitar chords.

Creeley thought about her mom. She thought about her brother. She thought about her father wrenching on old cars. She imagined Monty Emeril rotting to death in a prison cell. When she was done thinking about all that, she reminded herself:

God. When I started, I didn't know a damn thing.

But now I know it all.

Now, I know everything there is.

Acknowledgments

To the readers of this book—thank you for your passion for words and stories and free expression. None of this exists without you...the reader. To my wife, Lesley, and my son, Charlie, for making time for me to write. I love you both. Thanks to all those in my life who knew I was writing and never thought once to discourage me. Sometimes, not saying no is all the yes somebody needs. Thanks to all my family and friends. You know exactly who you are. Thanks to all my writer/artist friends...I'd fill many more pages if I listed everybody. You know exactly who you are. And, lastly, thanks to the team at Run Amok Books for the time, patience, and expertise: Krysta Winsheimer, Vern Smith, and Gary Anderson...This book doesn't hit like it does without you. Thanks for believing in this story. And to all the writers: If you're out there and you're writing a story...Keep writing. The world dies without books.

About the Author

Matt Phillips lives in San Diego. His novels include *Countdown, Know Me from Smoke, You Must Have a Death Wish*, and *Three Kinds of Fool*. His short fiction has been featured in *Shotgun Honey, Mystery Tribune, Retreats from Oblivion*, and elsewhere.

www.ingramcontent.com/pod-product-compliance
Lightning Source LLC
Chambersburg PA
CBHW030150310726
48970CB00005B/1667